Diva's Last Curtain Call

Diva's Last Curtain Call

A Kendra Clayton Novel

ANGELA
HENRY

sepia™

DIVA'S LAST CURTAIN CALL

A Sepia Novel

ISBN-13: 978-0-373-83044-2
ISBN-10:   0-373-83044-0

www.kimanipress.com

Printed in U.S.A.

Acknowledgments

I'd like to thank the readers who've embraced this series,
my friends and family for their continued support, my agent,
Richard Curtis, and my editor, Glenda Howard,
for making more Kendra books possible.

PROLOGUE

Vivianne DeArmond couldn't contain the nasty little smile that spread across her face as she dragged the box out from its hiding place under her bed. She felt a little like Pandora as she opened the box and ran a trembling hand over the stack of papers inside, tracing the letters with her fingertip. She wasn't trembling with fear but anticipation, because she couldn't wait for what was in the box to cause the chaos and damage that it inevitably would. She just hoped she'd have a front-row seat when the drama unfolded. After all, she certainly deserved it.

She pulled out the plastic square that was wedged between the stack of paper and the inside of the box and looked around her room for a hiding place. Pulling open the double doors of her closet rather dramatically, Vivianne peered inside the cavernous space. She spied an old box of junk on the top shelf and grabbed it, a little too enthusiastically, and felt a twinge of pain in her lower back as she lowered the box to the floor.

Harriet, her assistant and friend of more than fifty years, had warned her she was playing with fire and would end up burned, too. And on some level, Vivianne knew it, but just didn't care. What did she have left to lose? Her career? That had been over for years. No one cared about seeing Vivianne DeArmond in a movie anymore. All anyone wanted to see these days were bleached-blond airheads with surgically enhanced bosoms and IQs to match their shoe sizes who couldn't act their way out of a wet paper sack. If she were still acting, the only roles Cliff, her ex-agent and ex-husband, would be able get her would be playing maids and grandmothers and what fun was that? Vivianne was still a very beautiful woman and felt she could easily pass for forty-five. But it was damned hard for a forty-five-year-old white actress to find good parts, so a sixtyish black actress, no matter how fine she might still be, who didn't want to play a maid or a granny, was basically shit out of luck. Cliff wanted her to read for the part of Glenda the Good Witch for a big-bucks remake of *The Wiz*. Vivianne wasn't interested. The last time Cliff had talked Vivianne into coming out of retirement and auditioning for a role it had been for the part of Dominique Deveraux on the prime-time soap opera *Dynasty*. Vivianne had nailed that audition. She owned that part. When the producers had decided on Diahann Carroll, she'd been devastated, especially when she'd found out that she'd never really had a shot at the role and had only been given a chance to audition as a courtesy to Cliff.

Vivianne's acting days were over. But at the height of her career, she'd really been something. Vivianne had had a mutual love affair with the camera that had ended in the late seventies with her small role in a low-budget horror movie. Cliff had called it a cameo. Vivianne knew it was just bit part. She'd even had to share a trailer with her stunt double. The humiliation of that experience had been enough to send her into retirement. Nevertheless, Vivianne was about to reinvent herself in a move that would serve two purposes: It would give her a much-needed career change and sweet revenge. She'd make her big announcement when she received her award at the Starburst Film Festival. She couldn't wait.

Vivianne rummaged through the box until she found an object that offered the perfect hiding place. She slid the plastic square inside, returned the object to the box, and slid the box to the back of her closet. Pleased with herself, she pulled the necklace of rectangular squares from inside her dress and squeezed it so hard the rectangles' edges almost cut her palm. Harriet didn't have a thing to worry about, Vivianne thought. Because Vivianne had all the insurance she needed to shield herself when the shit hit the fan.

CHAPTER 1

"Baby. Hey, baby," said the brother in the acid-green track suit and gold chains who was desperately trying to get my sister Allegra's attention. Allegra and I were having lunch at Estelle's, our uncle Alex's restaurant that I hostess at part-time. Actually, it would be more accurate to say we were *trying* to have lunch. Ever since we'd arrived, not a minute had gone by without someone approaching our table to talk to Allegra or get her autograph. Many people stopped by just to bask in the glow of my sister, and up until now, she'd been loving every minute of it. Now don't get me wrong, I'm not jealous of my beautiful baby sister. Really, I'm not. Well, maybe just a little. But these folks were interrupting my mealtime, and that is just not cool.

Allegra frowned and rolled her eyes before turning to reply to the persistent man who'd been trying to get her attention for the past five minutes. He didn't seem at all fazed by the fact that she'd been totally ignoring him.

"Yes, can I help you?" she asked, flashing him a low-watt smile and flipping a piece of her long honey-highlighted hair over her shoulder.

"Yeah," the brother said, grinning with a mouthful of yellowish, crooked teeth. I cringed as he came over to our table. Up close I could see that his face was a mass of razor bumps and my own face hurt just looking at him.

"Ain't you that Freaky Deaky chick? The one from that video?" Allegra's smile froze on her face at the mention of her first acting gig and the unwanted nickname that had resulted from it. I had to quickly turn away before she caught the big grin that had suddenly popped up on my mug.

Eight years ago, right after she graduated from high school, Allegra had hopped a bus to L.A. to pursue her dream of becoming an actress, a singer or a model. She wasn't real picky. In fact, whatever would allow her to do what she does best, which is being the center of attention, was fine by her. Almost immediately upon arriving in town, Allegra landed the starring role in a singer named Antoine's first music video. The song was called "Freaky Deaky." It was an annoying little ditty set to the music of "Old MacDonald," and even included the *e-i-e-i-o*'s. Amazingly, it became an instant hit and even spawned a dance craze.

The Freaky Deaky dance was a combination of the Hustle and the Twist, with some Funky Chicken thrown in for good measure. For about four months, dance floors in clubs all across the country were filled with foolish-looking people who were frantically spinning and clapping, twisting and flapping as though their underwear had caught on fire. Not only was the dance ridiculous looking, it could be hazardous to those unfortunate enough to be dancing near the uncoordinated or directionally challenged. Antoine, a rather homely brother with an overbite and a high-top fade, Freaky Deaked his way to the top of the charts, and my sister, with whom he conveniently fell in love and made one of his backup singers, was his Freaky Deaky queen.

But as with all good things, and even the not so good ones, it didn't last long. Antoine's next single, "Googley Woogley," tanked, and he and Allegra's fifteen minutes of fame, as well as their relationship, was over. And that was just fine by my parents, who had quickly grown tired of being asked about their Freaky Deaky daughter. It was fine by Antoine, too. Seems Antoine's overbearing mama was the one who wanted him to be a star. Antoine wanted to be a dentist and left the limelight willingly for dental school.

Allegra cleared her throat and took a sip of water before replying. "Yes, that was me. But that was a long time ago."

"Oh, I wasn't tryin' to crack on you, girl. That song was the jam back in the day. I just wondered if it was you, that's all. You still fine as hell. You ever get another job?"

Unable to suppress a giggle, I coughed to try and play it off as Allegra swung around to glare at me.

"I'm on *Hollywood Vibe*," she replied smugly, turning up her capped smile to its full brilliance. Antoine was her dentist now.

"What's *Hollywood Vibe*? Is that some kinda vitamin? I bet that's some good shit. Can I get some? Is that how you stay so fine?" asked the man. He was hanging over our table trying to look down Allegra's top. She leaned back in her chair and I grabbed my steak knife in case I had to protect my sibling.

"Hellooo. *Hollywood Vibe* is an entertainment news show, thank you. You know, like *Entertainment Tonight.* I'm one of the correspondents."

I couldn't believe my sister was more insulted that he didn't know about her current claim to fame than she was at the fact he was trying to get a peek at her boobs. An ample bosom is the only thing Allegra and I have in common besides DNA. Allegra is tall and slim like my mother, Uncle Alex and my late grandfather. She's undeniably the beauty in the family while I got the smart label and, depending on which way my scale is swinging, the chunky label.

Allegra's admirer was looking confused. "Naw, I ain't hip to the *Hollywood Vibe* thang, girl. See, I just got out the joint last week. I just wanted to holla at you," he said, glancing nervously at me as I tapped the steak knife against my plate, no doubt reliving some unpleasant prison experience. "You stay fine, you hear," he said and then puckered up and made a loud kissing noise that sounded like a fart. We both rolled our eyes as he walked away.

"Just got out the joint my ass," I said, tossing the knife on my now-cold steak. "The loony bin is probably more like it."

"I get approached by all kinds of nuts, Kendra. It's just a hazard of the business," Allegra said nonchalantly, flipping another strand of hair over her shoulder. Unlike me, with my short, no-nonsense do, Allegra wore her hair long and bone-straight with those honey-blond highlights.

"None of them are dangerous, are they?" I asked starting to feel concerned. Allegra had a way of tap dancing on my nerves, but the thought of anybody hurting her scared me to death.

"You sound just like Mama and, no, none of them are dangerous. I'm a lowly correspondent on a second rate entertainment news show, not Halle Berry." We both laughed.

"It won't always be that way. You're going places, Allie. This *Hollywood Vibe* thing is just a stepping stone." I was doing my best to be supportive, but I instantly regretted my comments.

"That's why you've got to help me, Kendra," Allegra whispered, looking around to make sure no one was listening. The nearest people to us in the restaurant were several booths away and would have had to have bionic hearing to be able to hear what we were saying.

"Vivianne DeArmond is going to ruin my career before it even gets off the ground. That's why I need your help." Allegra dropped her chin to her chest and her long hair fell around her face like a curtain. It was a sulky little move that never failed to get her her way with the men in our family. She did it so much that it had become a reflex. Being away from home for so long she'd obviously forgotten that this ploy had never worked on me. I stared at her silently until she remembered this fact and lifted her head up, giving me a sheepish look.

"Don't you think you're being a little melodramatic?" I asked calmly. Allegra sighed angrily and snatched her napkin off her lap and threw in on her plate.

"Hell, no, I'm not overreacting. I could lose my job, Kendra. I was sent here to get an interview with a has-been actress who hasn't made a movie in twenty years and is being awarded a lifetime achievement award by a two-bit film festival that nobody has ever heard of. She's acting like she's Greta Garbo with all this 'I want to be alone' crap. Her assistant won't let me anywhere near her. She should be happy anybody would want to interview her ass. Who the hell remembers Vivianne DeArmond, anyway?"

I did. Vivianne DeArmond might not have been the greatest actress in the world, but she was one of the first black actresses to make a mark in Hollywood and was easily one of the most beautiful. She'd been born Annie Burns in Willow, and she was one of our few claims to fame. Even though she wasn't nearly as well known as Lena Horne and Dorothy Dandridge, Vivianne DeArmond had starred in numerous independent films in the fifties and sixties and was a favorite of experimental French filmmaker, Jacques St. Marchand. Her most famous role was in St. Marchand's 1959 cult noir classic, *Asphalt City,* in which she played femme fatale Pearly Monroe. Vivianne's last role had been a blink-and-you'll-miss-her part in a low-budget horror movie in the late seventies called *Demon Kitty,* about a spinster who discovered her beloved tabby cat was possessed by the devil. Vivianne played a voodoo priestess who tried to exorcise the demon from the cat. She's on screen for all of five minutes before she's killed when the possessed feline, who incidentally looked about as menacing as Garfield in a snit, coughed up a giant flesh-eating hairball on her. It was an extremely undignified end to an otherwise respectable career.

"Why would *Hollywood Vibe* send you here to get an interview with a woman who doesn't want to be interviewed? Wouldn't they have known this before they sent you out here?" Allegra shifted nervously in her seat and wouldn't look me in the eye. "All right, Allie, out with it. What have you done?"

"Look, when I got this gig I thought they'd just be sending me to cover movie premiers and award shows and I'd get to wear designer gowns and rub elbows with directors and producers who might be interested in casting me. Turns out they actually want me to come up with story ideas. So, in the last production meeting, they asked me what stories I was working on. I didn't know what to say," she said, giving me a pitiful look. I started to ask her how Vivianne DeArmond's name came up, but she cut me off before I got a chance.

"Then I remembered you calling me the night before to ask me if I'd be making it home for Lynette's wedding and you mentioned the film festival and old washed-up Vivianne DeArmond getting an award. So, I told them I was from the same town as Vivianne and about her award and that I knew her and before I knew it—"

"They sent you out here to interview her only you can't get an interview because you *don't* know her and she doesn't want to be interviewed," I said, interrupting her.

"How was I supposed to know the executive producer is one of her biggest fans? They plan to feature my interview in a 'Whatever Happened to...' segment. I've done everything I can think of to get an interview, and she won't talk to me. You'd think she'd want to help another homegirl out."

"In a perfect world, maybe. But why do you thinks she owes you, someone she doesn't know from a hole in the wall, the time of day? You have no one to blame but yourself for this one, baby sister." She shot me a dirty look and turned to stare angrily out the window.

"I know I screwed up," she said finally, after picking at her half-eaten salad. "But, that doesn't change that fact that I still need to get that interview. Are you going to help me or not, Kendra?"

"And what exactly do you think I can do to help you get this interview?" Allegra perked up considerably and I felt a familiar feeling of dread creep up on me.

"Well," she whispered, leaning in close and gesturing for me to do the same. I did so reluctantly. "I know that Rosie's Cleaning Service cleans Vivianne DeArmond's house twice a week. I was thinking we could get hold of some uniforms and go to her house when the other cleaners are there. You can keep Vivianne's dragon-lady assistant busy while I approach Vivianne about interviewing her for the show." Allegra sat back and rubbed her hands together and smirked, obviously pleased with herself. She reminded me of a cartoon villainess who'd just sprung a goofy master plan to conquer the world on a reluctant henchman…me. I couldn't help it. I started laughing.

"What the hell is so funny?" she said, reverting to full neck-rolling, eye-popping, sister-girl mode.

"I'm sorry, Allie. But that's the stupidest thing I've heard in a long time," I said, wiping tears of laughter from my eyes.

"And why is that?" she asked in an icy tone that made me stop laughing immediately.

"First off, where are we going to get a hold of some of Rosie's uniforms? Secondly, don't you think the other cleaners are going to notice we don't belong there and blow the whistle on us? Thirdly, what's going to happen when Vivianne DeArmond realizes we're in her house uninvited and calls the police? Sorry, Allie but this little plan is only going to get us both arrested and you fired."

Believe me, it wasn't that I was above such behavior. I'd snuck into my share of places that I had absolutely no business being. But those were special circumstances involving murder and mayhem. Trespassing in the home of a reclusive actress to help my self-absorbed little sister get an interview that she'd lied to her boss about being able to get was something else entirely, especially since I'd promised my grandmother and my man to stay out of trouble.

"Then what do you suggest I do since you're so damned smart?" she asked, glaring at me. Allegra can get quite nasty when she's not getting her way. But I was still her big sister and not about to let her intimidate me.

"Why don't you just admit to your producer that Vivianne is being difficult and won't let you interview her?" I said, starting to feel mighty testy myself.

"Because I already told Noelle, my segment producer, that I lined up the interview. Besides, I'm not so sure Vivianne doesn't want to be interviewed. It's that assistant of hers, Harriet Randall, that won't let me anywhere near her. If I could just get her alone."

"Well, from what I've heard, Vivianne DeArmond is a first-class diva. Just tell your producer she changed her mind at the last minute."

"No! Haven't you been listening? I can't do that. Noelle is due in from L.A. tomorrow morning and she called and told me how excited her boss is to see my segment. I can't blow this, Kendra. My career depends on it."

"Then I really don't know what else to tell you, Allie." We stared at each other for a few minutes before she stood up and grabbed her purse.

"So, that's it then? You're really not going to help me?"

"Allie, I—" I began before she angrily threw up her hand cutting me off.

"Oh, just forget it, Kendra. I'll get the interview my damn self. I can see now that nothing has changed."

"Meaning what?" I had a good idea what she was going to say, but I could feel myself tensing up anyway.

"Meaning you're still jealous of me, aren't you? You can't stand the fact that I have an exciting career and a bright future ahead of me while you're stuck in this crappy little town working two dead-end jobs and getting nowhere fast."

I could hardly speak. How dare she talk about my life like that? I might only be a part-time English instructor with a GED program, supplementing my income hostessing at the very restaurant we were now eating in, but that didn't give her the right to trash my life. I was a teacher. I helped people get their general education diplomas. To date, her only achievement had been helping to create a goofy dance craze with a bucktoothed one-hit wonder.

"Oh, really," I said, crossing my arms and forcing myself to laugh when I really wanted to choke Allegra 'til she turned blue. "I seem to remember that *my* so-called dead-end jobs allowed me to loan *your* broke ass money when you were about to have your phone turned off last month. And furthermore—" Before I could finish, Alex walked up next to Allegra and put a hand on her shoulder. His face looked grim, but his voice was soft as butter. Alex never raises his voice, but I could tell he was angry over the scene we were making by the way his nostrils were flaring. He looked like a pissed-off horse.

"Ladies, what's the problem?" he asked, looking from Allegra to me and back again.

"Sorry, Uncle Alex, I gotta go. I'm a woman on a mission," Allegra said, giving Alex a quick peck on the cheek and tossing me a dirty look before heading out the door.

"It's so *moving* to see all the love flowing between my two nieces," he said sarcastically.

I stuck my tongue out at him.

When I arrived home a few hours later, I saw that Allegra's stuff was gone. No big surprise. I wasn't pressed. She'd only been staying with me because Mama wouldn't give her a key, let her come and go as she pleased and expected her to be in the house by the time she went to bed, which was around ten o'clock. Mama had an excellent memory when it came to the misconduct of her children and granddaughters and hadn't forgotten the time when she'd caught a sixteen-year-old Allegra dry-humping the captain of the football team on her good living-room couch. Allegra still hadn't shaken the "fast" label that Mama had tagged her with after that incident, which wasn't helped at all by the whole "Freaky Deaky" episode, nor had she earned back Mama's trust enough to be issued a key. So, she'd decided to stay with me. I figured she'd gone back to stay with Mama, claiming that I, her jealous, less-than-fabulous sister, was making life hard for her. But an evening of watching Lawrence Welk reruns with Mama and she'd be on my doorstep once again.

I spent the rest of my afternoon making the final arrangements for my best friend Lynette Martin-Gaines's bridal shower later that evening. Lynette and her fiancé, Greg Hull, were getting married in a week and I, being the maid of honor, was hosting her shower at the Red

Dragon Chinese Restaurant's party room. I was expecting about twenty-five of Lynette's friends and family members to show up and prayed everything would go off without any major drama. The source of my concern was three of Lynette's bridesmaids—Georgette Combs and Celeste and Cecile Warner—whom I hadn't hit it off with when I'd met them at Lynette and Greg's engagement party. The three had tried unsuccessfully to stir up conflict in the form of a fist fight between Lynette and me. I was hoping against hope that they wouldn't be able to make it to the party, but to my extreme disappointment they were the first three to RSVP.

I'd just stepped out of the shower and was lathering lotion on when my phone rang. It was Carl, my sweetie.

"Hey, I just got out of the shower. Why don't you come over and put lotion on my—"

"Uh, Kendra we need to talk," he said, sounding serious. Obviously this wasn't a social call. Carl's a lawyer and his lawyer vibe was radiating through the phone.

"Uh-oh. What's wrong?" I asked, feeling uneasy.

"It's your sister," he said simply. Envisioning Allegra lying dead in a ditch, my fingers clutched the lotion bottle so hard that half the contents spurted out onto my leg. I felt my throat start to close up, eliciting a strangled yelp that I barely realized had come from me.

"She's okay, Kendra," he said quickly. "I didn't mean to scare you."

"Then what's wrong?"

"I got a call from Allegra about an hour ago. She got

picked up by the police for trespassing on Vivianne DeArmond's property."

"What!" I shouted.

"Yeah. Apparently she was in Vivianne DeArmond's house, dressed as one of the cleaners, and was trying to interview her. Ms. DeArmond's assistant called the police."

"Where is she now?" I said through gritted teeth. I couldn't believe she'd actually gone through with her knuckleheaded plan.

"Well, I managed to convince Ms. DeArmond not to press charges. The police gave her a strong warning to stay away from Vivianne DeArmond and released her into my custody. An officer escorted us back to Ms. DeArmond's house, so Allegra could get her rental car, and I followed her to your grandmother's."

"Thanks, Carl. I swear I don't know what I'm going to do with her."

"Don't be too hard on her, Kendra. I seem to remember a certain person who's trespassed herself on plenty—"

"All right, babe. I'll talk to you later," I said, hanging up before he could take me on a trip down memory lane.

I finished getting ready for the bridal shower. As I pulled the dress I was planning to wear to the party out of the closet, my hand brushed against the hideous Smurf-blue, sequin-encrusted maid-of-honor dress with the big bow on the back that Lynette had picked for me to wear in the wedding. Usually, I shuddered every time I looked at the monstrosity. But I was too busy fuming about Allegra almost getting arrested, as well as feeling a little hurt that she'd called Carl instead of me. Then another more disturbing thought popped into my head, and I put my thumb clean through the thigh of a brand-new pair of panty hose.

Why in the hell did Allegra have my man's phone number?

CHAPTER 2

Lynette's shower was in full swing by eight that evening. The Red Dragon's party room was decorated with silver and white balloons, and the tables were adorned with purple silk tablecloths and beautiful floral arrangements of purple peonies and lilies. The guests had cooperated for the most part and were wearing the hats I'd picked up at the thrift store. Instead of the standard goofy paper party hats, I'd opted for vintage ones with feathers and bows. Alex had generously donated hors d'oeuvre trays from the restaurant, and Mama had made an assortment of desserts, including her famous lemon cake. I was pleased with the way everything had turned out. Not that I was getting much of a chance to enjoy it. I'd spent most of my time attending to every detail and making sure the guests and the bride to be were having a good time. Every once in a while I'd glance over at Georgette Combs and the twins, Celeste and Cecile Warner, who were huddled together in a far corner, to make sure they were behaving themselves. Aside from the alcohol-loving twins complaining bitterly to anyone who'd listen that, "It ain't no real party without liquor," and Georgette accidentally popping balloons with her freakishly long talonlike finger nails, they seemed to be behaving themselves.

"Where's Allie, Kendra?" Asked an annoyed voice behind me. I turned slowly, not really wanting to deal with the asker of the question, Mama, whom I'd purposely been avoiding since the party started. As far I knew, she didn't know about Allegra being picked up for trespassing, and I wanted to keep it that way. I also didn't feel like getting into why she'd left my place to stay with Mama.

"I haven't seen her since we had lunch earlier," I replied truthfully trying my best to look innocent. Mama eyed me suspiciously and I felt myself start to sweat. "You know how Allie is, Mama," I said quickly. "She probably just wants to make an entrance."

I sincerely hoped she hadn't ignored the warning the police had given her and gone back out to Vivianne DeArmond's house. Surely she wasn't that stupid, was she? Then I thought back to when Allegra was little and saw *Willie Wonka and the Chocolate Factory* on TV, after which she asked for an Oompa Loompa for Christmas for three years in a row. To this day, she's still a little fuzzy as to why she couldn't have one. My heart sank.

"You haven't done anything to upset her have you?"

"What?" was all I managed to get out.

"I noticed her stuff sitting on my back porch when I left for the party. I hope you two aren't arguing, 'cause she's only in town for a short time, Kendra. I hope you're not ruining her visit."

I could feel myself start to do a slow burn. Why did she

automatically think any problem between Allie and me would be my fault? Unbelievable. I didn't trust myself to speak. Fortunately, I saw Lynette standing in a corner all by herself looking sad and a tiny bit like Little Bo Peep in her big straw party bonnet. I excused myself, rather coolly, and went to see what was up with my best friend who wasn't looking anything like a happy bride to be.

"Everything okay?" I asked, grabbing Lynette's hand and giving it a squeeze.

"Of course. Everything looks great, Kendra. Thank you so much," she said, perking up. But her smile looked strained and didn't reach her eyes.

"Then why are you over here in the corner looking pitiful?"

"Girl, I'm just thinking about all the stuff I have to do before next week and I'm wondering how I'm going to get it all done. India's dress needs to be altered again. This is the third time. She's grown two inches and gained ten pounds since her first fitting. Monty's pouting because he's going to miss his friend Derrick's birthday party at Go Cart Land, which happens to be the same day as the wedding. And my mother is working my last nerve as usual. Men have it so easy. All they have to do is show up." It sounded reasonable enough, but I couldn't shake the feeling that whatever was bothering Lynette had nothing to do with her kids and mother.

"Oh, is that all," I said, laughing, "I thought maybe Talon Woman and the Double Lush Twins were giving you a hard time." She gave me a half-hearted laugh as we looked over to the far corner of the room and watched Georgette, Celeste and Cecile gorged themselves on food. Both twins had crumbs cascading down the front of their shirts and Georgette's mouth was smeared with cocktail sauce. We both cringed and quickly looked away as the twins took turns taking swigs from what looked like a forty-ouncer of beer that Celeste had pulled from her big purse.

As Lynette and I stood talking, her mother Justine joined us and I noticed Lynette visibly tense up. Justine had opted not to wear one of the party hats and her long, curly, black weave was hanging down her back like a horse's mane, as usual. She was wearing a tight denim jumpsuit and her feet were crammed into high-heeled, open-toed mules that were too small and left almost an inch of her heel hanging off the back. Her makeup was dramatic and overdone, as was her usual style. Justine was in her fifties but prided herself on looking much younger. She'd been known to tell her boyfriends that Lynette was her sister. Justine was holding a plate of food and eyeing it suspiciously, as though the food was plotting to make her fat.

"Hey, Ms. Martin. You having a good time?" I braced myself for her answer. Justine is moody as hell and you never knew if she's going to kiss you or cuss you out.

"Doing just fine, Kendra. You really outdid yourself with this party, girlfriend. Everything looks so nice," she said, a tad too sarcastically for my taste. Upon arriving at the party, Justine had made her distaste over the vintage hats I'd brought known by the way her face frowned up.

"No telling whose head those hats have been on," I'd overheard her saying to Lynette's future sister-in-law, Liz.

"Thank you," I replied, ignoring her tone.

"I just hope this isn't all for nothing. Lynette's first marriage lasted about as long as it takes a relaxer to grow out of my head!" She threw her head back and laughed loudly at her own joke.

I expected Lynette to be pissed, but instead she looked like she was about to cry. Justine was referring to Lynette's first marriage to Lamont Gaines. Lynette and Lamont had eloped right after we graduated from high school. The marriage lasted five years and resulted in two children, Lamont, Jr., and India.

"I hope my baby girl has better luck this time around. Greg's a good man, not like that other rooty-poot Negro she was married to, so maybe she'll be able to hold on to this one. I guess we'll see, won't we?" She flounced off to go bug someone else. Before I could console my friend, who now looked even sadder and more pitiful than before, I heard a loud buzz of greetings and excitement as Allegra made her grand entrance.

Much to my dismay, most everyone in the room had gathered around my sister, who was wearing the hell out of a figure-hugging fuschia halter dress. Her highlighted hair was a vision of poker-straight perfection and fell to her shoulders. Three-inch ankle-strap sandals made her even taller than her normal height of five foot nine. Her makeup was minimal, as she had nearly flawless skin, and only needed a little lipstick to accentuate her full lips.

In other words, Allegra was a goddess. I tugged self-consciously at my sleeveless, green silk wrap dress that, until my sister had made her appearance, I'd thought I looked really good in. Suddenly I felt as green as my dress, which bugged the hell out of me. Usually, I'm proud of my sister. But ever since she'd arrived in town I was realizing how much easier it was to be proud of her when she was clear across the country in L.A.

I waited until Allegra had finished her hellos and was putting her gift on the gift table to approach her. She looked less than thrilled to see me.

"Carl called and told me what happened. What in the world were you thinking?" I whispered. Mama was staring at us from across the room so I planted a smile on my face.

"Look, I told you how much I needed that interview. You wouldn't help me so I did what I had to do," she replied sweetly. She sure wasn't acting like someone who'd been picked up by the police and was in danger of losing her job.

"So, what are you going to do now?" I asked.

"Don't worry, sis, I've got it all under control," she said, smiling. I gave her a doubtful look.

"Please tell me you aren't going near Vivianne DeArmond again. If she wanted to be interviewed, she wouldn't have let her assistant call the cops on you."

"You know, you really need to loosen up, Kendra. That's part of your whole problem," she said, walking away from me to congratulate Lynette. I started to follow her, but Mama joined them and I decided to keep my distance. If Allegra thought I was a tight ass now, wait until I grilled her about how she got Carl's phone number.

"That your sister?" asked a voice behind me. I turned to find myself face-to-face with Georgette, Celeste and Cecile. Great. This was all I needed.

"Yes," I answered, trying hard to be polite. I just didn't like these women and, despite all my efforts to exclude alcohol from the party, the twins were noticeably drunk.

"Wow. You guys don't look anything alike," squeaked Georgette in her high-pitched Minnie Mouse voice.

"Yeah, y'all got the same mama and daddy?" slurred one of the twins. I couldn't be bothered to try and tell them apart even though one had red hair.

"That's usually how it works," I replied sarcastically.

"Well, we can see who it worked out better for in the looks department, huh?" said the other inebriated twin. All three walked away laughing as I felt my face burn.

Later that night, after the shower was long over, I sat in my apartment with my bare feet propped up on the trunk that served as my coffee table, nursing a glass of wine and thanking God that the whole ordeal was over. I had hired a group of male strippers to perform at the shower as a surprise to Lynette. I should have known not to hire strippers sight unseen, especially ones called O Boys. When a group of five elderly black men dressed in suits arrived, whose combined age had to be close to five hundred, I assumed they'd taken a wrong turn and were looking for the main restaurant.

"Sir, the restaurant is that big building out front," I said politely to the man nearest me. He squinted at me though his bifocals.

"No, this is the right place. This is the party room and we're here to party, girly girl," said the man shaking his narrow hips.

I could do nothing but stare as they plugged in a boom box and started stripping off their suits to the sounds of James Brown's "Get Up Offa That Thing." I found out what the O stood for: *old*. Apparently they didn't have enough money for the two extra letters on their business card that I'd found tacked up on the community bulletin board at B&S Hair Design and Nail Sculpture, when I'd gone to get my hair cut a month ago. Each garment of clothing the men shed revealed toothpick arms, spindly legs, wrinkled skin, sunken chests, gray hairs and G-strings exposing flat asses that wouldn't have held a dollar bill even if any of us had wanted to place one between their saggy butt cheeks. And to top it off, they couldn't dance, at least not any current dances. We all watched in silent amazement while the old dudes formed a line and started trying to do the Freaky Deaky. The drunken twins decided they wanted to get in on the act, too, and started dancing and stripping, as well. The party quickly turned to chaos. But at least it seemed to bring Lynette out of her funk and she laughed until fat tears rolled down her cheeks. In fact, the only ones who weren't laughing were Mama, who looked mortified, and Allegra, who probably thought I'd put them up to doing the dance that launched her C-list career. Mama glared at me until

Allegra, who was more than happy to leave, led her out of the party room and took her home.

I was half-asleep when I heard a knock at my door. I quickly answered it. It was Carl. He'd called when I'd got home and I told him all about the shower fiasco. He took one look at my face and gave me a sympathetic chuckle. Instead of speaking, he pulled me into his arms and I buried my face now into his chest enjoying his warmth and breathing in his signature scent, Obsession for Men. Then we started kissing and shedding clothes. I shoved him down on the couch, straddled him, and was reaching behind my back to unhook my bra when my door flew open revealing Allegra, with all of her luggage.

"Hey, sis, I'm back," she shouted and then froze upon seeing Carl and me in a state of aroused undress. We all stared at each other for a few awkward seconds until Allegra mumbled an apology and headed back to my bedroom with her stuff. Her openly appreciative glance at Carl's partially nude body wasn't lost on me, especially since he couldn't seem to keep his eyes off her, either.

The next morning I was with Mama sitting in Cartwright Auditorium, named for Willow's first mayor, Jacob Cartwright, awaiting the start of the Starburst Film Festival Committee's Lifetime Achievement Award ceremony for Vivianne DeArmond. I looked around the packed auditorium at the other attendees and was surprised that the crowd consisted of people from all walks of life and spanned many generations. Having been out of the spotlight for over twenty years apparently hadn't diminished Vivianne's memory as far as her loyal fans were concerned. We were currently watching a film retrospective of her career which, I was amused to notice, didn't include any mention of *Demon Kitty*. Before the start of the ceremony, Vivianne had signed autographs for her numerous fans, some who'd come from out of state, for about an hour in the auditorium's lobby. I didn't stand in the long line for an autograph, but I did get a good look at Vivianne, or Vivi as she's known to her fans, and was stunned to see how gorgeous she still was at sixty-five.

She was the epitome of graciousness, dressed in an elegant cream-colored pantsuit that accentuated her caramel-colored skin. Her suspiciously still-dark-brown hair was piled in curly disarray on top of her head with long tendrils framing a wrinkle-free, heart-shaped face. For someone who was known for her diva ways, she was on her best behavior and being quite personable and charming to her fans. The only time she got testy was when a nerdy-looking middle-aged white guy with thick horn-rimmed glasses tried to come behind the table she was sitting at and hug her.

"I don't think so, young man," said Vivianne with a look of disdain. She looked at the man's outstretched hand as though it was a wasp trying to land on her shoulder. "Please step back behind the table or I refuse to give you an autograph." Her graciousness apparently didn't extend to being touched.

The poor nerdy guy looked as if he might cry, but he

complied with the diva's demands and stepped back behind the table. He rushed off looking quite embarrassed after getting his autograph.

It was after this that her assistant, Harriet Randall, a squat sour-faced black woman with the demeanor of an army sergeant, called a halt to the autographs and led Vivianne away to her dressing room. Allegra hadn't exaggerated when she'd described Harriet. It was no wonder she couldn't get an interview.

When I'd gotten up that morning, after a sex- and Carl-free night spent sleeping on my couch, Allegra was already dressed and gone, leaving my bedroom looking as if a tornado had torn through it. I really wasn't in the mood to be bothered with her anyway, but I couldn't help wondering where she was off to so early in the morning. After a breakfast of cold cereal, I picked up Mama, who was still acting a little frosty over the shower, and we headed off to the ceremony. I was worried Allegra would show up, trying to get an interview, and get herself in trouble again. But, by the time the ceremony started, I was relieved that she didn't appear to be anywhere around.

"Your mom is gonna be so sorry she wasn't able to get home for this. She's a big Vivi fan, too," Mama whispered during the retrospective, causing some die-hard Vivi fans to shush her.

My parents lived in Florida and had recently left to go backpacking around Europe, a dream trip they'd been planning for over a year. Witnessing an aging actress get an award hardly compared to the trip of a lifetime. But I nodded in agreement anyway.

"I thought Allie was going to be here," said Mama.

"She's probably here someplace," I replied, ignoring the irritated disembodied sighs coming from around me. Mama was craning her neck and peering through the dark auditorium trying to spot her granddaughter. I was so tempted to tell her about Allegra getting caught in Vivianne's house, but decided it wasn't my place, and, besides, that would be tattling.

The film retrospective ended and the lights came back on. People were on their feet applauding and chanting "Vivi! Vivi! Vivi!" I looked toward the front of the auditorium expecting to see Vivianne smiling and waving like a beauty queen. But she was nowhere to be seen. Then a loud piercing fire alarm sounded and cut through the cheering and clapping like a knife. I didn't see or smell any smoke. Was this a joke? Everyone was looking confused and I heard a chorus of groans and cursing as we were instructed to leave the auditorium quickly by an annoyed-looking member of the film festival committee. As I was guiding Mama through the jostling crowd, I happened to turn and look down the long hallway that led to the basement dressing rooms used by performers. I saw Allegra run up the basement steps looking dazed and terrified. I called out to her, but in the loud commotion she didn't hear me, and I watched as she turned and rushed out a nearby exit. Once outside, I looked around for her and spotted her rental car tearing out of the parking lot.

I did not have a good feeling about this. Since Allegra had come from the direction of the dressing rooms, then she must have been trying to see Vivianne again. And Harriet Randall must have called the police again. At least that was the only excuse I could come up with for my sister looking so scared. I was relieved that Mama hadn't seen her, but I noticed she was still scanning the crowd looking for her.

"I wonder how much longer we're going to have to wait to get back in?" asked Mama, after we'd been waiting in the parking lot for fifteen minutes.

Most of the other attendees were also still waiting but many people had left in huff. I really wanted to leave myself to find out what was up with Allegra but Mama, being a movie buff and proud of Vivianne DeArmond's connection to Willow, wouldn't hear of it. The fire department had arrived five minutes earlier and we were waiting for the all clear, when a nervous-looking male film festival committee member addressed the restless crowd.

"Um, excuse me ladies and gentlemen," began the man in a gruff voice, looking like he might throw up. What in the world was going on?

"Due to an unfortunate circumstance, the award ceremony has been cancelled. We're going to have to ask that you all leave the premises at once," the man said, wiping sweat from his bald head with a handkerchief.

After a minute of stunned silence, everyone started talking at once. The committee member had a crowd of angry people surrounding him that he was unsuccessfully trying to placate.

"I came all the way from Pittsburgh for this," exclaimed one angry woman, pointing a chubby finger at the man's chest.

"I took off from work to be here today," said a handsome older black man wearing a T-shirt that read: Viva Vivi! But the committee member remained mum as to why the ceremony had been cancelled.

Some people, not needing to be told twice, jumped in their cars and took off. I noticed one of them was the nerdy-looking man who'd tried to hug Vivianne during the autograph signing. He looked around nervously before hopping in a beat-up white VW van and taking off. I'd heard about many instances of Vivianne's diva behavior, including holding up production on a movie set for hours after getting a paper cut while going over her script, and wondered if she was up to her old tricks again. I prayed that's all it was.

"Oh, come on, Kendra. Take me home. I don't have time for this mess. I've got stuff I could be doing." I silently followed Mama to my car, unable to shake the uneasy feeling that something was terribly wrong and wondering what my sister had to do with it.

This feeling intensified as Mama and I were pulling out of the auditorium's parking lot and a couple of police cars and an ambulance arrived.

"I wonder what happened?" asked Mama, looking back. I didn't reply. My mouth was suddenly very dry.

When I pulled up into Mama's driveway, Allegra's rented black Toyota was parked with the front bumper scraping the closed garage door. Mama hopped out and inspected the damage to her garage door. Besides the scrape in the paint, the aluminum door was dented, and looked to have been knocked off track. I could tell she was highly pissed.

"I bet that silly girl wasn't even paying attention! Always looking at herself in the mirror. And she *will* be paying to get my garage door fixed! You can bank on that." I followed Mama through the side gate into the backyard where we could hear someone crying hysterically. It was Allegra. She was sitting on the porch step sobbing. When she spotted Mama, she flew off the porch straight into her arms.

"Allie? Baby what's wrong?" Mama said, patting Allegra's back and giving me a bewildered look. We both knew this couldn't be about a broken garage door. Allegra usually tries to sweet-talk her way out of any wrong doing she's guilty of. She tried to talk, but we couldn't understand a word she was saying through her hiccupping sobs.

Mama tossed me her house keys. "Go get her some water." I went to do as I was told and took a big gulp of cold water myself before going back outside. I was almost too afraid to know what was wrong.

After taking a few sips of the water, Allegra finally calmed down enough to talk.

"It was so horrible, Mama," she said shaking her head at the memory. "Vivianne DeArmond. She's...she's—" She started to sob again. Mama had had enough and grabbed her by the shoulders giving her a good shake.

Allegra twisted free of her grasp and blurted out, "She's dead, okay! Somebody killed her!"

Mama gasped and stared at me.

"Come on. We need to go inside," I said, ushering my still-crying sister and my shocked grandmother into the house.

Once we were all seated around the kitchen table, Allegra finally told us what happened. As it turned out, I was right to be uneasy.

"I found a message written in the dirt on the hood of my rental car yesterday after Carl and I left the police station and I went back to Vivianne's house. It was—"

"Police station? What in the world were you doing at the police station?" Mama interrupted. Allegra's eyes got big and she looked at me. Crap. I wasn't about to let her drag me into her little scheme from yesterday. It had been *her* master plan, so she could explain it to Mama.

"Allegra can explain that to you when she's finished. Go ahead," I said, gesturing for her to continue.

"She better explain," Mama mumbled.

"Uh, anyway, like I said, there was a message on my hood. It said 'Call me', and there was a phone number. So, I called the number and it was Vivianne DeArmond. I couldn't believe it! She told me she wanted to give me an interview but she could only spare me a few minutes and she didn't want to be on camera. She told me she could talk to me this morning at eleven-thirty before she accepted her award. She said not to be late or to tell anyone about the interview." She stopped talking and took another sip of water.

"I got to her dressing room on time and knocked on the door. But no one answered so I walked in anyway. She was lying on floor. She was dead!"

"Are you sure she was dead, Allie? Maybe she just fainted," Mama said.

"No, she had a knife in her back and there was blood on the floor and on the walls," Allegra said. She wrapped her arms around her as if she was suddenly cold.

"What did you do after that?" I asked, hoping maybe she'd told someone about Vivianne before fleeing a murder scene.

"What did I do? What do you mean what did I do? The fire alarm went off and I got the hell out of there and came straight here. What was else was I supposed to do? I wasn't going to stick around, especially after what happened yesterday." Allegra looked at me again and Mama puffed up.

"One of you needs to tell me what exactly happened yesterday, and I mean right now!"

When she realized I wasn't going to do her explaining for her, Allegra told Mama all about sneaking into Vivianne's house and getting picked up by the police. I made sure she didn't leave anything out. Mama sat shaking her head and was silent for along time.

"So you just took off and didn't even bother telling anyone or trying to get help?" Mama asked incredulously.

"I was scared, Mama, the police will think I had something to do with it because of what happened yesterday."

"Oh, Allie." Mama sighed, shaking her head.

"What!" She huffed, looking at both of us like we were the crazy ones. Apparently, I was going to have to enlighten her.

"How do you think this is going to look when the police find out you were there and fled the scene? I saw you leave the auditorium and I know I couldn't have been the only one who did." I realized my mistake immediately when Mama's head whipped around and she shot me a venomous stare.

"Well, why in the devil didn't you tell *me* you'd seen your sister? You knew I was looking for her."

"I didn't want to worry you because I didn't know what was going on," I said meekly.

"Like I'm not worried now?" She leaned back in her chair dramatically and pressed a hand to her forehead like we were going to be the death of her. Anyone wondering where Allegra gets her drama gene wouldn't have far to look.

After a few uncomfortable minutes of silently watching Mama frown and shake her head and Allegra stare stony-faced and teary-eyed out the kitchen window, I made a suggestion that should have been obvious to anyone with good sense.

"Come on. We need to go to the police station so Allie can give them a statement." Mama mumbled in agreement and we got up from the table but Allegra just sat there and looked at us like she didn't understand English. We waited for her to get up but she didn't move.

"Allegra Janine Clayton, get your behind up from that table so we can go get this straightened out!" Mama said in a voice that dared my sister to disobey and took me back to childhood. In my case it had usually been, "Kendra Janelle Clayton, get your behind out there and cut me a switch!" I cringed at the memory.

But Allegra still didn't budge. Uh-oh. I thought Mama might combust.

"Did you hear me, girl?" Mama leaned down and got right in Allegra's face. Her voice was a low snarl.

"You want me to go cut a switch?" I offered hopefully, but was only answered with dirty looks from both of them.

"All right, if that's the way you want it. I'll just call the police and have them come over here." Mama headed for the wall phone in the pantry. Allegra burst into tears again.

"I don't wanna go to jail, Mama. I didn't do anything!" she wailed, as tears flowed freely down her face and a trickle of snot dripped from her nose. She ran a hand over her face smearing the tears and snot. Eew! She certainly didn't look like much of a goddess now.

My grandmother stared at me in defeat. She'd never been able to stand seeing Allegra in tears. If it had been me she'd have dragged me to the police station by the scruff of my neck. But I sensed now wouldn't be a good time to point this out. We both sat back down.

"Allie, this is exactly why you need to go down and tell them what happened. Now, how's it going to look if they have to track you down? Then you're really going to look guilty," I said softly, handing her a tissue from my purse.

She shook her head no and poked her lip out slightly like a sulky toddler. I groaned and laid my head down on the table.

"Come on, baby," Mama said, getting up and putting an arm around my stubborn little sister. She gently attempted to pull her to her feet. Allegra stiffened up and didn't move for a moment. It almost looked like Mama was trying to drag a reluctant dog by its leash. "Let's get you cleaned up. Then we can figure out what we're gonna do, okay?" Allegra finally stood up and allowed herself to be led to the bathroom. Mama tossed me a look that said "Think of something" over her shoulder. But I was way ahead of her.

Allegra might not want to listen to what we had to say, but there was one person who I knew she'd listen to. Even though I didn't want to think about the looks the two of them had given each other the night before, I got on the phone and called Carl anyway.

CHAPTER 3

In the year that Carl and I had been dating, I'd yet to really see him in full-on lawyer mode. It was fascinating to watch. Barely ten minutes had passed from the moment he'd arrived to the time he'd convinced Allegra to go with him to the police station, but, then again, Allegra loves men. She's one of those women who sees other women as competition and doesn't have many female friends. She had always gotten along much better with men since she didn't care whether they dressed better or were thinner than she was. Carl was apparently no exception. Standing in the middle of Mama's kitchen dressed in a charcoal-gray suit that framed his six-foot-one frame well, with a burgundy silk tie that had been loosened, a crisp white shirt against chocolate skin, and smelling good to boot, Carl was the very image of tall, dark and handsome, my sister's favorite type. Allegra quickly dried her tears and adopted an air of innocent fragility that made me want to kick her.

"So, does this make you my lawyer now?" Allegra asked, looking at Carl with big doe eyes. I sucked my teeth and Mama cut me a Your-sister-could-be-in-trouble-so-cut-the-crap look.

"Well, let's not jump the gun, Allegra, I'll certainly be present while you give your statement. But I imagine that should take care of it. Once you explain what happened, that should be the end of it. Now, you've told me everything, right?" Carl asked. We all looked at Allegra.

"There's nothing more to tell. I told you everything that happened," she said, getting up from the table and putting her water glass in the sink. Carl and Mama seemed satisfied she was telling the truth. I wished I shared their satisfaction. I knew better than anyone how sneaky Allegra can be. I prayed she'd told Carl the truth.

"Oh, and Kendra," Carl said, addressing me for the first time since he'd arrived. He must still be a little pissed over me abruptly changing my mind about jumping his bones the night before and sending him home with a boner. But there was no way I was having sex with him with my sister in the next room. Plus, after ogling her, I had a pretty good idea who he'd be thinking about while making love to me. He should be happy I didn't give him a fat lip to go along with his stiffy.

"I wouldn't be surprised if the police contact you and your grandmother for statements since you were both at the auditorium when the murder occurred. You two might want to come down to the station with us and go ahead and talk to them and get it over with."

"But we were in the auditorium. We didn't see a thing," Mama said.

"Doesn't matter. They're going to want to talk to everyone who was there," Carl said fixing his tie.

"And how would they even know we'd attended the ceremony?" I asked. The last thing I wanted to do was talk to the police if I didn't have to. There was a certain Willow police detective named Trish Harmon who wasn't a big fan of mine, and the feeling was very much mutual.

"We had to reserve our tickets for the ceremony, remember, Kendra? I bet our names are on a list. Carl's right. We need to go on down to the station with him and Allie." Mama got up and reached for her purse.

The doorbell rang and we watched as Mama hurried off to answer it. She returned seconds later with a white woman who looked to be in her late twenties. She had short, spiky hair a shade of bright red that couldn't possibly occur in nature, was rail-thin, and dressed in jeans, a white T-shirt and high-topped tennis shoes. When she spotted Allegra, she instantly smiled, revealing small white, pointy eyeteeth that made her look like a bride of Dracula.

"There you are," the woman said, walking over to embrace Allegra. But I noticed Allegra didn't seem all that pleased to see her visitor.

"Everyone, this Noelle Delaney, my segment producer at *Hollywood Vibe*," Allegra said, quickly pulling out of the embrace and causing Noelle to give her a curious look. We all exchanged subdued hellos.

"I'd just checked into my hotel when I heard about what happened to Vivianne DeArmond. It's all over the news. They said she was murdered. I've been trying to call you. Your cell phone must be turned off."

"I think I left my phone in my rental," Allegra mumbled, looking at the floor.

"Where's the crew? Out back?" Noelle asked, walking over to the back door and looking out into the empty backyard. I assumed she was talking about Allegra's camera crew, whom she'd sent back to L.A. Allegra looked panicky and remained silent.

"Please tell me you got the interview before someone stuck that knife in Ms. DeArmond?" Noelle asked, like it was no big deal, then seeing the shocked looks on all our faces tried to clean it up. "I'm sorry. I didn't mean to sound so insensitive. I'm just tired. I worked twelve hours yesterday then had to hop a plane out here at the crack of dawn. I'm running on empty."

"Ms. Delaney, Allegra is the one who found Vivianne's body," I said, since Allegra seemed to have lost her tongue.

"Oh, my God! Are you kidding? You found her? You poor kid! Are you okay?"

Someone once told me that Hollywood was home to legions of insincere and phony show-biz people. I was now a witness to this fact as I listened to the concern that spewed from Noelle lips and noticed that her words didn't quite match the glitter of excitement in her green eyes. She looked as if she'd just hit the entertainment-news mother lode.

Allegra finally spoke up and explained what had happened that morning, conveniently leaving out being picked up for trespassing the day before. When she told Noelle about having to go down to the police station to make a statement, Noelle looked a little worried, but I figured it had more do with negative publicity for *Hollywood Vibe* than concern for my sister.

"Can I ride to the station with you guys? I told my cab to go. I should probably be there, too," said Noelle.

"Sure, but it'll be a tight fit with all of us in my car," Carl said, looking at me for some reason. I'm no skinny Minnie, but surely he didn't think I'd be a danger to his car's shocks. I knew I was being overly sensitive, but why was I feeling like he didn't want me around?

"No problem. My car's here. I'll drive myself and meet you guys there." I watched as they all left and tried not to blow my top when I looked out the window and saw Allegra give Carl a seductive smile as he held the car door open for her. Flirting was as natural as breathing to my sister, but I didn't appreciate her doing it with my boyfriend.

I was pulling the back door shut when I heard a shrill chirping sound from inside my purse. It took me a second to realize what it was. It was my cell phone. Carl had given it to me for Christmas. I'd accepted the gift graciously, because I knew it had cost him a lot of money. But I don't need a cell phone, a new car, most definitely, but not a cell phone. I rarely used it, and especially not during peak calling hours, which, of course, it was now. This had better be important I thought, pressing the talk button.

"Hello."

"Kendra, it's me," said a small voice I barely recognized as my best friend's.

"Lynette?"

"Are you busy? Can you come over here, please?" I heard what sounded like sniveling.

"What's wrong? Is it one of the kids?"

"No, they're fine. I just…I just really need to talk to someone," she said dissolving into tears. Between her and my sister I was going to drown in a sea of tears.

"Lynette, honey, I'm on my way someplace important, but I'll be by just a soon as I—"

"The wedding's off, Kendra! I know you really didn't want to wear that dress anyway. So, now you don't have to."

"What happened?" I asked, but I was answered by the sound of the dial tone bleeping in my ear. I couldn't believe she'd hung up on me. Damn! Why did everyone's problems have to hit on the same day?

Figuring Allegra and Mama would be tied up with giving their statements, and hoping I wouldn't be missed for a while, I hopped in my little blue Nova (see, I told you I needed new car) and headed over to Lynette's.

Lynette and her kids lived with her mother Justine in a brick tri-level on Pickett Avenue. Six years ago, after catching her husband Lamont in bed with their babysitter, Lynette had moved back home and filed for divorce. Living with her mother was supposed to be temporary. But Justine usually found one reason or another to discourage Lynette from moving out. Free child care was the biggest reason Lynette had stayed at her mother's. Justine worked part-time and was able to take care of her grandkids while Lynette worked. The arrangement kept her from having to entrust her children to the care of strangers. I didn't blame her. After all, her last babysitter had fucked her husband.

I parked in front of the house and knocked on the door. Lynette answered it wearing a ratty-looking terry-cloth bathrobe. She'd recently taken out the braids she'd worn for the past two years and was wearing her long hair pulled into a fat braid that hung down her back. Thick gym socks were on her feet. She blew her nose on a wadded-up tissue and stepped aside to let me in.

"Now, what's all this about the wedding being off? Did you and Greg get into an argument?" I asked, looking around. No one else appeared to be home except Justine's terrier Coco who spun around in circles at my feet for attention. I bent down and stroked her back.

"Where's everyone at?"

"Ma's at work and the kids went to King's Island with the church youth group," she said, sinking down on the couch.

"Okay. So tell me what happened." I sat down next to her.

"Nothing happened," she said shrugging, "I just can't go through with it, that's all."

"Why?" I'd reached my tears-and-drama quota for the day with Allegra and had little sympathy left.

"Because I'm no good at marriage, that's why. Look what happened to my first marriage."

"Is this about what your mother said at the shower? She was just trying to be funny."

"No, she wasn't, Kendra. She was serious and she's right. I don't know if Greg will be any happier with me than Lamont was." She dabbed at the tears than had started to flow down her face again.

"Lynette, you and Lamont were teenagers when you ran off and got married. You were just kids. What the hell did the two of you know about being married?"

"There was more wrong with our marriage than us just being young," she said, looking uncomfortable. I waited for her to elaborate but she just blew her nose. I looked at my watch. Allegra, Carl, Mama and Noelle were probably at the station by now and wondering where the hell I was. I felt bad for my friend but I didn't have time for this.

"Meaning what?" I asked. I immediately regretted sounding so impatient when Lynette jumped up suddenly and glared at me.

"Excuse me if my problems are bothering you. I can tell you don't really want to be here so why don't you just step!"

"Look! I'm sorry, Lynette. You asked me to come over and I did. But now you're talking in circles. Just sit down and tell me what the hell is going on."

"All right," she said, plopping back down on the couch. "Sex, Kendra! The problem is sex!"

Uh-oh. I looked at her dubiously. "What about sex?" I asked. Did I really want to know about this? It didn't appear that I had a choice.

"Well, you know I'd never been with anyone before I married Lamont, right?"

"Yeah," I said, nodding for her to continue.

"I couldn't wait for our wedding night. I thought it would be like something out of a dream."

"And it wasn't," I said. I couldn't really blame Lynette for thinking her first time was going to be a multi-orgasmic delight. We'd both bought into that heaving-bosom-throbbing-manhood romance-novel crap as teenagers. But Lynette had never told me that her wedding night had been anything but wonderful.

"It was terrible. I mean, you can't expect a teenage boy to be a red-hot lover but, damn. He was pitiful, Kendra. It hurt. He had no rhythm in his stroke, and two minutes into it he'd start moaning and screaming like a girl and sweating like a pig. I had to fake these loud-ass dramatic orgasms just to get him to stop. Otherwise, he could go on forever. It was worse than watching paint dry. And in the five years we were married, it never got any better."

I had to look away so she wouldn't see me laughing, but I failed miserably. I'd never got to know Lynette's ex-husband Lamont Gaines very well, but I didn't have a hard time imagining his six-foot-four, two-hundred-and-forty-pound butt moaning and screaming like a porn star en route to the money shot.

"I'm glad you think my pain is so funny," she said, but I saw her own lips twitching and didn't feel so bad.

"The night I caught him with the babysitter I knew what was up before I even unlocked the door. I could hear his ass all the way down the hall." We were both laughing now.

"What happened after you caught him?"

"He had the nerve to tell me it was all my fault 'cause I wasn't satisfying his needs. But, hell, there was only so much I could stand. I would make up any excuse not to have to be with him. It's a wonder I managed to get pregnant once, let alone twice."

"Why didn't you tell me about any of this before?"

"I was too embarrassed. I just wanted to forget about it." I guess I couldn't blame her for that.

"Okay, I get it. Lamont was a piss-poor lover. What's that have to do with Greg?"

"There hasn't been anyone since Lamont, Kendra." It was a moment before it dawned on me what she was saying.

"You mean you and Greg haven't—" I began incredulously.

"Made love. No. We've never been together." I looked closely at her to see if she was kidding, but she was dead serious.

"Wow! You've been together for two years. I just assumed you two had been getting busy all this time. What's the problem?"

"It's not a lack of desire. I want Greg. I just keep thinking about how it was with Lamont. I feel so inexperienced. With Lamont, all I had to do was lie there with my legs open. It was all about him. I could have been a hole in the mattress for all he cared. I've never even had an orgasm, and I'm afraid Greg will be disappointed and be sorry he married me," she said in a small voice.

"You haven't told Greg about any of this?"

"No. When we first met I lied and told him I didn't

believe in premarital sex. He wasn't happy at first, believe me. I think he thought he could change my mind. We almost broke up. But after a while he got used to taking a lot of cold showers."

"Lynette, you really need to be discussing this with Greg. He's crazy about you, girl. I'm sure he'll understand. He's a great guy and—"

"I know he's great, Kendra. You don't need to tell me that. I'm just trying to save him from being disappointed."

"He's not going to be disappointed, Lynette. The man has waited two years for you. Doesn't that tell you something?" Lynette gave me a strange look and even though she didn't disagree, she didn't look quite convinced, either.

"How did life get so complicated?" she asked, getting up and tossing her soggy tissues in the wicker wastebasket by the TV. I watched as she picked up a framed photo from a group of pictures sitting on top of the TV. The picture was of the two of us as Girl Scouts taken when we were twelve. We were in our uniforms and had just gotten back from selling Girl Scout cookies when Justine decided she needed to immortalize the moment. The picture showed two slightly chubby, sulky-looking preteen girls whose chocolate-smeared lips and crumb-covered sashes bore testament to the fact that we'd eaten more cookies than we'd sold. Clearly, Justine had been trying to teach us a lesson.

"Remember those Girl Scout camping trips we used to go on and all the fun we used to have?" she asked, eyes gleaming. I took a quick peek at the clock on the wall before answering. I really needed to get going.

"Of course I remember," I said with more enthusiasm than I felt. I'm not the outdoors type and could remember nothing at all *fun* about sleeping in a tent, being eaten up by insects, and dining on burnt-up hot dogs and half-cold baked beans. The s'mores were nice, though.

"That was back when life was uncomplicated. We didn't really have anything to worry about, did we, Kendra?" She was looking sad again and I decided to excuse myself from her pity party or I could easily be there all afternoon.

I got up and gave her a big hug. "Why don't you come over tonight and we can order pizza and have a bottle of wine?"

She shrugged and smiled in half-hearted agreement. I gave her hand one last squeeze and told her I needed to get going. When I got to the door, I looked back and saw she was still staring at the Girl Scout picture with a funny look on her face.

When I finally arrived at the Willow police station about ten minutes later, Mama was sitting on a bench in the lobby while Noelle was about twenty feet away in a corner talking on her cell phone. When she spotted me, Mama purposefully looked at her watch and frowned.

"Where have you been? We got here almost forty-five minutes ago."

"Sorry. Something came up. Have you given your statement yet? Where's Allie?" I asked, looking around.

"She and Carl have been in with that Detective Harmon

for about a half an hour. I already gave my statement. It only took five minutes. Now, what came up?" I was toying with telling her my car wouldn't start but didn't feel like lying.

"Lynette was—"

"Lynette? What could possibly be going on with Lynette that's more important than you being here for your sister?" Clearly nothing short of death and dismemberment was going to be a good enough excuse for me being so late.

I started to say something when I spotted Carl and a sullen-looking Allegra, who was dressed in a big baggy gray sweat suit emblazoned with the letters WPD, which I assumed stood for Willow Police Department, and flip-flops. Noelle abruptly ended her call when she spotted them and we all rushed up to them.

"Where are her clothes? Has she been arrested?" Mama asked Carl in a shrill voice.

"No. But there was some blood on the bottoms of her shoes so they took them and her clothes for blood analysis," said Carl. He had a comforting hand on Allegra's lower back. I knew she was upset but I was bothered by it all the same.

"They said I can't leave town and I need to make myself available for further questioning," Allegra said. She wasn't crying anymore but looked like she was in shock.

"I'm sure that's just routine, right?" asked Noelle.

"They just want to cover all the bases," Carl told us. Mama and Noelle visibly relaxed but Allegra was staring at me.

"Where the hell were you? I thought you were going to follow us. We were here a good fifteen minutes before that detective called us in. Why weren't you here?" Now everyone was looking at me. I couldn't lie cause I'd already told Mama where I'd been. So once again I started to explain. And once again I didn't get far.

"I find a dead body and have to come down here and get grilled by the police and have my good Calvin Klein suit and Ferragamo pumps taken into evidence. I could lose my job and your ass is more worried about some petty-ass problem Lynette is having? I'm your sister, Kendra. You should have been here for me!" She turned and buried her face into Carl's chest and started sobbing.

I chalked it up to frustration over everything that had happened that day and struggled not to take it personally. But when I put a comforting hand on her shoulder she jerked away from me. Mama was nodding her head in agreement, and neither Carl nor Noelle would look me in the eye. Great.

"I'm sorry, Allie. I didn't realize it would take so long," I said meekly. She continued to ignore me.

"Well, there's no need to be worried about your job just yet," Noelle said, brushing past me to stand next to Allegra. "I just got off the phone with Bob McLean, the executive producer, and he's consulting with *Hollywood Vibe*'s lawyers. He didn't seem to think this was any reason for you to be let go."

"Then why is he consulting the lawyers?" Allegra asked. She'd turned to face Noelle and I couldn't help but notice that her big sobbing routine had produced no tears whatsoever. The big faker! Noelle didn't seem to have an answer for her and turned a shade of red almost as bright as her hair.

"Oh, forget it! I just want to get out of here before anyone sees me looking like this."

We all watched my sweat-suit-clad sister as she rushed across the lobby toward the police station's revolving doors. Her flip flops slapped loudly against the linoleum floor. We started to follow her, but everyone froze when an older black woman, as short and squat as a fire hydrant, wearing a black suit and black-and-white spectator pumps, came charging into the lobby. Her hair was pulled back severely into a bun that was several shades darker than the rest of her hair and screamed *hairpiece*. When she spotted my sister, her already sour expression turned to sheer rage and she pointed a stubby finger at Allegra.

"You little bitch! You killed Vivianne! I know you did it!" shouted the woman I now recognized as Vivianne DeArmond's assistant, Harriet Randall. She flew at Allegra and started swinging her big black patent-leather purse, catching my sister upside the head and knocking her to the floor.

"Why couldn't you just leave her alone!" Harriet screamed and started to raise her purse again to hit my sister who was cowering on the floor in a fetal position with her arms raised over her head to shield herself.

Mama, Carl, Noelle and I all ran to Allegra's aid. But it was my almost-seventy-three-year-old grandmother, who I never realized could move so fast, who got to Harriet first and yelled, "Now, hold up, heifer!" and tackled the woman to the ground. Mama and Harriet were rolling around on the floor slapping at each other. Harriet had Mama by her throat, but Mama grabbed Harriet's hairpiece and gave it good tug. It came off in her hand and she tossed it over her shoulder where it landed at Noelle's feet. She jumped back like it was a rat infected with cooties and stepped on my foot, causing me to yelp in pain and my eyes to water. Harriet wasn't at all fazed about her altered hairdo and hadn't forgotten her main target. She kept trying to crawl over to pummel Allegra some more, but Mama kept pulling her out of reach. I ran over and Carl and I tried to pry the two brawling women apart. Carl had Harriet under the armpits trying to pull her to her feet and I had Mama's arm. Mama was still spitting mad but allowed me to help her to her feet. But Harriet fought Carl off like he was a mugger and slugged him hard in the stomach, causing him to double over. She'd raised her lethal purse again to bash him on the head when some police officers, who must have been on a doughnut break, finally ran over to subdue her.

"She's crazy!" yelled Allegra, who had gotten up off the floor and was cowering behind Noelle.

"Murderer!" screamed Harriet, still lunging for Allegra. She bit the hand of one of the officers as they wrestled her to the floor and were attempting to cuff her.

"I didn't kill her. We had an appointment for an interview! Why would I kill her?" Allegra screamed back.

"Liar! I handled all of Vivianne's publicity. If she had granted you an interview, it would have been through me!"

The officers finally got the cuffs on Harriet and dragged the enraged old broad to her feet.

"Get her out of here," said the unfortunate officer with Harriet's teeth marks in his hand gesturing toward Allegra.

Mama grabbed Allegra and started to march out of the police station with me, Noelle and Carl in tow. When we reached the revolving doors we were met by a barrage of flashbulbs going off in our faces as a dozen or so reporters confronted us, hurling questions at Allegra.

"Were you the one who found Vivianne DeArmond's body?" asked a sweaty fat guy with in a too-tight suit.

"Is it true that she was stabbed?" asked Channel Four's star news reporter, Tracy Ripkey, whose big blond bouffant do looked a little dented as she tried to squeeze through the crowd to stick her microphone in Allegra's face.

"Can you still do the Freaky Deaky?" asked a smarmy-looking guy in dirty jeans and a T-shirt who wasn't a member of the press, just some fool trying to be funny.

At the sight of the cameras, Allegra instantly perked up and opened her mouth to speak before Mama glared her into silence.

Noelle yelled, "No comment," and gathered protectively around Allegra, who looked longingly at the reporters, and hustled her into Carl's car.

Later that evening, Carl and I were soaking in my tub. It was a tight fit with the two of us and we'd sloshed water on the bathroom floor, but I wasn't complaining. Allegra had gone back to stay with Mama. This was the closest I'd felt to Carl since before my sister arrived in town, and I had started to feel a little neglected.

"You never did give the police your statement. How much do you want to bet Harmon and Mercer come knocking on your door?"

I groaned. They were the last two people, besides my sister, that I wanted to talk about. I didn't have much of a problem with Detective Charles Mercer. He was a nice enough guy and usually pleasant to me. But his partner, Trish Harmon, had about as much charm and warmth as a head of iceberg lettuce. Hermits have more people skills than she does.

"I'll go talk to them tomorrow. I've had enough drama for one day."

"Poor Vivianne DeArmond. The woman was supposed to get an award and ended up with a letter opener in her back. Damn, that's a shame," Carl said, massaging my sore foot. There was still a faint impression from where Noelle had stepped on me.

"A letter opener? I figured she'd been stabbed with a knife."

"No. It was a letter opener."

"That's weird. I mean, if you're planning to stab someone, you don't plan on doing it with a letter opener. You'd use a knife."

"I know I would. But what who said the murder was planned? It could have been a crime of passion."

"I wonder if it was Vivianne's letter opener?"

"Does it matter? Dead is dead whether she was killed with a knife, a letter opener or a pitchfork."

"No. I was just thinking out loud."

"It's too bad your sister wiped that message off her hood. It could have backed up her story about the interview. The fact that Harriet Randall is claiming she knew nothing about the interview adds a new wrinkle to Allegra's story."

"Can't they check phone records to see that Allie really did call Vivianne?"

"Yes, but there will only be a record that a phone call was made and how long it lasted, not what they talked about. The police could think she was calling to harass Vivianne."

"It's going to kill Allie if she ends up losing her job over this mess."

"Once the results on her clothes come back showing they're blood-spatter free, she should be in the clear," Carl said confidently.

I lowered myself farther into the hot sudsy water and wished I shared his confidence.

CHAPTER 4

I dreamt that I was running through the halls of Cartwright Auditorium in my Mickey Mouse nightshirt. A hooded shadowy figure was chasing me with a sharp knife. The halls of the auditorium were mazelike with twists and turns like a serpent's back. I couldn't find my way out and felt myself panicking. The shadowy figure was gaining on me. Then a loud ringing fire alarm echoed through the halls, and my pursuer stopped abruptly and pulled off the hood. It was Allegra. She covered her ears as the ringing got louder and louder. I woke suddenly, tangled up in my sheets, sweating and very much alone. Carl was gone. I could still hear the ringing. But as I slowly came fully awake, I realized it wasn't a fire alarm—it was my phone. I untangled myself and answered it.

"Hello."

"Kendra?"

"Yeah. Who is this?" I mumbled, looking at the clock on my bedside table. It was nine o'clock in the morning. It was Sunday. The day of rest. I take that *rest* part very seriously.

"It's Greg, Kendra. I'm sorry to wake you, but is Lynette over there with you?" I sat straight up in bed.

"She's not over here, why?"

"Apparently, she told her mother she was spending the night with me. I haven't seen Lynette since before her bridal shower Friday night. If she's not at home, and she's not with either of us, then where the hell is she?"

Should I tell him about the conversation I had with his soon-to-be-wife yesterday? It really wasn't my place to tell him about Lynette's sexual hang-ups. He'd find out about that himself soon enough. At least, I hoped he would. Lynette must have been more upset than I realized. I felt awful. If I hadn't had my hands full with the Allegra situation, or been getting my freak on with Carl last night, it would have dawned on me that Lynette had never come by for the pizza and wine I'd suggested. Where in the world could she be? I finally told Greg an edited version of my conversation with Lynette, leaving out any mention of the sex issue, and told him his fiancée was experiencing a case of stress-induced wedding-day jitters. I was hoping he'd buy it and I could track Lynette down and slap some sense into her. He did buy it, but it didn't make him any less worried.

"I can't believe she's getting so freaked out about our wedding. We've been going to church counseling and everything."

"Really? I didn't know that." If Lynette was still having doubts even after going through counseling, she must really be in a bad way.

"It's mandatory. The minister who's marrying us wouldn't do it until we completed these mandatory counseling sessions. We had our last one last week."

"I thought Reverend Merriman was marrying you guys?" Robert Merriman was the pastor of St. Luke's Baptist Church, the church Mama still attended regularly and that I'd grown up in but rarely attended anymore. If Reverend Merriman wasn't marrying them then that could only leave a couple of other people.

"Reverend Merriman had a conflict and couldn't do it on the date we picked out. Morris Rollins is marrying us at Holy Cross."

Uh-oh!

Morris Rollins was the very attractive, popular, charming and charismatic minister of Holy Cross Church, a towering testament to modern architecture that many older folks in town thought was an eyesore. Rollins and I had made each other's acquaintance last year when a student of mine at Clark Literacy Center was wrongly accused of murdering one of Rollins's loved ones. Despite the fact that he was old enough to be my father and had buried his second wife last year, there was an undeniable attraction between us that I found to be very disturbing. Carl knew Morris Rollins, too, and occasionally did legal aid work for Holy Cross Ministries, which made my attraction to the good reverend even more annoying.

"Kendra, are you still there?" Greg asked, snapping me back to attention.

"Sorry, Greg. What did you say?"

"I was wondering if Reverend Rollins might have heard from Lynette. I mean, if she's stressing about the wedding, maybe she called Reverend Rollins to talk."

"I guess it's a possibility. Why don't you call and ask him?" I said, even though I was pretty sure Lynette wouldn't have called Morris Rollins.

"See, here's the thing, Kendra," Greg said in a tone that indicated he was about to ask me to do something I wasn't going to want to do. "I never let on to Justine that Lynette wasn't with me. Justine's on her way over to drop off Monty and India because she's going to Columbus to visit her sister. I don't want the kids, and especially Justine, to know there might be a problem with Lynette." He paused and I knew it was coming. "Would you be able to go over to Holy Cross sometime today and talk to Reverend Rollins and see if he's heard anything from Lynette?"

Damn. What could I say? I sure as hell wasn't about to tell him I was afraid I'd end up naked and sweaty with Morris Rollins if I lingered in his presence too long. Not that the thought wasn't extremely appealing. I'd never felt the need to confide my lust for Rollins to anyone, not even Lynette, who knew about most of the men I'd lusted after, and I wasn't about to confess now.

"Of course, I'll—" Greg cut me off when I heard the faint sound of his doorbell in the background.

"Thanks, Kendra. Gotta go. Call me." He hung up before I could finish lying to him about how it would be my pleasure to grill Morris Rollins about Greg's runaway bride.

I showered and headed over to Mama's to see how things were going with my sister, the suspect. I certainly didn't want Allegra or Mama to accuse me again of not being supportive. Plus, I was hoping to snag a couple of Mama's homemade waffles. I was putting off my trip to Holy Cross. I'd started to call the church to talk to Rollins over the phone instead, but then realized he was probably delivering his Sunday sermon.

I had turned onto Orchard Lane and was headed for Mama's driveway when I noticed a man and a woman sitting in a green Honda parked three doors down from Mama's house. I wouldn't have given them a second glance if it hadn't been for the woman's hair: short, red and spiky. It was Allegra's producer, Noelle Delaney. The man she was with was a very light-skinned black man with short dreads. I drove past slowly and could hear them screaming at each other through the Honda's rolled-up windows. They didn't notice me at all. It wasn't any of my business, so drove on, pulled into the driveway and parked behind Allegra's rental.

When I walked into the kitchen, Mama was sitting at the table drinking a cup of tea with the Sunday paper spread out in front of her. She was still dressed in her church clothes. She attended St. Luke's sunrise service at six-thirty every Sunday morning. I thought back to what I'd been doing at six-thirty that morning. Oh yeah, being chased through my dreams by her knife-wielding granddaughter. I knew she wouldn't appreciate me sharing that dream with her.

"Why are you here so early? I haven't even started dinner yet." She was referring to the fact that I eat at her house every Sunday.

"Just came by to see how Allie's doing. She up yet?" I asked, heading toward the stairway that led to the second-floor bedrooms. Mama looked up from her paper and gave me a slightly confused look.

"Allie's not here. Carl came by and took her out to breakfast to cheer her up." My head whipped around so fast I almost got whiplash.

"I figured you knew and just didn't want to get up. I know how you like to lay around in the bed all morning," she said quickly, getting up from the table.

I couldn't speak. Allie was my sister, not his. If she needed cheering up, I'd be the one to do it. And why hadn't Carl asked me to go? Don't I need breakfast just like the next person? And just when was this little rendezvous planned? He didn't leave me a note or anything. Just rolled out of my bed that morning to take Miss *Hollywood Vibe* to breakfast. I know I was asleep, but he could have at least left me a note.

Then a vision suddenly flashed in my mind of Allegra calling Carl and sounding pitiful. I bet she even cried a little, and Carl, being the kind of man he is, probably suggested getting together to discuss her legal options. I'd be willing to bet my next paycheck that it was Allegra who wanted to go to breakfast and told Carl not to wake me. Priceless.

"Why don't I fix you some waffles?" Mama walked into the pantry and I could hear her opening and closing cabinets while I stood and fumed. My sister was after my man, and all my grandmother could do was offer me food? How well she knew me. But not this time. I'd suddenly lost my appetite.

"No, thanks," I said through gritted teeth. I walked out the back door. Mama called out after me.

"And don't go bothering Carl and Allie, Kendra. I'm sure they have some serious business to discuss and your sister needs to focus on getting herself out of this mess, you hear me?" she said to my retreating back. I didn't bother answering her.

Instead, I hopped in my car and backed out of the driveway. I drove by the green Honda, which was still parked in the same spot. Only this time, Noelle and Mr. Dreads were kissing passionately. I only caught a glimpse of them before the Honda's windows fogged up. Well, at least someone's having fun, I thought miserably.

I arrived back at my apartment close to eleven o'clock. I wrestled with the idea of trying to track Carl and Allegra down but decided in my current mood it would be a very bad idea. I had at least an hour to kill before services at Holy Cross were over and I could talk to Morris Rollins. Given the murderous feelings I was harboring toward my sister, I decided I was in need of a little spiritual healing. I changed out of my jeans and T-shirt and put on the green silk wrap dress that I'd worn to Lynette's shower along with a pair of strappy high-heeled sandals, sprayed on my favorite vanilla-scented cologne and headed off to church. As usual, Holy Cross's parking lot was packed, and I had to park a block away.

Church services were in full swing and I could hear the

choir singing a spirited rendition of "Go Tell It on the Mountain" when I walked into the church's open glass atrium. The double doors to the main church hall were closed and I eased one side open and slipped in. I found a space at the end of a pew in the back. A few people gave me curious glances, but most paid me no attention at all and kept right on singing and clapping along with the choir. When the choir finished, everyone sat down, and Reverend Rollins took his place behind the pulpit. Almost as tall as a basketball player, Rollins was a sight to behold in his black ministerial robes. He was brown-skinned and bald. I could see the diamond stud in his ear twinkling from all the way in the back of the church. I noticed he was no longer wearing the goatee he'd had when we'd first met, and now wore a neatly trimmed beard and mustache. He smiled at the congregation and I felt the familiar fluttery feeling in the pit of my stomach that I got whenever I saw him, which is why I made sure it wasn't often. I heard some disembodied sighs floating in the air around me and knew I wasn't the only woman who was appreciating the reverend's attributes. Morris Rollins wasn't conventionally handsome, but he definitely had that certain something that made you look twice.

"Brothers and sisters," he began in his deep, soothing, hypnotic voice. "Today, I'd like to talk to you about something that plagues each and everyone of us. Something that no man woman or child is immune to. Brothers and sisters I'm talking about…temptation," he said, staring, it would seem, right at me.

"Tell it," cried out an enthusiastic sister fanning herself vigorously and nodding like a bobble-head doll.

Temptation? The man must have been reading my mind.

An hour later the service was over and Rollins was in the atrium greeting his flock. I stood apart from the crowd watching him work his charm and magic on each and every one of his congregation. Some people were pulled into big bear hugs, while others got hearty pats on the back. All the women got a kiss on the cheek and the children got tickled or tossed playfully into the air. Every few minutes he'd glance over at me waiting for him and smile. I could feel myself start to fall under the spell of that smile and had to remind myself why I was there. After about twenty minutes, he was finally able to pull himself away.

"Kendra," he said taking my hands into his. His hands were warm and his smile had turned slightly devilish. Lord help me. "How are you?" He pulled me into a Lagerfeld-scented embrace, holding me a little longer than necessary.

"I'm fine, Reverend Rollins," I said, gently extricating myself. He laughed heartily and I could feel my face flush.

"I haven't seen you in a while. Come on into my office and tell me how you've been," he said putting a hand on my shoulder and guiding me into his lavish office.

I sat on the gold love seat in front of his large round desk and remembered the first time I'd been invited into his office, a visit that had almost had me turning into mush. I noticed he still had the picture of him, his daughter, Inez, and his recently deceased second wife, Nicole, displayed prominently on his desk. I glanced up and saw that the mural depicting him in the pulpit delivering a sermon was still painted on the ceiling.

"Can I assume that you've finally taken me up on my offer to join Holy Cross?" he asked hopefully.

"Actually, I needed to speak with you about a friend of mine who you recently counseled." He looked curious so I continued.

"Lynette Martin-Gaines? She and her fiancé, Greg Hull, are getting married here next Saturday."

"Oh, Lynette and Greg. Yes, I did counsel them. But you know I can't discuss that with you, Kendra."

"I know. It's just that Lynette has been experiencing cold feet over the wedding and she's sort of taken off. You haven't heard from her, have you?"

"You mean, she ran away?"

"Exactly."

"No. I haven't talked to Lynette since her and Greg's last counseling session about a week ago. You don't think anything serious has happened to her, do you?" he asked, looking concerned.

"I'm hoping that she just needed some room to breathe and took off for the day to be alone. But Greg is worried and asked me if I'd come talk to you. So, here I am."

He leaned back in his chair and stared at me without with speaking for a few seconds. I couldn't read his look and it was making me uncomfortable.

"You're probably right," he said finally. "I'm sure that's all it is. But how about you? Are you okay?" He was looking at me like he wanted to give me another hug. The last time I was in close proximity to Morris Rollins we'd ended up in a lip lock. I could feel myself getting hot just thinking about that kiss.

"Me? I'm fine, why?"

"I saw you and your family on the news last night coming out of the police station. The police don't think your sister had anything to do with Vivianne DeArmond's murder, do they?"

"Allegra was the one who found Vivianne's body." I could have told him more but didn't feel like getting into it. Rollins whistled, shook his head, and stared at me again. I shifted around uncomfortably on the love seat and wouldn't meet his gaze.

"Are you worried?" he asked.

"A little," I replied truthfully. "Because you know how the police can get things wrong. They get stuck on one idea and don't want to think about anything or anybody else." I was not so subtly referring to the murder investigation that had first brought us in contact with each other last year.

Morris Rollins was one of the reasons the police had been looking in the wrong direction during that investigation. He'd had a good reason, at least as far as he was concerned, but I was still pissed at him for almost letting an innocent young man go to prison. It was something that still hung in the air between us like a thick fog.

"Can I ask you something?" he asked softly, leaning forward in his big leather chair. I nodded slowly, not really sure if I wanted him to ask me anything.

"Your sister found a dead body and your soon-to-be-married best friend has gone AWOL. So, why is it that you're the one looking like your dog just died?"

His tone was serious, but his eyes were laughing at me. I smiled as I suddenly realized how tensed up I was, and I instantly relaxed. The Allegra/Carl/Lynette situation apparently had me more stressed than I knew.

"That's better," he said. "You have such a beautiful smile."

"Thanks," I said getting up from the love seat to make my getaway. It's been my experience that whenever a man starts praising my attributes, some sort of proposition usually follows.

Rollins was a widower and free to proposition whomever he wanted. But even though my relationship with Carl was being put to the test, I'm a one-man woman. I didn't need the kind of drama in my life that juggling men can bring. Plus, I knew if I ever gave it up to Rollins, it would be like taking a hit off a crack pipe. You think doing it one time won't hurt you, but before you know it, you're hooked and wandering the streets, strung out with crusty lips.

"Now, where are you running off to? At least let me take you out to dinner. It's been so long since I've seen you," he said, standing up and coming around to sit on the edge of his desk directly in front of me. I could tell by his amused expression that he knew I was trying to get away from him. So he grabbed my hand and pulled me gently toward him.

He was giving me such a warm smile I found myself hypnotized and didn't resist as he wrapped his arms around me. My cheek was pressed against his shoulder and he was rubbing my back. This was *not* what I came here for, but I couldn't move. Being in his arms felt just a little too good, which was horrible, not because I felt guilty, but because I didn't. Clearly it was time for me to go.

"Maybe some other time, Reverend Rollins. I need to see if I can track down Lynette and make sure she's okay," I said softly and started to step out of his embrace, but he wasn't quite ready to let me go.

"I hope you know I'm going to hold you to that," he said, hugging me again and planting a warm, lingering kiss on my cheek.

His beard tickled and I giggled. He took that as encouragement and leaned down to kiss me on the mouth. But I quickly pulled away.

"Take care, Reverend Rollins, and please give me a call if you hear from Lynette," I said, walking out of the office, leaving him staring after me looking more than a little disappointed.

I decided to drive around to see if I could spot Lynette's car before calling Greg to report back on my visit to Holy Cross. I was sitting at the traffic light on Main Street when I spotted a young black man with short dreads, sporting faded jeans and a tight blue polo shirt. He looked to be in his twenties. It was the same man that I'd seen sucking face with Noelle Delaney. I watched as he crossed the street in front of my car and walked into Denny's. There was something so familiar about the guy now that I'd gotten a chance to get a good look at him. I knew I'd seen him someplace other than hugged up in that Honda with Noelle. But I couldn't put a finger on where it had been. It was now almost one and I hadn't eaten. So I pulled into Denny's parking lot and decided to kill two birds with one stone: My nosiness and my appetite.

Denny's was pretty crowded with after-church folk. While I was waiting to be seated, I spotted Mr. Dreads in a nearby booth sitting with a well-dressed older white man who looked to be in his sixties, and a fortyish white woman with long, bleached-blond hair. After indicating my preference for a table, I was happy when I found myself seated in the one right across from Mr. Dreads and his companions. I placed an order for a tuna melt and fries and sipped my water so they wouldn't realize I was listening to their conversation.

"Quit your bitching, Kurt. Your mother's dead and all you can do is bug me for money? I already told you I'll buy you anything you need. But I'm not giving you any cash. You're not snorting up, shooting up, or drinking up my money," said the older man. The man was balding and had the sallow liver-spotted skin of old age. But he was dressed to the nines in an expensive looking gray pin-striped suit with a white shirt, red tie and diamond tie tack. I saw a gold nugget ring shining on his finger each time he took a sip of his coffee.

"Since when was Vivianne ever a mother to me? Hell, just 'cause she's dead don't suddenly make her mother of the year. You sure weren't talking that mother shit when she was alive and well," said Mr. Dreads, aka Kurt.

My ears perked up big-time. Were they talking about Vivianne DeArmond? Could Kurt be Vivianne's son? I stole a glance and saw that Kurt's pale face was grim and unsmiling. He had gray eyes and freckles ran rampant across his face. I couldn't see much of Vivianne DeArmond in him at all.

"Kurt, honey, don't cuss at your father," said the blond woman, rubbing Kurt's arm. The woman was attractive. Her strong jawline and high wide forehead kept her from being pretty. But too much time spent in the sun, heavy makeup and over-bleached hair made her look hard, as well. The plunging neckline of her purple top revealed cleavage that was way too deep and her breasts in general had the big and unnaturally round look of surgical enhancement. Why any woman would want boobs bigger than her head was beyond me. She smiled at Kurt and it softened her face, but not much.

"Then tell him to stop picking on me," Kurt said, jabbing a finger in his father's direction. "Damn, I just got out of rehab last month. I'm finished with alcohol. How many times do I have to tell you that?"

Kurt's father laughed. It was a loud angry snort that didn't have much to do with being amused.

"I've heard all this before, remember? The first time around it was cocaine. Then you moved on to prescription painkillers, this last time it was alcohol. What's it gonna be next, Kurt, huh? I bet if you could mainline Kool-Aid you'd do that, too, wouldn't you?"

"Cliff, please," pleaded the blonde in a whisper. She looked around, aware that they were causing a scene. "Can't you see how hard he's trying? Leave him alone."

"Stay out of this, Stephanie. You're part of his whole problem. You baby him too much. Twenty-five years old and never had to work hard a day in his life. I get him jobs and he messes them up then expects me to hand out money to him like it grows on trees in the backyard—"

"Aw, forget it," Kurt said, cutting him off. "I don't need this bullshit." He slid out of the booth. "Soon as the funeral's over I'm going back to L.A. and you won't have to worry about me asking your ass for another dime ever again." He stalked toward the door, but his father wasn't finished yet.

"I'll believe that the day I sprout wings and fly to the moon!" Kurt turned and flipped his father the finger before walking out the door. Cliff leapt out of the booth to follow him. Stephanie quickly grabbed his arm and pulled him back down into the booth. He angrily slapped her hands away.

Everybody in the restaurant stopped eating and stared at Cliff as though he had, in fact, sprouted wings, and Stephanie, who I assumed must be his wife, glared at him as if she wished he would indeed fly away.

"Was that really necessary? Why do you have to be such a bully?" Stephanie said. I watched as she got up and hurried after Kurt. I was doubtful she'd catch up to him in her tight white miniskirt and four-inch gold pumps.

I was looking out the window trying to see them when the server set my food in front of me. By the time I'd salted my fries and taken the first bite of my tuna melt, I glanced out the window again and saw Stephanie and Kurt talking. Cliff was watching, too, and made a disgusted noise as she slipped something into Kurt's hand on the sly. The way Kurt's face lit up, I knew it was money. He gave her peck on the cheek and then sprinted across the street. Seconds later, he was out of sight, and Stephanie came back into the restaurant. She'd barely sat down before Cliff starting bitching.

"How in the hell is that boy supposed to learn any responsibility when you keep babying him?" Cliff face was bright red and I feared for his blood pressure.

"What?" Stephanie replied innocently. Her heavily madeup eyes widened in faux shock. She looked like a startled clown.

"I know you gave him money, Stephanie. For God's sake, even Vivianne knew not to give Kurt any money."

Uh-oh. I instinctively knew those were fighting words. Anyone with sense should know not to compare one's former spouse favorably with their current spouse, at least not unless that person didn't mind sleeping with one eye open. I peered over at Stephanie and saw her visibly stiffen.

"You're absolutely right, Cliff. Vivianne never gave Kurt anything. Not love, time, attention or money. The only thing she loved more than herself was the damn camera. I'm the only mother that boy has ever known and I'm going to make sure he's happy." Stephanie buried her face in her napkin.

"Dammit, Stephanie, Vivianne's dead. I didn't mean it that way and you know it," Cliff said sheepishly while stirring his coffee.

"Yes, you did," she said blowing her nose. "I don't care that she's dead. And I'll tell you another thing, Clifford Preston. I wouldn't be so high and mighty if I were you, because you've had some filthy little habits of your own. Haven't you?"

Now it was Cliff's turn to stiffen. Stephanie shrank back against the booth. Cliff stood up and tossed money on the table. "I'll be in the car. Don't be long." I watched as he stalked out of the restaurant. Five minutes later, Stephanie left, as well.

I pondered what I'd just overheard as I was finishing my lunch. So Vivianne DeArmond had a son. Interesting. I knew Vivianne had been married but hadn't been enough of a fan to know she had a son. And apparently Vivianne and her son hadn't been close. Did Kurt try and hit her up for money, too? And had he got mad when she'd said no? Mad enough to plunge a letter opener into her back? Maybe I should mention this when I gave my statement to Harmon and Mercer. Then another big question came to mind. Why hadn't Noelle Delaney mentioned her connection to Kurt? You'd have thought that at some point during all the madness of yesterday she'd have mentioned she knew Vivianne's son. I didn't re-member seeing a wedding or engagement ring on Noelle's finger or a wedding band on Kurt's, so why the big secret? I intended to find out.

CHAPTER 5

It was after eight o'clock that evening and Allegra, Noelle and I were sitting on Mama's porch drinking lemonade and digesting the huge Sunday meal of pork roast, sweet potatoes, macaroni and cheese, green beans and peach cobbler we'd just consumed. By the time I'd finally seen Carl and Allegra it was dinner time. My uncle Alex and his girl-friend of the past eight years, Gwen Robins, were also present. We all crowded around Mama's dining-room table. I knew it wasn't the time to bring up the breakfast rendez-vous. Plus, I'd calmed down considerably since that morning.

Still, I kept watching the two of them closely to try and detect any evidence of illicit activity: lustful looks of longing, lipstick-smeared collars, hickeys, wadded-up condom wrappers falling out of pockets. I even dropped my napkin on the floor on purpose to make sure they weren't holding hands under the table. Nothing. It was almost as though they were ignoring each other on purpose. After dinner, Mama had gone to play bridge at a friend's house and Alex, Gwen and Carl had gone to watch a Reds game on Alex's big-screen TV. That left just us girls. Good. Now, I had to figure out a way to bring up Kurt.

"Your grandmother's an awesome cook," Noelle said to no one in particular. Thinking back to the way she'd practically licked her plate I knew she was being truthful.

"Thanks," said Allegra and I simultaneously. We looked at each other and smiled. Now that Carl wasn't around I was more relaxed. Being paranoid is tiresome and takes up way too much energy.

"Have you heard anything more from *Hollywood Vibe*'s lawyers?" Allegra asked, turning to Noelle.

Allegra and I were sitting in the two wicker rocking chairs facing the street while Noelle was sitting on the porch's wooden railing facing us with her tennis-shoe clad feet dangling over the side. All anyone had to do was push her and she'd fall ass-backwards into the bushes below. When Allegra asked her about the lawyers, Noelle abruptly stood up like she was aware her answer might earn her a shove into the bushes.

"No, I haven't heard anything from the lawyers, but I did speak to Bob McLean." I remembered Noelle saying Bob McLean was *Hollywood Vibe*'s executive producer.

"And?" Allegra asked when Noelle failed to elaborate.

"And Bob is very concerned about what effect Vivianne DeArmond's murder and your involvement in it could have on *Hollywood Vibe*'s reputation. You know how hard he's worked to make the show a legit source of entertainment news. After that whole Ross Abbott incident, he's got a right to be concerned."

Ross Abbott was a bad-boy actor, well-known for his roles in action-adventure movies, who got married as often as most people change their underwear. Usually stories in the press about Abbott concerned his exhaustive love life. But *Hollywood Vibe,* in a new-kid-on-the-block effort to scoop all the other entertainment news shows, had broken a story about Ross Abbott wearing a full set of dentures, a toupee and lifts in his shoes. Abbott had promptly sued the show for slander and had even gone so far as to have himself measured in his stocking feet during a press conference to prove that he was truly the five feet ten inches he claimed to be. He also made his dentist and his hairstylist, a flamboyant little man named Mr. Billy, sign sworn affidavits that his thick brown hair and big white chompers were indeed all his. Needless to say he won his case. One of Abbott's disgruntled ex-girl-friends, who was rumored to have been sleeping with Bob McLean, had given *Hollywood Vibe* false information and the show took a big hit. They became the laughing stock of the entertainment world. Late-night-talk show hosts joked that *Hollywood Vibe*'s news coverage was short, bald and toothless. Now, a year later, they were just beginning to put the fallout behind them. Allegra looked as if she couldn't decide whether to cuss, cry or throw up.

"Once the test results come back on your clothes, I'm sure that will be the end of it," I said, hoping to put my sister's fears to rest. Noelle nodded in agreement.

"Yeah. That's what Carl said this morning. I guess we'll

see, won't we?" Allegra stood up and headed into the house. She flung the screen door open a little too forcefully and it slammed shut behind her. Noelle stared at me awkwardly. I smiled to show I wasn't mad at her. I wanted her in a good mood for her forthcoming grilling.

"This is so awful. You think she'll be okay?" Noelle asked, as she nervously sipped her lemonade.

"She'll be fine once she can put this behind her," I said.

"I can't imagine why Vivianne DeArmond's assistant didn't know about their interview. I wonder why she didn't tell her?"

"Harriet Randall's a pretty forceful woman. Maybe Vivianne wanted to do an interview and Harriet objected. Maybe that's why Vivianne didn't tell her," I said.

"Well, I certainly wouldn't want to be on that woman's bad side. She's nuts."

I certainly couldn't argue with her on that one. After a few minutes of chatting about nothing in particular, we fell back into an uncomfortable silence. No sense in putting it off any longer. My curiosity was killing me.

"I didn't know Vivianne DeArmond had a son," I said casually. Noelle's glass stopped halfway to her mouth. Her cheeks turned slightly pink and she took a big gulp of lemonade. I waited for her to say something, but she didn't comment, just turned to stare moodily out into the street.

"He's friend of yours, right? How's he handling his mother's death?" I persisted.

Noelle turned and gave me a quizzical look. "What makes you think I know Vivianne DeArmond's son?"

"I saw the two of you in your rental this morning. The way you two were going at it, I got the impression you knew each other pretty well."

She shook her head slowly and looked at me like she had no idea what I was talking about and was wondering what kind of idiot I was. For a split second I thought I might have been mistaken. Naw. I know what I saw. I'd fogged up plenty of car windows myself. The last time being with a certain sexy reverend.

"I really don't know what you're talking about. Yes, I knew Vivianne DeArmond had a son. But I've never met him. So it couldn't have been me you saw this morning. Coming here for dinner is the first time I've been over here today." She was giving me one of those show-biz smiles. The kind that didn't reach her eyes. Despite her attempt at acting nonchalant, I could tell she was pissed. But why?

"Really? That's funny."

"Why?" The phony smile was gone replaced by an annoyed frown.

"Because I never said it was *this* street that I saw the two of you parked on. It's amazing you'd know that if it wasn't you I saw."

By now her face had turned bright red and her lips were pressed together so hard they disappeared. She opened her mouth to say something. I knew it wasn't going to be anything nice and leaned forward in my rocker ready for her verbal beat down. It didn't come. Before Noelle could say a word, Allegra walked back out onto the porch. She had a big heaping bowl full of peach cobbler and ice cream. Now I knew just how freaked out she must really be. She ate a lot when she was stressed, which was another big difference between us. I never needed a reason to eat a lot. I just needed to be conscious.

Allegra was too preoccupied with her dessert to notice the tidal wave of animosity that her producer was throwing my way. She sat back down in the rocker and didn't look at either one of us. Noelle set her glass on the railing and smiled at my sister. Considering how mad she'd just been I was amazed she was able to snap back so quickly.

"Allegra, I need to take off. I've got conference calls to make about some stories for next week's shows. I'll give you a call later, and don't worry. Everything's going to be okay. You'll see."

Allegra's mouth was full of ice cream and cobbler, and she merely waved as Noelle hurried down the porch steps, hopped into her rental and took off.

"I'm so glad she's gone. That chick gets on my nerves," she said after Noelle pulled away from the curb.

"You don't like her?"

"She's not as bad as some of those phony asses at *Hollywood Vibe*. But I can only stand so much of her and I don't trust her all. She started out as the assistant to the producer that got fired last year after that Ross Abbott mess. People say she was working behind the scenes to make sure he got blamed for it. She was after his job from the beginning. But that's Hollywood for you. You've got a ton of people all after the same small piece of the pie. It's cutthroat like you wouldn't believe, Kendra."

"Is that why you were so afraid to tell her you were having trouble getting the interview?"

"Damn right. I wasn't the first choice for this job, Kendra. They'd already offered it to some chick who'd been a runner-up in the Miss America pageant. She had to turn it down cause she was hospitalized for anorexia. Then they were going to give it to some rock star's daughter. She turned it down because they wouldn't pay her enough. Then it was offered to some has-been soap-opera star. She took the job but quit after one day when she got the lead role in some off-Broadway play. I was fourth on the list. I'm a black woman trying to get ahead in Hollywood. That means I have to be twice as good as those white girls just to get half as far."

"Why didn't you tell me?"

"Because I wanted everyone to think I was the star of show, when in reality, I'm just scrambling to keep ahead of the pack. You have no idea how many people I have nipping at my heels wanting to be where I am and waiting for me to mess up," she said miserably. "And it looks like they're about to get their wish."

I didn't know what to say to her. In light of what she'd just told me, telling her not to worry seemed insensitive. Then I wondered how much, if anything, she knew about Noelle and Kurt. I wanted to know just what the two of them were up to and if it could have anything to do with Vivianne's death. I told Allegra about seeing Cliff, Kurt and Stephanie Preston at Denny's.

"I heard they were in town to see Vivianne get her

award. Did you know Cliff used to be Vivianne's agent, as well as her husband?"

"No," I replied honestly.

"He's the founder of the Preston Agency. It used to be as big as William Morris. Cliff Preston is the reason Vivianne DeArmond was able to have a career as a leading lady at a time when black actors were hired to play maids, mammies and chauffeurs."

"How do you know all of this?"

"I found out when I was doing research to prepare myself for interviewing Vivianne. Rumor has it Cliff Preston's talent agency is on its way to being as dead as disco. He was really in town to try and get Vivianne to take a part in some new movie. I think he figured if he could revive Vivianne's career from the ashes then his business would pick up and maybe he'd get some big-name clients again."

"What about their son, Kurt? What's his deal?" Allegra rolled her eyes and gave me an incredulous look. "What?" I said, as she shook her head and laughed.

"You really didn't recognize him, did you?"

"No. Should I have?"

"Remember that stupid show that was popular about ten years ago called *Ninja Dudes?*"

I thought for a minute and then realized that's why Kurt Preston looked so familiar to me. Kurt had been an actor, too, though his career had been short-lived. He'd probably been about fifteen at the time he'd appeared on *Ninja Dudes* back in the late eighties and I couldn't remember ever seeing him in anything after that.

"You mean that awful show about the widower in Hawaii who adopts three teenage boys of different races who surfed by day and were crime-fighting ninjas at night?" Okay. I watched a couple of episodes. So what?

"Yeah. He played the black son named Jabari who wore sunglasses all the time and only got to say stuff like, "Dudes, let's roll, or "Dudes, chill out." I don't think they ever gave that poor guy more than three words to say at a time," Allegra said, laughing.

With his gray eyes and freckles, Kurt Preston looked more like a Jerry than a Jabari to me. But I guess that's Hollywood for you. They probably made him wear those sunglasses to hide his eye color.

"What happened to him after the show?" Like I needed to ask. From what I'd overheard at the restaurant, Kurt had become active in pursuits of the pharmaceutical kind.

"Well, I think Cliff tried to get Kurt more acting jobs, but by the time the show was canceled, he was heavily into drugs. He's been in and out of rehab so many times they should name a wing after him. I've seen him in a couple of commercials, but that's it. He sure hasn't had the career his costar Ross Abbott has had. I hear Kurt and Ross are still good friends."

Ross Abbott? I'd forgotten he'd been on the show, too. He'd played Todd, one of the other ninja dudes. It was his first role, the one that started his career as an action hero. Was this the reason Noelle didn't want anyone knowing about her and Kurt? In light of the *Hollywood Vibe* scandal, it certainly wouldn't look good if Noelle was dating a good friend of a man who'd sued the show, especially since there had been talk that Noelle was involved in the firing of her predecessor. I started to ask but Allegra wasn't finished with her story.

"Vivianne was forty when she had Kurt and by the time he was five, she and Cliff were divorced. Cliff got sole custody of Kurt because Vivianne was deemed unfit. He raised Kurt with his second wife, Stephanie, an ex-Vegas showgirl who's twenty years younger than him. Kurt and Stephanie are really close. Vivianne stopped acting not long after she lost custody of Kurt."

"Why?" I asked. Allegra shrugged.

"No one really knows for sure. One theory is that she could no longer get leading-lady roles and her ego couldn't take it. Another theory is she had a nervous breakdown after losing custody of her child. I guess we'll never know now."

I was finishing up my lemonade, and Allegra had eaten her last spoonful of ice cream, when an unmarked black Crown Victoria, the kind used by homicide detectives on the Willow police force, pulled up and parked in front of the house. I felt a cold knot forming in the pit of my stomach as I watched detectives Trish Harmon and Charles Mercer emerge from the vehicle and approach the house. I heard Allegra groan.

Trish Harmon and I had butted heads before during two other murder investigations. She thought I was stubborn, obstructive and foolish. I thought she was humorless, cold and about as flexible as a corpse in full rigor. I figured we were about equal in our dislike of one another. I noticed she'd let her hair grow out a little from her normal mannishly short do. But she was dressed as drably as usual in a gray suit with a long pleated skirt that I'd seen her in before. Charles Mercer, her chubby sidekick, was looking pleasant, if a bit uncomfortable in his tight blue sport coat and tan dress slacks. I grabbed Allegra's hand protectively and we both stood as the detectives walked up the porch steps.

"Miss Clayton, we need you to come down the station with us to answer some more questions," Trish Harmon said, addressing my sister. Allegra squeezed my hand so hard it went numb.

"What's this about?" I asked Harmon. She ignored me. No big surprise.

"You can either come willingly, Miss Clayton, or we can arrest you," Harmon said to my sister when she failed to move. Allegra gave me a panic-stricken look as Trish Harmon grabbed her opposite wrist and started to lead her in the direction of the porch steps. I pulled my sister's other wrist and Allegra was pulled between Harmon and me, arms and legs outstretched like a piece of caramel taffy.

"Hey. You can't just drag her off with no explanation," I complained, tugging her back toward me.

"Yes, we can. Your sister was told to make herself available for questioning and we've got lots of questions for her," Harmon said, calmly pulling Allegra back to her. Uh-oh! What happened? What did they want to talk to her about?

"You don't have to drag her off like a common criminal. Get your hands off her," I snapped, holding my ground and tugging my stunned-looking sister back to me.

"We can always arrest you for obstruction. In my opinion, you're long overdue for a jail cell and I'd love to fix that," Harmon fired back through gritted teeth.

Mercer was watching the tug of war between his partner and me with amusement. But after a couple of minutes he finally decided enough was enough. He walked over and gently pulled Allegra free of our grasping hands.

"Your sister isn't under arrest, Miss Clayton. We just need her to come down to the station to answer a few questions, that's all. There's no need to worry," he said, leading Allegra down the steps to their car. I believed him like I believed in Santa. I started to follow but Allegra, who'd suddenly regained her composure, stopped me.

"It's okay, Kendra. I haven't done anything wrong. Call Carl and have him meet me at the station." I watched helplessly as they ushered her into the backseat. Harmon turned and tossed me a venomous smirk.

"Don't you say a single word to them until Carl gets there! Do you hear me?" I called out before they slammed the car door shut.

I went into the house and called Carl and told him to meet me at the station. What in the world could they want to talk to Allegra about now? Did Harriet Randall convince them that Vivianne hadn't agreed to an interview? There was no proof whatsoever that Vivianne had granted Allegra an interview. She'd wiped the message from Vivianne from her car. She'd been the one who called Vivianne, not the other way around. Vivianne's own assistant didn't even know about the interview. Plus, Allegra had been picked-up for trespassing in Vivianne's house. In light of the conversation I'd just had with my sister about how she was struggling to stay ahead of the pack, I was beginning to wonder just what Allegra was capable of if she were desperate enough. I knew my sister was no murderer. But in her quest to hold on to her job, had Allegra lied about Vivianne's note on the car? Had she shown up at the award ceremony, hoping to catch Vivianne alone in the attempt to get an interview? And when she discovered her dead, had she had to come up with an excuse as to why she was there? I honestly couldn't say I wouldn't put it past her.

I'd been sitting in the near-empty lobby of the police station, with its beige linoleum floors and uncomfortable age-scarred wooden benches, for an hour when it dawned on me that I hadn't touched base with Greg about Lynette. I pulled out my cell phone and dialed his number. He answered it on the first ring and his anxious-sounding hello answered my question about whether Lynette had come home.

"It's me, Greg. Any news?"

"She called to check on the kids. But she didn't sound good," he said with a heavy sigh.

"Where is she? What did she say?"

"She said she needed some time to herself to think. She wouldn't say where she was. She sounded weird, Kendra. I've never heard her sound like that before. I asked if she wanted to cancel the wedding and she started crying and hung up on me."

I knew I should tell him everything about my last conversation with Lynette, but I could think of no comfortable way to do it. Even Lynette was having a hard time telling him about her sex hang-ups. What exactly was I supposed to say?

"Kendra, I need you to do me a huge favor."

"What's that?" I asked with dread. I had enough on my plate with Allegra.

"Please help me find her. The wedding is six days away. I'll try and stall Justine as long as I can. You know what she's like. I don't want her to know Lynette has taken off. But we've got to find her. There's all kinds of last-minute wedding stuff to take care of and the kids will be asking questions. I'm really worried about her."

"So am I, Greg, so am I. Look, I'm off on spring break this week. I'll see if I can track her down tomorrow, okay?"

"Thanks, Kendra. I'll let you know if I hear from her." He hung up without saying goodbye.

Wonderful. Not only did I have a sister who'd gotten mixed up in a murder, I also had to deal with my best friend, the runaway bride. Could this day get any worse? Yes, it could.

Two hours later, Carl and Allegra emerged from the

interrogation room looking like they'd been through hell. Allegra walked straight past me into the nearby women's restroom without speaking. Carl looked at me and shook his head.

"Out with it," I demanded, not sure I really wanted to know.

"They found Allegra's fingerprints on Vivianne DeArmond's purse. They found the purse in the Dumpster behind the auditorium"

"Huh?" Not a very literate response, I know. But I was stunned. "How in the hell did her prints get on that purse?"

"Allegra said when she walked into the dressing room, she tripped over the purse, which was on the floor. She picked it up and when she walked around the corner, she saw Vivianne lying in a pool of blood. She said she was too shocked to move. Then when the fire alarm went off she dropped the purse and ran. She can't explain how the purse got in the Dumpster."

"Well, they didn't arrest her so they must have believed her, right?"

"It would have helped if she'd have remembered picking up the purse in the first place when she made her original statement. Now, with her prints on the purse plus the fact that there is no evidence proving she was granted an interview, her story is sounding like bullshit." Carl ran a hand over his face and sat down on the bench I'd just vacated.

"She didn't have a purse when I saw her at the auditorium after the fire alarm went off," I said. But truthfully, remembering back to seeing Allegra coming up the steps from the auditorium's basement, I only recalled the terrified look on my sister's face, not whether or not she was carrying anything with her.

"You're her sister, Kendra. I don't think what you saw is going to hold much weight with Harmon and Mercer. I just wish there was some proof that Vivianne had really consented to that interview."

If Allegra had lied about the interview and now the purse and ended up going to jail, she wouldn't have to worry about going alone because my foot would find a permanent home in her ass.

"But what about Allie's clothes? Have the tests come back yet?"

"No. Their crime lab is understaffed and backed-up. They had to send the clothes to the state crime lab, which is even more understaffed and backed-up. I'm not sure when we'll get those results."

"So what is her motive supposed to have been for killing Vivianne?" I was talking to Carl, but my sister emerged red-eyed from the restroom and answered for him.

"They think I showed up at Vivianne's dressing room uninvited to try and interview her. She told me no and threatened to call the police. When she turned and headed for the phone, I flipped out and grabbed whatever happened to be closest to me, which was the letter opener, and stabbed her in the back. They also think I was trying to make it look like a robbery by taking the purse and tossing it in the Dumpster. I swear I dropped that purse when the alarm went off. I don't even know where the Dumpster at Cartwright Auditorium is."

"The only reason why they haven't arrested her is because her prints weren't on the letter opener. It was wiped clean," Carl said.

"Was there anything missing from the purse?" I was hoping that no money in the purse could point to someone desperate for cash, like Kurt Preston.

"They wouldn't tell us," Carl said. I told him about the argument I'd overheard between Kurt and Cliff Preston. Carl perked up considerably.

My cell phone rang and I answered without thinking. It was Mama. Just great! I'd been waiting to tell her about Allegra being taken in for questioning until after it was over. I knew she'd just rush down the station and be worried to death, and in the process, annoy the hell out of me. I knew she had a right to know what was going on with her granddaughter. But don't I have a right to some peace?

"Is your sister with you? I'm about to go to bed and if she's not here in the next twenty minutes, she'll get locked out and will have to stay with you."

"We're on our way," I told her. I wondered how ready for bed she'd be when we told her the latest news?

I spent the night at Mama's. I had no choice. It was a weird night. After we arrived and told her all about what was going on, she was beyond pissed. I couldn't tell who she was the maddest at: me for not calling and telling her what was going on or Allegra for getting herself into such a mess or Carl for not being able to do more to get my sister out of her mess. She ranted and raved for a while and then told Carl to go home and me and Allegra to go to bed. She must have forgotten I had a place of my own because when I started to walk out with Carl, she grabbed me and told me to go to bed in a voice I didn't dare disobey. I had a switch-cutting flashback and hurried upstairs behind Allegra. If it wasn't for the memory of Mama's hissy fit ringing in my ears, it would have almost been like old times. Allegra and I were sharing the same room we'd stayed in years ago when we used to spend the night as kids. The twin beds even had the same spreads they'd had all those years ago, white, with little blue— faded now—cornflowers. Cute.

I couldn't sleep and slipped downstairs to watch TV with the sound turned down low so as not to wake Mama. At three in the morning I was still awake. I decided to see if there was any peach cobbler left. The house was dark and quiet. So quiet that the sudden sound of a cat yowling from somewhere outside made me jump. I walked into the kitchen. The only light came from moonlight streaming in through the gaps in the closed curtains and the glow of the fluorescent light over the kitchen sink that Mama always left on.

I headed into the pantry and spied the foil-wrapped cobbler dish on the counter. My mouth started to water. I reached for the dish and detected movement to my left behind the curtains of the small window that looked out over the back porch. I turned and was frozen to the spot as the movement continued. Someone was on the back porch. I listened and could hear the creak of footsteps. I grabbed either side of the lacy curtains, yanked them open, and looked out. I was face to face with a black ski-masked face, pressed against the window. My heart jumped into my throat blocking the scream that was welling up inside me. The person in the ski mask turned and I could hear pounding footsteps running. For some unknown reason that still escapes me to this day, I flew across the kitchen toward the back door. My hands were sweaty and my fingers fumbled first with the deadbolt then the latch on the screen door. Once I had it unlocked, I raced out onto the empty porch, tripped over a pot full of tomato plants, smacked my head against the porch's wooden railing and knocked myself out cold. Damn! And all I'd wanted was some cobbler.

CHAPTER 6

Mama found me conked out on the back porch. The too-tight nightshirt I'd borrowed from Allegra had ridden up exposing my cotton granny panties to the cool night air as I hung half-on, half-off the porch. Mama thought I'd been sleepwalking. I hadn't walked in my sleep since I was a kid. My parents used to wake up in the morning and find me everyplace but in my bed: once in the backseat of our car, another time in the basement laundry room and one place that I've yet to live down—Duke, the dog next door's dog house. But I hadn't been sleepwalking. I'd startled an intruder.

"Just let me throw on some clothes and I'll take you over to the E.R. You need to let them check you out," Mama said, handing me a bag of ice.

"Forget the E.R. You need to call the police. Someone tried to break in here," I pleaded. Mama wasn't convinced.

"What do I have that anybody would want?" She made a sweeping gesture around the room with her hand.

"Maybe someone wanted to find out if there was anything valuable in here?"

"So someone tried to break in and you ran after them?"

"Yes!"

"In your nightgown with no shoes on?" she asked looking skeptical.

"Yeah," I replied in a small voice.

"And if you'd caught the person what would you have done, spit on them?"

I shrugged. What would I have done? What in the world had I been thinking?

"I know you were up watching TV. What were you watching?"

I glared at her and mumbled the title.

"I didn't hear you," Mama said sweetly.

"Friday Foster," I said loudly.

"Hmm. Would that be that old Pam Grier movie where she gets caught up in some kinda murder conspiracy?" I nodded.

"Well, there you have it. You watched that movie, and with everything that's going on with your sister, had some crazy dream you were chasing after some imaginary intruder in your sleep. You were sleepwalking and tripped and fell."

"Mama, I swear I wasn't sleepwalking. I know what I saw."

"And I know what I heard," she said, firmly.

"You heard the intruder, too?" I asked excitedly.

"No. I heard you snoring. You were asleep, Kendra. Now, do you want to go to the E.R. or not?" She gently placed a warm hand on my head making it feel instantly better.

"No," I replied. Could I have really been asleep?

"Then I suggest you go back to bed. It's almost four in the morning and I'd like to get a couple of more hours sleep. God only know what the morning will bring."

How right she was.

Mama, Allegra, and I were eating breakfast when Noelle called with bad news. Until she was cleared of all suspicion in Vivianne's murder, Allegra had been suspended from *Hollywood Vibe*. Little sister did not take it well.

"I cannot believe they are doing this to me," she wailed, as big sloppy tears ran down her face. She pounded her fists on the table, almost spilling my milk.

Mama and I tried to console her but she pushed us away. She wasn't about to let us ruin her full-blown tantrum.

"I bet that bitch Noelle didn't even stand up for me. If they want to fire someone it should be her ass!"

"Watch your language, Allie. I know you're upset but this isn't helping. And they haven't fired your butt yet. Try and see it from their point of view," Mama said.

"This is just so unfair. I didn't do anything. Why is this happening to me?" Allegra stretched her arms up over her head toward the ceiling and shook her fists. All she had to do was vow never to be hungry again and she could have put Scarlett O'Hara to shame. All this melodrama and it wasn't even eight-thirty yet.

"What do you mean Noelle's the one who should be fired?" I asked. Allegra sighed and lowered her arms, settling into a nice subdued funk.

"Noelle's got a gambling problem, a serious gambling

problem. Cards, slots, horses, sports, you name it. If there were two little kids racing on their bikes, she'd bet on it. She's always broke. Once, she even came to work all bruised and beat up and I heard it was because she owed some guy a lot of money for a gambling debt she couldn't pay. She's already been to rehab a couple of times but I don't think it took."

"You think she's still gambling?" Mama asked.

"She gave me a ride home from the studio a couple of weeks ago when my car was in the shop. Her car had old scratch-off lottery tickets all over the floor and backseat. I saw some betting slips sticking out of her visor."

"As long as she does her job, why should *Hollywood Vibe* care about how she spends her private time?" I asked before Mama could.

"Because I suspect she's been using money from her expense account to pay her gambling debts. She's also been using her company cell phone to place bets. And it's awfully funny that a lot of people at the studio have had money stolen in the past couple of weeks. Noelle's probably resorted to stealing to feed her habit."

Mama and I looked at each and shook our heads.

"I'm not going down without a fight. *Hollywood Vibe* is not gonna just kick me to the curb," Allegra said getting up from the table. I didn't like the sound of that.

"What are you planning on doing?" I asked.

"I'm going to let the public know I'm innocent. My fans need to hear the truth from my lips. I'm going to hold a press conference right here on the front porch."

"Oh no you're not," Mama said, vigorously shaking her head. "You're going to lay low and keep your mouth shut. Whoever killed Vivianne might think you saw something and come after you."

In an effort to back Mama up and prove I hadn't been sleepwalking, I opened my mouth to speak up about my encounter with the ski-masked intruder. But Allegra held up her finger to my mouth like she was shushing a child.

"Why would the killer do that?" Allegra said angrily. "I'm the one they're suspicious of. If I was the person who killed Vivianne I'd lay low and let the police think I did it. Wouldn't you?" she asked, turning to me. She did have a point. But I knew better than to say so in front of Mama, who was looking like she wanted to beat someone.

"As long as you are staying under this roof, you will do as I say. And I say there will be no press conferences held on my front porch, back porch or any point in between. Do you hear what I'm saying, girl?"

"Fine. I'll go stay with Kendra then," Allegra said, sounding very much like the spoiled child she still was. She turned to walk out of the kitchen.

Mama angrily reached out toward Allegra as she passed, as though she was about to snatch a handful of honey-blond hair out of her head, but a loud knock on the back door made us all jump. It was Carl. You'd have thought it was Santa finally bringing her long-awaited Oompa Loompa, the way my sister's face lit up like a Christmas tree. She sashayed over to give Carl a hug. Now, I wanted to snatch her bald, too.

* * *

Even though I was on spring break that week from my job at the Clark Literacy Center, I still had to work at my other job as a hostess at Estelle's, my uncle Alex's restaurant. Estelle's, with its exposed brick walls, black-and-white checked tile floor and antique jukebox in the far corner, was named after Mama and had been a popular hangout with the students, faculty and staff of nearby Kingford College since it had opened several years ago.

It was early afternoon and business was slow. Kingford College was also on spring break. You could tell this by the way the locals were out in force, happy to have their town back even for a brief time. There were only a few people in the restaurant and I spent most of my shift folding napkins and silverware together, and staring out the restaurant's large front picture window, watching people who had to have fewer problems than me walk past.

"What's your problem?" asked Joy Owens, one of the other hostesses who'd just arrived to relieve me.

Joy is all of four foot eleven and usually wears her burgundy-tinted hair pulled back into a knot at the back of her head with bangs that cover her eyes and make her look about sixteen. Not a shy, innocent, debutante sixteen, either. More like a worldly, hard assed sixteen. Despite her teenage looks, Joy is actually a twenty-two-year-old art major at Kingford College.

"No problem, Joy. How about you? You having a nice day?" I asked with exaggerated politeness.

"I saw your sister on the news the other day. She's sure got a big problem. Hope they don't put her fine ass in jail. Do the words *prison bitch* mean anything to you?" she asked with a sneer.

"Do the words *kiss my ass* mean anything to you?" I responded, smiling sweetly. I wasn't about to let her annoy me. Joy is easily the most unpleasant person I've ever known. To say she doesn't live up to her name would be like saying King Kong was just big-boned.

"Now, see, I was about to tell you something about your girl Lynette. But since you got such a shitty attitude, you can forget it." I watched as she started to stalk back to the locker room.

"What about Lynette?" I called out before she could get too far. She turned and gave me a Grinchlike smile that made me wonder what in the world she was up to.

"I saw her over in Springfield this morning looking crazy as hell," Joy said, laughing spitefully.

"Where in Springfield? When was this?" I asked suspiciously.

"Downtown by the marketplace. She was sitting on one of those benches where people catch the city bus. I saw her this morning when I was coming from my girlfriend's crib."

"When did Cory move to Springfield?"

"Cory?" she said with an angry snort. "I cut her ass loose three months ago. You know that crazy bitch almost killed me."

Joy's ex-girlfriend, Cory, had accidentally, or so she

claimed, backed over Joy with her car almost a year ago after a heated argument. Joy still walks with a slight limp as a result. I guess I wasn't surprised they'd broken up. But then again, I wasn't surprised anyone would hit Joy with their car, either. What did amaze me was that Joy, with her perpetually frowned-up face and less-than-sparkling personality, was able to get a girlfriend in the first place.

"Did you say anything to Lynette?"

"Why would I say anything to her ass? She ain't my friend," she replied, like I'd just asked her something completely unreasonable. "Look, you made me late clocking in," she said in disgust, gesturing to the clock on the wall behind me. I ignored her as a group of people walked into the restaurant in search of a late lunch. After seating them, I grabbed my purse and was off to Springfield in search of my best friend.

Springfield was a small city located about a fifteen-minute drive from Willow. My father, Ken Clayton, is originally from Springfield but moved to Willow after marrying my mother Deirdra. Yes, my name is a combination of theirs. They moved to Florida five years ago after my father took early retirement from his job as mail carrier.

Once in Springfield, I headed down South Limestone Street toward downtown. I drove past South High School with its impressive white domed top, hung a left onto Spring Street, and turned right onto South Fountain Avenue. I decided to park my car at the marketplace, a massive three-story brick building built in the 1890s that used to be a farmer's market and housed city hall's offices. The old marketplace building certainly looked much better than Springfield's current city hall building with its outdated 1970s architecture that reminded me of a giant parking garage. Much like Willow, Springfield had once had a thriving downtown that had become a shadow of its former self after some major businesses pulled up stakes and left town or went under altogether. The big, hulking, abandoned buildings littering Springfield's downtown reminded me of the fossilized remains of huge prehistoric beasts. You could still see how grand they used to be, despite all the broken windows and graffiti making them look all the more sad and derelict.

I made a shortcut through the marketplace, ending up on the side that faced High Street. I spotted the benches that Joy had been talking about near the bus kiosks, and walk over to see if I could spot Lynette, though I was still doubtful Joy had actually seen her. What in the world would Lynette be doing in Springfield? I looked around for her or her black Nissan Altima. I saw about a dozen or so people lounging on or standing near the benches waiting for buses. Even though the buses had yet to arrive I thought I still detected a whiff of bus exhaust. Some of the people waiting looked like students, others were dressed in the uniforms of fast food restaurants and were obviously on their way to or from work, most were elderly people with shopping bags full of groceries. None of them was Lynette.

For the next forty minutes I walked all over downtown

Springfield hoping to spot my best friend or her car with no luck. It was hot. Sweat was trickling down my back, and my feet were beginning to ache even though I had on my running shoes. I felt like an idiot for listening to Joy. She was probably still laughing. Having realized I'd wasted enough time on my fool's errand, I headed back to my car, once again cutting through the marketplace to the parking lot. Numerous small shops had taken up residence inside the marketplace. You could find everything from handmade jewelry, antiques, leather goods and scented candles to decadent desserts, deli sandwiches and roasted peanuts. The smell of freshly baked brownies stopped me on my way out to the parking lot and led me into a bakery called Just Desserts. I bought a well-deserved—in my opinion—chocolate brownie with walnuts and thick chocolate icing and sat at a small table by the window to eat it. From where I was sitting, I could see people entering and exiting the building. I'd put the last morsel of the moist brownie in my mouth and was licking chocolate icing from my fingers when I noticed a white VW van pull up to the curb outside. A familiar-looking man got out and entered the marketplace with two equally familiar people greeting him as he walked in.

The man was white, middle-aged, balding and wore polyester pants in a revolting shade of avocado green. His yellow-and-red short-sleeved Bermuda shirt looked straight out of the fifties, as did his thick black horn-rimmed glasses. I recognized him as the man who'd tried to hug Vivianne DeArmond during the autograph session at the awards ceremony. Seeing the man wasn't much of a big deal but it was the red-headed woman and the light skinned young black man with her that surprised me. They were none other than Noelle Delaney and her hot-lipped lover boy—or should I say lover dude, Kurt Preston. Kurt was holding a medium-sized box that Mr. Bermuda Shirt was looking at in much the same way as I'd eyed my brownie. He started to take the box from Kurt, but Noelle stepped in front of him and held out her hand. Bermuda Shirt looked momentarily confused then pulled out a wad of money from his pocket, peeled off several bills and handed them to Noelle. Noelle counted the bills quickly before stuffing them in her purse. She gestured for Kurt to hand over the box. Bermuda Shirt looked like he'd been given a key to the city.

Well, well, well. How interesting. I could feel my curiosity racing into overdrive. I moved over to a table nearer to the door and strained to hear their conversation. But there was no conversation. I was disappointed to see Noelle and Kurt leave. Bermuda Shirt walked over and pressed the button for the elevator. I watched as he got on and disappeared behind the closing doors. I couldn't stop wondering what was in the box Kurt had given him. I knew no one lived in the marketplace and figured the man had a shop someplace on one of the upper floors. I walked up to the bakery's counter and bought a half dozen more brownies to take home, hoping also to get a little info.

"Would you happen to know a bald man who wears

horn-rimmed glasses and drives a white VW van? I think he has a shop here in the marketplace," I asked the slender woman who handed me my box of brownies. I wondered if it was willpower or a speedy metabolism that kept her so slim around so many goodies.

The woman thought for a minute before a look of recognition spread across her face. "You must be talking about Mr. Cabot. I don't know his first name. But I think the name of his shop is Cabot's Cave. It's up on the second floor."

"Thanks," I told her and headed out to the elevator, wondering what a shop called Cabot's Cave sold.

There wasn't much on the second floor of the marketplace. There was a large banquet room, an antique shop and a used book store. Most of the second floor was made up of empty spaces that were being renovated. Paint cans, tarps and rolls of carpet lined the halls. I could smell turpentine and wood shavings. Cabot's Cave was the last shop at the end of a short hallway. The door of the shop was light blond wood with a large frosted-glass panel in the center. The words *Cabot's Cave* were painted on the glass in big gold block letters trimmed in black. Underneath that, was the name of the proprietor, Donald Cabot, and a phone number. Hanging from a hook on the wall by the door was a plastic sign that read: Closed. The store's hours were handwritten on small piece of white cardboard taped at eye level above the doorknob: Open Tuesday thru Saturday 10am—6pm Closed Sundays & Mondays. I knocked anyway. For a second I thought I heard movement behind the closed door but no one answered. Apparently, I was going to have to wait to find out what Cabot's Cave sold and what was in the box. I pulled a pen from my purse and wrote the shop's phone number on top of the brownie box. I headed back to my car, stuck the Isley Brother's Greatest Hits in my tape deck, and headed back to Willow to the sounds of "Footsteps in the Dark."

Mrs. Carson, my landlady and Mama's best friend, was sitting in her usual spot on the front porch when I got home. Today, I was surprised to see her dressed not in her usual striped house dress and slippers but a royal-blue warm-up suit and white tennis shoes. Her gray hair was braided in its usual crown on the top of her head. A large tapestry purse with a thick black strap sat on her lap. A big gift bag with a pink pony on the front and a profusion of white tissue sticking out of the top sat at her feet. Mahalia, her Siamese cat, was pawing at the pony's yarn tail.

"What you got it that box, missy?" she asked as I approached the porch.

"I'll tell you what's in the box if you tell me where you're going looking so cute." She rolled her eyes, but I could tell she was pleased by the compliment.

"Today's my great grandbaby's first birthday. They're having the party at that Chuck E. Cheese's place and I'm waitin' for my ride," she said with a grimace, which indicated to me that spending time in a restaurant full of screaming kids wasn't exactly her cup of tea.

"Which one?"

"Loreen's girl, Sienna. I just hope that baby's sorry daddy stays away. Did you know he was a thief? He'll steal the wax right outta yo' ears if you don't watch him. I'ma have my eye on that boy if he shows up. Better not start no mess if he knows what's good for him."

Seeing as how Mrs. Carson's favorite son, Stevie, was also sticky-fingered, I was amazed she was being so judgmental. I ignored her comments and opened the box revealing the brownies. She reached inside, grabbed the biggest one and took a bite.

"Not bad. Mine are better, though."

"Have fun at the party," I told her as I walked up the steep steps to my apartment. I had the key in the lock and was about to open the door when Mrs. Carson called out to me.

"Kendra, that Reverend Rollins came by here lookin' for you. Said it wasn't nothing important and he'll stop back by. I hope you ain't steppin' out on that nice Carl, are you?"

"No. It's nothing like that," I called out, opening my door. Since it wasn't anything important, meaning not about Lynette, then why was he stopping by?

"Good! 'Cause that Carl's a cutie and anyway I heard Morris Rollins was running 'round with that Winette Barlow. You know, Crazy Frieda's sister-in-law?"

Huh? I almost dropped the box of brownies. I turned to ask her to repeat what she'd just said, but a car horn sounded and I watched as my landlady hurried off the porch and jumped into a waiting car.

I'd met Winette Barlow last year when I'd been attending a funeral. Winette's deceased sister-in-law, Elfrieda aka Crazy Frieda, whom everyone in town had mistakenly thought to be a bag lady, was also laid out that day in the same funeral home. Much like Rollins, Winette was an attractive fifty-something widow. She was always stylishly dressed and very friendly whenever I'd run into her in public. I didn't have to think why he'd be attracted to her. I heard a purr that sounded like a busted carburetor and looked down. Mahalia slunk up the steps, leapt gracefully up on my railing, and looked at me with her almond-shaped blue eyes as if to say, "Well, *you* don't want him. So, what's your problem?"

Damned cat.

The next day I was back in Springfield. I kept a half-hearted eye out for Lynette, though I knew I wouldn't see her. I'd called Greg the night before and he hadn't heard another word from her. He'd lied to Justine and the kids, telling them Lynette was away on an overnight trip for work. He didn't know how long he could keep the news of Lynette running off from her mother. Greg and I had agreed that if Lynette didn't turn up the next day, we'd have no choice but to tell Justine. I wasn't looking forward to that conversation at all. In the meantime, Allegra had indeed come back to stay with me.

I was sitting on my couch with a bottle of wine and the box of brownies, having a pity party over a man I had no business being upset over, when my door flew open, revealing Allegra with all her crap—again. This time, I refused to give up my bedroom and made her sleep on the couch. My sister was understandably jumpy. Every time she heard a car door slam she would run to the window, convinced it was Harmon and Mercer coming to arrest her. Plus, she polished of the rest of my brownies.

"I needed them more than you," she'd told me when I spotted the empty bakery box. I'd only been out of the room a few minutes. She must have inhaled those last three brownies. Then I watched as she picked up the half-full wine bottle and chugged the rest of it wiping a trickle of wine from her chin with the sleeve of her shirt.

"Allie, it's going to be okay. Carl's a damned good lawyer. You have nothing to worry about." I gave her hand a reassuring squeeze.

"Yeah, I have to admit he looks like he'd be damned good," she'd said with a sly smirk, then let out a small belch.

"He is," I'd told her rather frostily. Then, having nothing left to say, I had gone to bed and dreamt about catching Allegra and Carl in my bed feeding each other brownies.

My sister was actually the main reason I was back in Springfield. I wanted to know what was in the box that Kurt had given Donald Cabot, and if it could possibly have anything to do with Vivianne's murder. I knew I had to help my baby sister no matter what, even if she did annoy the hell out me and was after my man. Once this mess was cleared up, she could go back to L.A. and leave me to live my boring life.

This time, when I arrived at Cabot's Cave, the door

was open. As I walked in, I could hear Percy Faith's "Theme from a Summer Place" coming from an old record player sitting on the shop's front counter. A slight breeze was coming from one of the shop's large open windows. Cabot's Cave wasn't cavelike at all. It was a large, light and airy space with a high ceiling, bright white walls and same the gleaming blond woodwork that the front door was made of. The shop was filled almost to the gills with old movie posters, vintage records, toys and other odds and ends connected either to the movies or television. Under one glass-topped display case there were vintage lunch boxes from the fifties, sixties and seventies. The two dozen or so boxes included the Flintstones, Howdy Doody, Star Wars and Scooby Doo. I even spied a yellow Josie and the Pussycats lunch box identical to the one I used to carry as a kid. My mouth fell open when I saw the price, and I wished I'd held on to mine. Who knew old lunch boxes would be so valuable?

I flipped through the albums and was inspecting a plastic-encased soundtrack to the movie *West Side Story* when Donald Cabot emerged from another room and greeted me with smile. Today he was dressed in a red-and-black two-toned bowling shirt with the words *Daddy O* stitched on the front pocket, and jeans cuffed and rolled up past his ankles. Red Chuck Taylor high-topped tennis shoes were laced tightly around his skinny ankles and made his already big feet look boatlike. The shop's lights made his bald spot look shiny and his eyes squinted at me from behind his thick horn-rimmed glasses. If pressed to describe what look he was trying to capture I'd have to say it was *Revenge of the Nerds* meets *Grease.*

"Hello. Are you finding what you're looking for?" he asked with such hope and enthusiasm I wondered how many customers he actually had on any given day. Was there a big market for memorabilia?

"You've got a lot of good stuff here," I replied, ignoring his question and making a sweeping gesture around the shop.

"Thank you," he said, grinning and turning slightly red. I could tell he was as proud of his shop as any mother would be of their child.

"You know, if you can't find what you're looking for here I can always try and track something down for you from another collector." I was about to tell him that wouldn't be necessary when I happened to glance over his shoulder and noticed a poster on the wall. I brushed by him and stared at what looked like an original poster for the movie that launched Vivianne DeArmond's career, *Asphalt City.*

The poster depicted a very young and beautiful Vivianne dressed in a tight black skirt, slit thigh-high on one side, and a yellow halter top. A black scarf was knotted around her neck. Black open-toed, high-heeled sandals graced her feet and large silver hoop earrings dangled from her ears. Her hair was long and wavy with one side falling over her right eye. Lush red lips pouted seductively as she leaned suggestively against a lamppost with her voluptuous breasts thrust out and straining against her top. The movie's tagline, "Love Her at Your Own Risk," screamed in red letters across the top of the poster, underneath the title.

"It was her most famous role," said Donald Cabot walking over to stand beside me. "Her other film work was quite special, as well, but she could never quite capture the intensity of emotion she projected as Pearly Monroe," he continued wistfully. I wondered what he thought about *Demon Kitty*.

A lot of people thought *Asphalt City* was a masterpiece. I thought it was one of the most depressing movies I'd ever seen. Vivianne played Pearly Monroe, a prostitute who seduces a naive young policeman, Sam Hart, and talks him into robbing and killing her vicious pimp and lover, Johnny Desmond. Instead, their plan backfires and Desmond kills the cop in self-defense. Pearly rats Desmond out to the police and testifies against him in court. Desmond is sent to the electric chair. After his execution, a destitute and guilty Pearly realizes she loved Desmond after all and can't live without him. The movie ended with her throwing herself off a bridge. The credits rolled as her trademark black scarf fluttered in the wind. Not exactly an uplifting tale, but Vivianne's performance was excellent. Plus, the fact that Vivianne was rumored to be romantically involved with the movie's very French and very married director, Jacques St. Marchand, didn't exactly hurt ticket sales.

"She deserved an Oscar for that role," Donald Cabot declared indignantly.

"Yes, she did," I agreed. "I saw you at the award ceremony for Vivianne DeArmond this past Saturday, didn't I?" I asked matter-of-factly. Cabot swung round and gave me a startled look.

"You were there?" he asked, surprised.

"Of course I was there. I'm a huge Vivianne DeArmond fan. I can't believe she's really gone." I shook my head and tried my best to look distraught.

"I cried like a baby when I heard about it on the news. Hollywood has lost one of its brightest stars. I just wish she could have done one more movie." He looked as if he was about to cry and I pressed on.

"And to think there was a killer roaming around the auditorium," I said to gauge his reaction. Just how much of a fan of Vivianne's was Donald Cabot? Did he try and approach Vivianne in her dressing room and get angry when she rejected him again? Could he have killed her?

"You know," he said, looking around as though the shop was filled with people and he didn't want to be overheard. "I tried to see Vivianne in her dressing room and that horrible assistant of hers was guarding that room like a sentinel. I wonder where in the world she was when Vivianne was murdered. If you ask me," he murmured, looking around again. "I bet she killed Vivianne."

CHAPTER 7

"Why do you think that? Did you hear them arguing or something?" I asked hopefully.

"Oh, no, nothing like that," he said quickly. "But I never saw that woman leave Vivianne's side the whole time she was at the ceremony. It's strange she would have left Vivianne alone and she's sure mean enough to be capable of murder." He was certainly right about that, I thought, as an image of a raging Harriet Randall being wrestled to the ground by the police flashed in my mind.

"Why were you trying to see Vivianne?" I asked.

"I wanted to invite her to my unveiling," he said, rubbing his hands together excitedly.

"Of your shop?"

"My new display. Come and see," he replied, ushering me toward the back of the shop from which he'd emerged only moments before.

I allowed him to lead me into a small room just off the shop's main area. He flipped a switch on the wall and I felt as though I'd stepped into a shrine. The entire room was wall-to-wall Vivianne. The walls were adorned with posters from every one of her movies, including *Demon*

Kitty. There were mannequins dressed in her movie costumes. I recognized the black skirt and yellow halter top from *Asphalt City,* and the midnight-blue evening gown she wore as torch singer Ginger Nolan in the movie *Club Savoy.* There were autographed pictures and movie props: the silk cushions she lounged on as scheming harem girl Yasmeen in the movie *Arabian Adventure,* the sparkling silver crown she wore during her guest starring role as alien Queen Zenobia on an episode of *Star Trek,* and the nunchacku she used as ass-kicking private eye Sassy Parker in the early seventies blaxploitation movies *Sassy Mama* and *Sassy Mama's Revenge.* There was even a crate full of copies of her unmemorable one and only album, *ViVi Sings,* which one harsh music critic said should have the word *badly* tacked on the end of the title.

I wondered what Vivianne would have thought of her entire career laid out in this little room. Would she have been flattered or, like me, wondering if Donald Cabot had a cage in his basement with her name on it? I could feel Cabot's eyes on me awaiting my reaction. I certainly didn't want to disappoint or offend him since I'd yet to get the information I'd come for.

"This is amazing. How in the world did you get all of this stuff? Is all this authentic?"

Cabot had been grinning until I asked about the authenticity of his display, then a frown eclipsed his face and he got a little huffy. "Of course it's all authentic. Most of it came from memorabilia auctions, and the rest I bought from private sellers."

I noticed some of the items weren't movie-related and must have been Vivianne's personal things. The movie stuff didn't have prices, but the personal items had tags on them. I looked at the tag on a cream-colored lace slip and had to keep my jaw from dropping. Donald Cabot was charging an arm and a leg to anybody who wanted a piece of Vivianne.

"I didn't realize this kind of stuff would be so valuable," I said.

"To be honest, there hasn't been much interest in Vivianne's memorabilia in quite some time. But now that's she's dead there's been renewed interest in everything to do with her. You're looking at the single largest collection of Vivianne DeArmond memorabilia in the world and it's only going to get bigger," he announced beaming.

"Really. Why is that?"

"Let's just say I've tapped into a new source," he said coyly. Based on what I'd witnessed yesterday, I knew who the new source must be.

"Am I the first one to see this new display?"

"Actually, I was quite honored to have Vivianne's ex-husband and former manager, Cliff Preston, attend a private viewing of the collection. He even brought his wife and son with him. He was quite impressed."

"Wow. When was this?" I asked excitedly. My enthusiasm may have been fake but not my interest in his answer.

"Hmm. Let's see," he said concentrating. "It was last Friday evening, the night before the awards ceremony. I was hoping he'd bring Vivianne with him but no such luck." He shook his head sadly.

"How'd he even know about your display?"

"Oh, I contacted him months ago when I first heard the Starburst Film Festival was going to be honoring her. It was long overdue in my opinion," he sniffed. "Anyway, I wrote and told him I was putting together a display and invited him to view it. I wrote to Vivianne, too, of course, but she never responded. I just know that assistant of hers probably never even gave her my letter." I nodded in commiseration.

I'd witnessed Kurt Preston and Noelle Delaney selling a box to Donald Cabot. It had obviously held some of Vivianne's things. I wondered if Kurt had known his mother's memorabilia would become so valuable once she was dead. Did he get tired of her refusing to give him money and come up with a deadly plan after seeing this display? Was Noelle involved, as well? She certainly needed money, too. If I was right and Kurt and Noelle had something to do with his mother's murder, I knew Harmon and Mercer would want proof. Even if they didn't believe me, at least they'd have someone else to be suspicious of besides my sister.

"To be honest, Mr. Cabot, I've come here because I have a small collection myself. I collect items owned by local stars. I'd like to buy something for my collection. Is everything here for sale?" I said looking around the small room.

"Everything is for sale. What would you like?" Donald Cabot said his face glowing with excitement.

"I'm not quite sure. Do you have any suggestions? Are

these all of Vivianne's things or do you have more that I haven't seen?" I asked carefully.

"This is everything. I think I may have just the thing for you, it came in yesterday. Vivianne was said to be quite the collector when it came to purses, although this is the only one I have," Cabot said gesturing toward a small black beaded evening bag perching on top of the white dresser used in Vivianne's romantic comedy *Nightie Night*.

I walked over and picked the bag up. It was an unusual triangle shape. The sides and bottom of the bag were stiff, silk-covered, and heavily beaded. The top was soft black cloth and closed completely when I pulled the velvet drawstring. It sort of looked like a small ornate laundry bag. I examined the price tag. Ouch. At a hundred and fifty bucks it wasn't cheap. Not surprisingly, it was the least expensive thing on display and I knew I had to buy it to prove to Cabot I was serious. Plus, the bag was pretty cute and I needed a new black one. I'd been looking on my usual trips to Déjà Vu thrift store without luck.

"I'll take it," I said holding the bag out to Cabot. He grinned like a Cheshire cat.

"Excellent, though I have to warn you, this wasn't used in any of her movies. This was a personal item, though she was photographed with it." He gestured to a black-and-white photo of Vivianne in a beaded evening gown with the purse looped around her wrist. "I just had the picture of her with the purse until yesterday. I was so pleased to actually add the purse to the display."

"Wonderful. It'll be perfect for my collection," I told his back as I followed him up front. "I'd be interested in seeing more of Vivianne's handbag collection. Would you happen to be able to give me the name of the person who sold you this one?"

He didn't answer me and I realized he was waiting for his money. I pulled out my checkbook and blew my grocery budget for a month. I held the check just out of his reach and he looked at me impatiently.

"Your seller? Do you know if he has any more of Vivianne's handbags?" I said, waving the check in front of his face. His greedy little eyes glittered behind his thick glasses.

"That information is confidential," he said reaching again for the check, which I still held out of his reach.

"You can't help me at all? I'm willing to pay top dollar." The mention of money practically made Cabot salivate.

"How about I tell my seller of your interest and see what else he may have?"

"I'd really like to talk to the seller myself if that's possible. Of course, you'll handle any sales that result from this meeting," I added quickly when I saw the scowl pop up on his face at the mention of meeting with his seller.

"Leave me your name and number and I'll see what I can do," he said, reaching out and snatching the check. I gave him my name and number and left with my new purse.

* * *

When I got home there was a gold Mercedes Benz parked in front of my duplex. I got out and walked up the front steps. Morris Rollins was sitting on the porch with Mrs. Carson. Just great. He was the last person I wanted to see. The two were laughing like old friends even though I knew Mrs. Carson didn't have a high opinion of Holy Cross and disapproved of Reverend Rollins's popularity with the ladies. I was tickled to see that even my seventy-two-year-old landlady wasn't immune to Rollins's charm. She was giggling like a schoolgirl.

"Here she is," said Mrs. Carson when they finally noticed me coming up the steps. Rollins stood up, making a striking figure even casually dressed in his tan pants and white crew-necked shirt. I could smell his Lagerfeld cologne as I approached the porch. I wondered if Winette Barlow liked the way he smelled, then realized it was really none of my business.

"Hello," I called out, forcing a smile.

"I've got some news for you about Lynette," he said, trotting down the steps to meet me halfway.

"You saw her?" I stopped and looked up at him. The sunshine made his brown skin glow.

"No. But she called and I know where she is. I thought we could go and talk some sense into her," he said, heading to his car and opening the passenger door for me. Why did I suddenly feel like I was stepping into a lion's den?

"Where is she?" I asked, getting in and sinking back

against the leather seat. Rollins got in, started the car and pulled away from the curb before answering.

"She's at the Heritage Arms. She said she knows you and Greg are worried and wanted me to let you know she's okay."

Was he kidding? The Heritage Arms was a roach motel on the edge of town that catered to cheating spouses, truckers, hookers and college students looking for a cheap place to host a party. I was familiar with the Heritage Arms because I'd lost my virginity there the summer before going off to college. I'd also had the misfortune of being attacked by a murderer a year ago in one of the Heritage Arms's less-than-luxurious rooms. I could think of a million other more desirable places to go and be alone, like a cave, for instance.

"When is she planning on coming home?"

"I didn't exactly get the impression that she was planning on coming home. She just told me to tell you guys she was okay," he replied, negotiating a turn. I groaned.

"She's getting married in four days. What is she thinking?" I'd been sympathetic to my best bud in the beginning, but now I was pissed.

"I don't think she's thinking at all. I think she's running scared. Sometimes that happens when people finally get what they want."

"Well, I could wring her neck," I said in exasperation. "She's got a wonderful man who loves her and wants to marry her and what does she do? She runs away."

"Most people have a hard time seeing what's right in

front of their faces," Rollins said softly. I glared at him after I realized it was a not-so-subtle dig at me and his loud, infectious laugh filled the car. I couldn't help but smile.

"Not me," I replied innocently. "I know Carl's a good man and I'm not running from him."

"Does that mean you and Carl are getting married?" he asked. His tone was casual but I saw his hands grip the steering wheel a little too tightly. He had a hell of nerve.

"Not anytime soon. What about you, Reverend? Is there a new lady in your life?" He didn't answer until he stopped at the next light.

"Would it bother you if there was?" he asked, turning to look at me. I could have sworn I detected a bit of sadness in his eyes. I looked away.

"Why would it bother me?" I questioned, sounding cold even to my own ears. He didn't respond and we drove in an uncomfortable silence until we were about to pull into the hotel's parking lot.

As we were pulling into the lot, I noticed a black Nissan Altima pulling out and speeding away. It was Lynette.

"There she is," I said, pointing to the black car. "Hey. Where's she going?" I reached across Rollins's lap and honked his horn. Lynette never looked back. "Follow her," I ordered Rollins, who put his foot on the gas sending me flying back into the passenger seat.

Lynette was driving as though she was in the Indy 500. Rollins's Mercedes was right on her tail. We were on a two-lane road with cars traveling in the opposite direction, and we couldn't pull along side of the Nissan. Rollins was honking his horn for her to stop, but she wouldn't look back. We were close enough for me to see the back of her head and her ponytail. Her car windows were rolled up and I could hear music blaring. She couldn't hear me. I yelled out the window again.

"Lynette! Pull over! Where are you going!" No luck. Finally there were no cars coming down the opposite side of the road and Rollins pulled alongside Lynette's car. I was practically hanging out the window waving my arms.

"Lynette! Lynette!" Just then I saw a blue pickup truck heading straight for us. There was no way we could pull into the other lane because of Lynette's car. I screamed. The driver of the pickup laid on his horn. Rollins grabbed my shirt and pulled me back in the car. He jerked the wheel to the left just in time and ran the Mercedes into a ditch on the side of the road. I groaned and laid my head against the dashboard. Rollins and I were both breathing heavily.

"You okay?" he asked rubbing my back in slow circular motions. I was going to be more than okay if he kept rubbing my back like that. I was going to fall asleep in his lap, not that he'd complain. Then I wondered if he rubbed Winette Barlow's back, too.

"I'm going to kill her," I said, sitting up abruptly, causing Rollins to chuckle. Little did he know I wasn't entirely referring to Lynette.

We drove back to the Heritage Arms and Rollins and I went inside to the motel's front desk to leave a message for Lynette to call, only to be told she'd checked out. Now I was really going to kill her. I didn't need this.

"Try not to be too mad at her, Kendra. Marriage is a big commitment. I bet a day or two away from it all is just what she needs to get her head on straight," Rollins told me on way back to my apartment. I certainly hoped he was right. At any rate, if Lynette wasn't back the next day, Greg could tell Justine himself.

"Thanks, Reverend Rollins," I murmured as I was about to jump out of his car.

"Let me know what happens," he said softly, squeezing my hand before I got out. I was relieved to see him go. The less time spent alone with him the better.

I was feeling restless and hopped in my car and headed over to Mama's house hoping to snag some lunch. Instead, I found myself unable to park at her house. There was a big van belonging to Channel Four news blocking the entrance to the driveway. My sister, dressed in a beige pantsuit with her hair pulled pack into a conservative French roll, was standing in the middle of Mama's big front yard giving an interview to Channel Four news reporter, Tracy Ripkey. I didn't see my grandmother anywhere and wondered if she knew what was going on. I also didn't see Noelle Delaney. Did Allegra even bother clearing this with her producer?

"What is it you'd like viewers to know about your involvement in the murder of Vivianne DeArmond, Miss Clayton?" asked Ripkey. Her big blond bouffant hairdo looked like a cloud of yellow cotton candy and must have been taking up too much camera space because a member of the camera crew silently motioned for her to move so they could get a closer shot of Allegra. My sister was looking solemn and righteous as she gazed into the camera and spoke.

"I'd like everyone to know that I am completely innocent. In fact, I'm a victim, too. Whoever killed Vivianne DeArmond is still out there free while I've been placed under a cloud of suspicion."

"Do you feel you've been treated unfairly by the Willow police department?" Allegra visibly shuddered. Her face crinkled up as if she'd caught a whiff of something foul.

"I think the Willow police department needs to be looking in every direction and not just at me."

"Can you tell us about finding Vivianne's body?" asked Ripkey.

"I can't comment on that due to the ongoing police investigation. But I will say that Vivianne was looking forward to our interview and told me she had an exciting announcement for her many fans."

An exciting announcement? This was the first I'd heard about any announcement. Was Allegra telling the truth or just trying to get more attention for herself? The only other person who could back up her claim was dead. How convenient.

"Do you have any idea what this announcement was?" asked Ripkey, trying hard to look cool and professional but failing big-time. The way her eyes were shining with excitement told me she knew she'd landed a big story.

"She never said," Allegra replied, shaking her head sadly. "I wonder if we'll ever know." Her bottom lip quivered and her eyes widened in childlike wonder. What a ham. I had to bite my lip to keep from laughing.

Ripkey wrapped up the interview and the camera crew started packing up their equipment. I walked over to Allegra, who was removing her microphone, and caught the tail end of the conversation.

"That was wonderful, Allegra. I'm sure we can run this as an exclusive tonight on the six o'clock news," said Ripkey excitedly. She thanked my sister profusely, and Allegra held up her hand in mock protest.

"Not a problem, Tracey. I wanted to tell my side of the story. Thank *you* for giving me the opportunity to tell it."

Tracey finally noticed me standing there and looked over at my sister, who continued to smile and ignore me. What was her problem now?

"I'm Kendra Clayton, Allegra's sister. Nice meeting you," I said, holding out my hand to the reporter when it became apparent no introduction would be forthcoming from Allegra. Tracey Ripkey's eyes lit up with a greedy gleam.

"Great! I'd love a quote from you, as well, Kendra. Can you tell me how you feel about what's going on with your sister?" she asked, fumbling for her microphone. Allegra glared at me and I finally realized she thought I was trying to steal her thunder.

"I'm sorry but I don't have any comment at this time."
I grabbed Allegra by the elbow before the eager reporter
could protest, and ushered her onto the porch. I could feel
Tracey Ripkey's disappointed stare boring into my back.
I waited a few minutes while they finished packing up and
left before confronting my sister.

"What was that all about? I thought Mama said you
couldn't hold a press conference here?"

"No. What Mama said was that I couldn't hold a press
conference on her front porch, back porch, or anywhere
in between. I was in the front yard, and besides," she said,
plopping down into one of the wicker chairs. "It wasn't
a press conference. I came over her to see Mama and she
wasn't home. That reporter and her camera crew showed
up and asked me for an interview as I was getting back
into my car to leave, and I figured, what the hell. Since
Hollywood Vibe doesn't have my back, why should I
keep my mouth shut and take this lying down?"

I glanced over at the driveway and noticed a red Honda
Civic instead of her rented black Camry. "Whose car is
that? I asked, gesturing toward the driveway.

"I had to rent another car. The police impounded my
other rental this morning. I don't know what they expect
to find," she said softly.

I didn't like the sound of that. This just wasn't getting
any better. They truly thought my sister had something
to do with Vivianne's murder. I was worried because I'd
yet to hear from Donald Cabot. What else could I do to
help Allegra? While we sat silently on the porch, Mama

arrived home with some groceries. We helped her unload and put them away as she heated up leftovers from last night's dinner for our lunch. We were all subdued and silent as we ate. Mama was reading the paper and I caught a glimpse of something about a memorial service for Vivianne as she folded it up. While Mama and Allegra washed up the lunch dishes, I took the paper and went into the bathroom to read. It wasn't really much of a story, just a notice about a private memorial service for Vivianne DeArmond being held at the Walker and Willis Funeral Home at six that afternoon. The service was by invitation only. Too bad, because I planned to be there, invitation or not.

I was parked in front of the three-story turn-of-the-century mansion that had been the Walker and Willis Funeral Home for the past fifteen years at four that afternoon dressed in a dark burgundy pantsuit with a black silk blouse. The black beaded purse of Vivianne's that I'd bought was looped around my wrist. I watched for about a half hour as people came and went. How was I going to pull this off? I needed to get in there and hide before Vivianne's service started. Then I could mingle with the family and maybe find out something that could help my sister. As I sat watching, a hearse pulled into the driveway that ran alongside the house. Roger Walker, one of the owners of the funeral home, came up out of the basement from an unseen side door. I could hear him fussing at the driver from where I was parked.

"I've been waiting for an hour, Sonny. Where the hell have you been?" demanded Roger, looking grumpy. Roger Walker was a tall, thin, chinless and eternally annoyed man in his early forties with big eyes that looked permanently startled. It was a good thing he mainly worked in the basement with the deceased and spent limited time with their families because his people skills were about as lively as the corpses he spent the majority of his time with.

"What's the big rush? This guy ain't got no place to be but in the ground," chuckled the tall and muscular Sonny, who looked too cool for school in his black shades with a toothpick dangling from the corner of his mouth.

"You're screwing up my schedule. We're backed up as it is, and you're out joyriding. I better not hear about you using the hearse to run that girlfriend of yours around town. Just 'cause you're Ticia's nephew don't mean you can't be fired." Sonny flipped Roger the finger when he turned his back.

Roger was busy helping Sonny unload the body from the back of the hearse, and I was tempted to sneak into the house through the open basement door while their backs were turned. But I knew the embalming took place in the basement and I wasn't about to try and sneak past any dearly departed souls. Plus, I'm not exactly the Road Runner. I was wearing high-heeled shoes and knew I wouldn't be able to zip across the yard and down the basement steps unseen.

Finally, I got out of the car and headed across the street. I walked up the front steps of the funeral home and walked inside. Like most old Victorian mansions, the foyer was small and dark and it took a second for my eyes to adjust. I could hear people talking and followed the sound to the front parlor where Roger's wife, Leticia, was talking to an elderly couple. Leticia was slightly over-weight and very attractive with such a pleasant and charming personality that people were constantly amazed she was married to Roger. I stood awkwardly in the doorway for a moment before she noticed and gestured for me to have a seat on one of the sofas in the back of the large room. I parked it on a brown leather love seat and waited while Ticia Willis-Walker finished her business with the elderly couple, who were looking mighty uncom-fortable, as though they knew it was only a matter of time before they made their last stop at Walker and Willis and didn't want to be spending any additional time there.

The room we were in was quite nice with comfy leather furniture and plush maroon carpeting. There were vertical blinds in the windows instead of curtains and the taupe walls were covered in Monet reproductions. Cut-glass bowls filled with scented potpourri sat on most of the tables around the room. Ticia must be trying hard to make the house feel like something much more pleasant than a funeral home, espe-cially since she, Roger and their two kids lived on the top two floors. In this room, at least, she'd succeeded.

Finally, the couple left, with a bundle of flyers on various funeral plans clutched in their hands, and Ticia turned her attention to moi. Now, my problem was: What the hell was I going to tell her?

"It's Kendra, right?" asked Ticia, smiling a little uncertainly and sitting down in the leather chair opposite me. She was dressed in a light-gray skirt with a royal blue blouse. A multi strand of silver beads hung around her neck and shiny silver hoops dangled from her ears. Her hair was short and natural and was beginning to go gray. I wasn't surprised she was unsure of my name since I'd attended very few funerals in my lifetime and wasn't at all unhappy that she didn't know me better.

"Yes, that's right. I'm sorry to stop by without an appointment, Mrs. Willis-Walker, but I had some time on my hands and wanted to talk to you about my situation." Just what my situation was I'd yet to figure out.

"Oh, honey," said Ticia softly, leaning forward and taking my hand. "You're not ill are you?" she looked alarmed and gave me a much-needed idea.

"Yes, I am," I began and slumped my shoulders. "I'm going to be having some major surgery soon and I just wanted to make some arrangements for myself, you know, to spare my family the ordeal in case things go…badly," I said, looking away dramatically. "I don't have a lot of money so I thought I'd come and talk to you about my options. You know what I mean, don't you?"

"Of course I do, honey," said Ticia, patting my hand. "I'm sure you won't be needing any arrangements for a very long time, but it's so thoughtful of you to want to spare your loved ones from having to make arrangements for you," she said, like she truly meant it, and then, ever mindful of the fact that she was in business to make money, added, "What kind of arrangements were you thinking about? We have a nice prepaid budget plan that includes a casket, burial plot, two floral arrangements and a nice headstone that includes up to ten words of engraving."

My life summed up in ten words or less. What in the world would I want on my headstone? Here lies Kendra Clayton, never wed, but always well fed. That was exactly ten words.

"Kendra, are you okay?" asked Ticia, sounding concerned that I might be about to expire on her nice leather love seat.

"I'm sure that plan will be fine," I said, giving her a weak smile. She got up to get me some brochures. I looked around for a possible place to hide. It was already going on five o'clock.

"There are two models of caskets to choose from with this particular plan. We have them in our showroom on display. Are you up to taking a look?"

No! I wanted to scream. Picking out my own casket was something I couldn't ever imagine myself being up for. But instead I said, "Are you sure you have time to show me? I read in the paper that Vivianne DeArmond's memorial service is being held here. Don't you have to get ready?"

"Everything is all set for the memorial. We're closing up in about a half hour to get ready for the guests. So, I still have some time. The showroom is just in the next room." She gently took my hand and pulled me to my feet.

I followed her out of the room and down the long hallway and glanced into another room along the way. There were chairs set up and the room was almost filled to capacity with floral arrangements. I caught a glimpse of a large photo of Vivianne sitting on an easel and realized this must be the room the memorial service was being held in.

"This way," said Ticia, standing aside to let me enter a room about the same size as the one we'd just left. But instead of being filled with tasteful furnishings, it was filled with about a dozen shiny new caskets with the lids closed.

"They're all so nice. How will I ever choose?" I said, hoping she'd didn't detected my tone of sarcasm.

"Actually, these are the two that you can choose from with the plan you'll be getting." She led the way down the aisle that ran between the caskets to the back of the room and gestured like a game-show hostess to two coffins, one on either side of her. Then she lifted the lids on both of them.

The one on her left was a plain, no-frills, dark brown casket made of what looked suspiciously like pressboard with a bright, gaudy, yellow satin lining, and the casket on her right was a dull stainless-steel affair lined in a garish red with black fringe on the little pillow. Not exactly the Cadillacs of caskets, but what can you expect on the budget burial plan? I guess I should be happy they weren't cardboard boxes, though that brown one looked a little suspect. I spied a gleaming mahogany casket trimmed in gold with beautifully carved flowers on the front. I went over and lifted the lid revealing the silky pale green embroidered satin lining. As far as caskets went, this one was a beauty. Talk about going out in style.

"How much is this one?" I asked with real enthusiasm.

"This is one of our top-of-the-line models. It's ten thousand dollars. We don't offer layaway," she added quickly, pissing me off. Layaway? That's a hell of a thing to say to someone who may not have much time left. Then, realizing I wasn't really dying and had no need of a casket, I chilled out and turned to give her a brave smile.

"Can I have a few minutes to make up my mind?" She looked at her watch, indicating that a few minutes would indeed be all I could have.

"No problem, Kendra. I'll be in my office at the end of the hall if you have any questions." I smiled my thanks and watched as she left the room, pulling the double doors closed behind her and leaving me to choose between the two equally ugly caskets in private.

Before I could fully focus on what I was going to do, I heard a loud voice from behind the closed doors.

"Aunt Ticia! Your husband's trippin' for real. You better check his ass before I do," I heard Sonny the hearse driver say as he passed by the showroom. I heard his loud voice get fainter the farther down the hall he got. I went over and pressed my ear to the door and could hear Ticia's voice scolding Sonny in hushed angry tones. I couldn't hear everything she was saying but caught the words *customer, showroom, shut up* and *your ignorant behind* and knew Sonny was getting a verbal beat down. I opened the door a crack, looked down the hall and saw Ticia grab

Sonny by the front of his shirt and pull him into her office and shut the door. More loud angry talk could be heard from behind the door. Great! This was just the opportunity I needed to find a hiding place. I quickly opened one of the double doors to the showroom and had started to leave when I spotted Roger Walker heading down the steps from the family's home on the top floors. I jumped back into the showroom and shut the door. The phone in the foyer rang and Roger answered it. I cracked the door again and heard him talking. I waited, but Roger didn't appear to be about to end his conversation anytime soon and I realized that wherever I hid would have to be in the room I was already in and the only place to hide was in one of the caskets. Crap!

CHAPTER 8

It was now or never as I heard the door to Ticia's office open. I hurried across the room and opened the lid of the pretty mahogany casket. Hell, if was going to have to hide in a casket, it was damned well going to be the prettiest one. I flung one leg up into the casket and then hoisted myself up the rest of the way until I was sitting inside. I looked over at the double doors and could see the shadow of two sets of feet underneath the bottom of the door. I pulled the lid shut and lay back in the soft, silky lining just as I heard the door to the showroom open.

"Have you made up your—" I heard Ticia begin then stop when she saw the room was empty. "Kendra?" I heard her say. "Now see, you scared my customer away with your big mouth. Boy, I oughta kick your behind!" Ticia said in a shrill, highly pissed-off voice. I had no idea the placid Ticia Willis-Walker could get so annoyed. Then again, the most mild-mannered person can snap when you mess with their money. "Go set up the guest book for the memorial service and then clock out before I wring your neck." I heard Sonny mumble something unintelligible then heard what sounded like the light being flipped off and doors being shut. Now, all I had to do was wait for the service to start.

It was hot inside the casket. I wanted to get out but kept hearing Ticia's voice in the hallway. I started to sweat despite the fact that I'd propped the lid open a crack with a roll of mints from my purse. I held my watch up to the dim light streaming through the lid and saw that it was quarter to six. I could hear more people in the hallway and realized the guests were arriving. After about ten more minutes, I was unable to stand it any longer. I opened the lid and started to get out when I saw one of the double doors to the showroom start to open. I quickly lay back down, closed the lid and held my breath. I could hear the voices of what sounded like boys, two or three of them. I couldn't be sure.

"We're not supposed to come in here. If my mom catches us I'm dead meat," pleaded the voice of one boy.

"DJ, man, let's bounce. I knew Creepy Clementine wasn't nothin' but a pussy," said another boy cruelly. I heard laughter from yet a third boy.

"Yeah, I ain't never seen a cat so afraid of his mama." Both boys were laughing now. I knew that Roger and Leticia had a teenaged son named Clement. That name, combined with the fact that his parents ran a funeral home, must make school a torture for poor Clement Walker.

"Okay, you can look around, but only for a minute. We're supposed to be studying," said Clement, trying unconvincingly to sound nonchalant.

"Hey, I wonder what it feels like to be inside a coffin,"

said the voice of the boy named DJ. "Hot and uncomfort-able," I was tempted to shout.

"I'll give you LaTonya Marshall's phone number if you get inside," said the other boy, sounding as if he was getting closer.

"No! I told you we aren't supposed to be in here," pleaded poor Clement.

"Tonya Marshall's digits? Hell, for a chance to tap *that* ass I ain't scared of no coffin or your mama, Clementine," said DJ. I almost had a heart attack as the lid to the casket started to lift then slammed shut.

"I said no! We gotta go," said Clement, sounding like he was about to cry.

"Hold this fool, man," commanded DJ of the other boy. I could hear a struggle and decided not only was it time for me to get out of the casket, I wanted to teach DJ and his friend a lesson. I waited for the lid to lift then said in a low, deep growl, "I love company!" I grabbed the shocked-as-shit DJ by his shirt and pulled him into the casket and held him tight as he started to struggle. DJ let out a shrill, high-pitched scream, much like an actress in a B horror movie, tore out of my grasp, leaving most of his T-shirt behind in my hands, and bolted from the room. I guess he won't be getting LaTonya Marshall's digits after all. Lucky girl.

Clement and the other boy ran into each other several times, like the Three Stooges minus one, in their attempts to get out of the room. Once they were gone, I quickly hopped out of the casket and had started to leave when

I heard footsteps rushing down the hall. I quickly opened the lid of a shiny black coffin nearest the door and jumped inside. If I'd known when I got up this morning that I'd be playing musical caskets, I'd have stayed in bed. The double doors to the showroom flew open. I heard Roger Walker's angry voice and Clement's scared breathless one.

"Over here, Dad. There was someone in there, I swear," said Clement, sounding near hysteria.

"Boy, you better not be lying to me. I don't need this mess."

"I'm not lying," said Clement.

I lifted the lid just a hair to see what was going on and saw Roger Walker standing over the mahogany casket. I watched as he lifted the lid, revealing it to be empty. His scowl could have curdled milk. I thought Clement might faint. It was my fault he was about to get into trouble and I felt really bad about what I'd done. But there was nothing I could do about it now. Besides, much to my horror, Clement wasn't about to let it go.

"See, here's DJ's shirt!" said Clement excitedly. Crap! I must have dropped the shirt in my haste to get out of the casket. "That monster ripped it right off his back. I knew I wasn't seeing things. It's probably still here in one of the other caskets."

"Monster?" said Roger skeptically. "What are you talking about?"

"It was this old ugly hag. She was dressed all in red."

An old, ugly hag in red? That little nerd! And it's called *burgundy,* thank you.

"I'll look on this side and you look on the other," said Clement as he went down one side of the room cautiously opening caskets one by one.

Roger was just staring at him like he was an idiot. I quickly closed the lid. I felt myself go cold and stiff with panic. Maybe by the time he got to the black casket I'd actually be dead, giving me a true reason for being here. I heard his fingers on the lid of my hiding place. The gig was up. Or was it?

"Have you two lost your minds?" said the voice of Ticia Willis-Walker, aka my savior, from the doorway of the showroom. "We got folks arriving for the memorial service and you two are running around like you don't have good sense. What are you doing in here?"

"Ma, I saw a—" began Clement. But his mother wasn't having it.

"Clement Mortimer Walker, you shouldn't have seen anything because you're not supposed to be in here, are you?"

Mortimer? That poor boy is screwed coming and going.

"No, ma'am," mumbled Clement.

"Then get your narrow tail up those steps before I put my foot in it, and get that homework done and don't ever bring those knuckleheads into my house again," she said through gritted teeth.

I heard Clement mumble, "Yes, ma'am," as he passed by my casket on his way out of the room. One down, two to go.

"Are you going to help me, Roger? I've got programs

to hand out and there are still more flowers arriving. I can't do this all by myself and what in the world did you say to Sonny?"

"Don't start on me Ticia. You act like you're the only one who works around here—" Roger and Leticia fussed their way out of the showroom. I heard the door shut behind them and was finally able to let out a sigh of relief.

I could finally get out. I'd changed my mind about attending the memorial service. I just wanted to go home. But I soon discovered it wasn't going to be that easy as I pushed on the lid of the casket. It was jammed. I pushed harder and harder, but the lid wouldn't budge.

I took a deep breath and tried to remain calm. Suddenly it seemed as if there wasn't enough air and my breathing became ragged. I started to freak out. I was screaming, though I doubted anyone could hear me. I felt the casket move ever so slightly with my frenzied efforts to get out. Maybe if I could rock it off of its stand onto the floor, the lid would pop open. I started rocking my body from side to side for several minutes. The heavy casket moved a little but not enough to tip it onto the floor. I was becoming sweaty and lightheaded and knew my efforts were decreasing my air supply. Tears of frustration welled up in my eyes. I didn't want to die. I could only imagine what people were going to think when they found my body. No. I wasn't going out like this. I had to get out. I closed my eyes, and was just about to start rocking again, when the lid to the casket opened. Air rushed inside and I gulped it in, noticing that it smelled of Lagerfeld cologne. I opened my eyes and found myself staring up at the handsome face of a shocked and speechless Morris Rollins.

"What are you doing here?" I asked feebly as he helped me out of the casket.

"What am *I* doing here? I came in here for some privacy to use my cell. Kendra, what's going on? Who put you in that casket?"

"You're here for the Vivianne's memorial?" He nodded and I quickly explained why I was there and what had happened. For a second he looked confused, as though he couldn't decide whether to laugh or yell at me. But the former finally won out and he leaned against one of the other caskets, his body heaving in an effort to hold in the side-splitting laughter that was dying to get out. I just glared at him, though the humor of the situation wasn't lost on me, and I could feel a smile tugging at my lips.

"Kendra, I swear, besides God you're the only person I'd want on my side if I ever get into trouble," he said, wiping his streaming eyes. That made me smile.

"Well, I should probably go. Thanks for saving me," I mumbled, turning to leave.

"No, wait," he said, stopping me. "Why don't you come to the memorial service as my guest? Least that way you'll have a legitimate excuse for being there and you can mix and mingle to your heart's content." It was an excellent idea, since I hadn't managed to find out a single thing to help my sister. But I knew there had to be catch.

"And that's all there is to it, huh? You'll let me be your guest?" I asked skeptically.

"Of course, you'll owe me a dinner, preferably a home-cooked one, as payment. I mean, after all, it's the least you could do. I did save your life," he said devilishly.

"Fine, let's go," I said, turning my back on his grinning face and leaving the room.

We headed down the hall where I could see well-dressed people being greeted at the door of the viewing room by Ticia Willis-Walker, who gave me a confused look as I walked up to her accompanied by Rollins. I spoke up before she could say anything.

"I'm so sorry, Mrs. Willis-Walker, for taking off earlier. I had a family emergency and had to run home."

"Not a problem, Ms. Clayton," she said, not really paying attention to me but to my handsome companion, who was giving her his biggest panty-melting smile. I hoped she was so bedazzled by Rollins that it wouldn't occur to her that I was trying to crash the memorial service of a woman whose murder my sister was being questioned about.

"I hope it won't be a problem, Leticia. Kendra and I have some church business to discuss so I asked her to be my guest for the service. I hope you won't make her wait for me in the car," he said gravely.

Ticia gave me a startled look and then patted my arm comfortingly. It hit me that she must be thinking that I was meeting with Rollins to discuss my possible funeral service. This was getting depressing.

"Go right in," she said handing us programs with a picture of Vivianne, gorgeous and smiling, on the front. It was a fairly recent picture that I'd never seen before. Vivianne was dressed in a green twin set, black slacks and pearls and was standing under a large tree with her arms crossed. I wondered if it had been taken on her property.

Most of the chairs in the room were already filled and we took seats in the back. I could see Cliff and Stephanie Preston sitting in the front row with Kurt slouching and sour-faced in a chair a row behind them. Harriet Randall was seated in the front row on the opposite side of the aisle. I noticed she was openly giving the Prestons dirty looks, but either they didn't appear to have noticed or didn't care. Vivianne's casket, a duplicate of the beautiful mahogany-and-carved-flower model I'd recently been hiding in, was sitting in front of the room. I was surprised to see it was closed and draped in a profusion of yellow roses and baby's breath. I wondered if something had been wrong with Vivianne's face that prevented having an open casket. I didn't recognize any of the other people in attendance and guessed by some of the youthful hairdos framing old faces, capped teeth and varying degrees of faded flashiness, that they must be ex-showbiz people. Many of them were stopping to hug a teary-eyed Cliff or nod at Harriet who, depending on their position on the entertainment food chain, either gave them a small tight smile or a queenly wave of her hand. A sudden image of Joy Owens in about forty years popped into my head when I looked at Harriet's grim face. Stephanie and Kurt got ignored all together. Kurt didn't seem to care but Stephanie looked hurt.

"Why were you invited?" I asked Rollins when we were situated in our seats.

"Harriet Randall is a member of Holy Cross. She asked me if I'd come for moral support." Harriet at Holy Cross? Or any church for that matter? But then again, a person who bit a police officer and bashed people with a patent-leather purse would definitely be a candidate for spiritual healing. Was she a murderer, too? Could Donald Cabot be right in his suspicion that Harriet killed Vivianne?

"Why wasn't the service at Holy Cross?" I asked.

"Because Vivianne was an atheist. She didn't want a church service. She also wanted to be cremated and have her ashes spread out under the big Hollywood sign in Los Angeles. But I don't think Harriet could bear not having a grave to visit. I'm going to let her know I'm here. You should probably keep your distance. I don't know if Harriet will recognize you as Allegra's sister. Just try and stay out of trouble, you hear me?" I gave him a mock salute and watched him head off to greet Harriet. Harriet showed the first signs of grief that I'd seen in her when Rollins put his arm around her in comfort. She buried her face against his shoulder and sobbed for a few minutes. Either Vivianne's death had finally hit her, or she was trying to cop a feel.

Once Harriet pulled herself together, the service started and a procession of friends and loved ones made their way up front to say a few words or share a story about

Vivianne. As I'd suspected, many of the people in attendance had some kind of ties to the entertainment business. One of Vivianne's former makeup artists, a freeze-dried-looking old broad named Suzette Keynes, with eyebrows that arched into the hairline of her white-blond wig, and wearing a leopard-print suit and pillbox hat that looked like museum pieces, told a long-winded story about how hard it had been to find the right makeup for Vivianne since cosmetics companies didn't cater to black woman at the time. What should have been a tribute to Vivianne ended up being an infomercial for a new line of makeup she'd created for older women called Special Effects. Harriet had to clear her throat several times and practically shake her fist at the woman to get her to shut up and sit down.

Vivianne's leading man in the movie *Sassy Mama,* a still-handsome and quite dapper seventy-year-old ex-actor named Felix Gerard, told the story of how he and Vivianne had had to put up some of their own money to finish the film when the production company that had produced it went bankrupt. He then went on to talk about the lack of good roles for black actors, which I thought was going to lead to praise for Vivianne's acting career and how she broke barriers in Hollywood. Instead, Mr. Gerard bitterly mused about how he'd almost beaten out Sidney Poitier for the role of Virgil Tibbs. Apparently, it was something he still had his undies in a knot over, and he ultimately had to be led back to his seat by his embarrassed wife.

After each person finished speaking, Cliff kept trying

to get up to say a few words, but Stephanie would pull him back down into his seat and give him a warning look like he was a little kid about to spill his milk. Finally, it was Harriet's turn. She'd stopped crying by the time she stepped in front of the podium and stared mournfully at the rose-covered casket before speaking.

"The movie world may have known her as Vivianne DeArmond, but I knew her long before Hollywood did. I knew her when she was just Annie Burns, a skinny little girl who grew up on a farm on the outskirts of town. I knew her back when she had her first role as a shrub in our second-grade play, when she was a cheerleader in junior high, when she went on her first date, and got her first job as a clerk at Foster's Five & Dime. Even when the bright lights of Hollywood, that shone with all the brilliance of fool's gold, lured her away from her home—" she cut her eyes in Cliff's direction "—she never forgot about me. And even after the career she loved so much chewed her up and spat her out, she still put aside her own pain to help me in my darkest hour. Yes, the entertainment world may have lost a bright light. But to me, Vivianne was simply my best friend and I'll miss her more than anyone will ever know."

I looked over at Cliff who was red-faced and furious-looking. Stephanie was rubbing his arm as if she was trying to calm him down. Kurt was asleep. What a loser. If he can't even be bothered to stay awake for his mother's memorial service then what else was he capable of? I quickly checked my cell phone to see if I had a message from Donald Cabot. No such luck.

An uncomfortable silence descended upon the room as Harriet returned to her seat. No one else took the podium and people were shifting around nervously. Ticia came forward from her place at the door and thanked everyone for attending, and announced that refreshments had been set up in the back of the room. A couple of people left but most stayed to socialize. Cliff was holding court in one corner and loud laughter soon filled the room. Harriet was deep in conversation with Rollins. Stephanie was talking to Suzette Keynes, who was pressing makeup samples into her hands. Kurt was the only one who wasn't mingling. He was in the back of the room at the refreshment table stuffing himself with cookies. He seemed as good a place to start as any and I took a plate and sidled up next to him.

"I'm so sorry about your mother," I said, as I filled my plate with cookies and cocktail mints. He turned to stare at me and I caught a flicker of recognition that quickly disappeared.

"My mother? Oh, you mean Vivianne," he said, dismissively looking over at the casket. "Sorry, it's just that we were never close. I saw her maybe once a year. Now she's gone and everyone thinks that changes our relationship."

"It's sad you didn't get a chance to work out your differences before she died," I said, popping a mint in my mouth. He looked at me closely again and I had to try hard not to squirm.

"Who'd you say you were?" he asked, looking me up and down.

"Sorry, I'm Nola Morgan. I was your mother's beautician," I said, holding out my hand and glancing over at Harriet, who was still talking to Rollins. He gave my hand a hard quick shake.

"I thought maybe you were a reporter. One snuck in here earlier today and tried to get a picture of Vivianne in her casket. That's why it's closed, now. I thought ole Harriet was gonna stroke out," he said giggling. I caught a whiff of marijuana, which would explain his munchies, at any rate, and his khaki-colored suit and blue shirt looked wrinkled, as though he'd slept in them. More loud laughter erupted from Cliff's corner and Kurt rolled his eyes. "That's my pops for you. Never misses out on an opportunity to tell a funny story about his glory days."

"I read someplace that he used to be Vivianne's agent."

"Yeah, about a million years ago. He was trying to get her to audition for a role in some big remake of *The Wiz* as Glenda the Good Witch. But Vivi was being difficult, as usual. She never missed an opportunity to make his life hell."

"Is the blond lady your stepmother?" I asked, around bites of oatmeal raisin cookie.

"My mom. Not my stepmother. She raised me, not Vivianne." He cast narrow eyes at the casket still occupying the front of the room.

"Is she in show business?"

"Used to be. Ex-Vegas showgirl. But she quit once she married Dad and became a full-time mother to me. She put me before her career. Not like some women I could name," he said and walked away.

Kurt certainly was angry with Vivianne, and he and Noelle needed money. If he'd channeled his anger into killing her, was it because he knew how valuable her memorabilia would become after her death or because she was never a mother to him? Either way, I had to be able to back up this info when I gave it to Harmon and Mercer. I sure wished Donald Cabot would call me. I was finishing up my cookie when I heard a voice behind me.

"Hello," said Stephanie Preston as I turned around. She was dressed in a steel-gray power suit with big shoulder pads that looked as if she'd stolen it from Krystle Carrington's closet. Her blond hair was pulled into a bun at the nape of her neck and her overly tanned skin looked less harsh in the soft lighting of the funeral home. Her makeup was still overdone however, with pancakelike foundation, heavy purple eyeshadow and black eyeliner. Her lips were frosty and pink and I noticed some of it was smeared on her front teeth.

"I'm Stephanie Preston." She held out her hand and I shook it.

"Nola Morgan, nice to meet you."

"So, you a friend of Vivianne's?" she asked, looking over her shoulder at the casket.

"Not really. More like an acquaintance. I did Vivianne's hair occasionally."

"Aw, I bet that was an experience," she said and laughed spitefully.

"Well, yes. Not to speak ill of the dead," I said, quietly looking around the room, "But you know what she was like. She could be quite demanding." I was hoping to keep the conversation going. I had the feeling Stephanie was looking for someone to vent to. And I wasn't wrong. She snorted and laughed again.

"I know about Miss Vivianne DeArmond all right. She's my husband's ex-wife, or I guess I should say *was*. I've never met a more vain, self-important and self-involved woman in all my life," she shook her head. "But I guess you couldn't really blame her for being the way she was, what with everyone telling her how beautiful she was all the time. But the one who really kills me is that best friend of hers," she said, nodding toward Harriet, who was now talking to Ticia.

"What about her?" I asked, feeling my curiosity perking up.

"Harriet Randall has absolutely no reason to act so high and mighty. You know, what with her husband having robbed that bank here about twenty years ago. Are you from here? I'd have thought you'd have known."

"Twenty years ago I was only nine years old. My biggest concern was mastering long division," I said smiling.

"Oh, of course, you'd have been too young to remember," she said, lightly smacking her forehead. "His name was Elgin Randall. He was a petty thief and robbed the bank Harriet used to work at. A guard was shot during the robbery. They never caught Harriet's husband. He's still on the run. They even thought she might have been in on the plot but could never prove it. Instead, they just fired her. That was not long after Vivianne had quit acting and moved back here to live in her family's old farm-house. She gave Harriet a job as her assistant, but it was the least she could do, considering," Stephanie said smirking.

"Considering what?" I asked. Stephanie motioned for me to lean in closer. I did.

"Elgin Randall was Vivianne's first love. They were engaged to be married when they were young but Vivi-anne wanted to be an actress and she left him practically at the altar and ran off to Hollywood. She met and married Cliff, but she never loved him. He launched her career and she felt grateful to him. Elgin was so heart-broken he ended up marrying Vivianne's best friend, Harriet, instead. I guess they were happy enough until Vivianne came back here to live. She and Elgin never stopped loving each other and started having an affair."

"How do you know?" I asked incredulously.

"Cliff told me a lot of it. But Kurt used to spend a couple of weeks with Vivianne in the summer when he was a kid, and he told me he saw her kissing Harriet's husband and even walked in on them in bed once. I always wondered if Harriet knew." We both turned to stare at Harriet as she rearranged the roses on top of Vivianne's casket.

That sure put a new wrinkle in things. Could Harriet have somehow found out her so-called best friend had been sleeping with her husband all those years ago? Was that the meaning of the letter opener in Vivianne's back? Vivianne had stabbed Harriet in the back figuratively and Harriet had returned the favor literally. I didn't have much time to think it over because Cliff had come over to join us.

"This is my husband, Cliff Preston. Cliff this is—"

"Nola Morgan," I finished for her. Cliff gave my hand a hearty shake. He was dressed in a black suit with a gold tie. Up close I could see his eyes were the same gray as his son's.

"She used to do Vivianne's hair." Stephanie stood a few inches taller than her husband and looked down at him affectionately.

"Really?" he asked, not looking convinced. "I've always known Vivianne to do her own hair. She had a pathological distrust of hairdressers after one messed up her hair so badly it fell out in patches. She had to wear a wig for months." He spoke easily, but his eyes told me he smelled a rat. Uh-oh! What could I say? I looked over at Suzette Keynes, who was chatting up Rollins and got an idea.

"You caught me, Mr. Preston," I said, laughing nervously. "The first time I did Vivianne's hair was last night for the memorial service. I do hair and makeup for most of the funeral homes in this area. I usually try to be on hand during the services for touch-ups and things in case they need me."

"You could have told me," said Stephanie, squeezing my arm. Cliff seemed satisfied, as well, and gave me a friendly smile.

"A lot of people get creeped out when I tell them what I do for a living. I've kind of gotten used to stretching the truth." They had no idea just how much.

"No big deal, young lady. I work in Hollywood, the land of illusion where nothing and no one is what they seem." We all laughed.

"I bet the movie business has really changed since Vivianne's day, huh?" I asked Cliff.

"Right you are, young lady, right you are. Movies these days are nothing but dreck in my opinion. All the great directors are gone. Now, everything is so overloaded with special effects people don't even need to be good actors anymore." He shook his head in disgust.

"Well, what about opportunities for black actors? Surely that's improved, right?" I asked quickly to derail his diatribe.

"Yes, more doors are open to black actors these days, but there's still a long, long way to go, both in front of the camera and behind," he said. "I'm proud to say that I recognized Vivianne for the talent she was when other agencies would only have let her through the door to clean their offices. But, still, I had to fight tooth and nail for every single part Vivianne got. That's one of the reasons she did so many independent films. The big movie studios were reluctant to cast a black woman as the lead in a major motion picture. Independent filmmakers were able to take more risks, and even then it didn't always work to Vivianne's advantage."

"How so?" I asked.

"Take Vivianne's big-break out role in *Asphalt City*. She played a prostitute. That role was her greatest triumph and her greatest tragedy. After that she was typecast and mainly got offered parts as prostitutes or whores, 'fallen women,' as Vivianne always put it. No one wanted to see her as anything but the femme fatale. It was a hard pill for her to swallow. She was a great actress and wanted to be able to show her range, but she rarely got the opportunity," Cliff said vehemently. Stephanie sighed irritably and turned to the refreshment table piling a plate high with stuff I knew she didn't want. Cliff cut his eyes at her but otherwise ignored her.

Even dead, Vivianne was obviously a sore spot for the Prestons. Stephanie didn't seem to mind talking about Vivianne as long as it was negative, but she apparently couldn't stand hearing anything remotely positive about her, especially coming from her husband. How much had Stephanie hated Vivianne? But that was going to have to be a question I'd ponder at a later date, because Harriet Randall had finally noticed me and come charging over to where I was chatting with the Prestons.

"And who might you be?" she asked without a trace of friendliness in her voice. She was wearing a brown dress with an orange-and-black scarf draped around her neck and held in place at her throat with a large, gold, star-shaped brooch. The same black hairpiece that Mama had ripped off her head at the police station was back in its place on her head. She was a short woman, but her pointy-toed, two-inch black pumps put her almost at eye-level with me. She was so close I could see the faint trace of a mustache on her upper lip and two coarse hairs sticking out of her chin. She also reeked of Chanel No. 5. I looked around like I didn't know if she was talking to me. I started to say something but Stephanie spoke up instead.

"Stop being so rude, Harriet. This young lady works for the funeral home. She did Vivianne's hair last night." Stephanie towered over Harriet, who refused to look up at her.

"Excuse me, but I don't need a lesson in manners from the likes of you," Harriet said, still not bothering to look up at Stephanie, who appeared furious.

"Now, what did you say your name was?" Harriet said taking a step closer to me. I remained silent. Where was Rollins?

"Harriet, calm down. You're causing a scene. I thought this evening was supposed to be about Vivianne," said Cliff.

Harriet did at least turn to acknowledge Cliff, and, as she did so, the scarf at her neck slipped and I noticed three faint scratch marks on the left side of her neck. I could tell she'd tried to cover them not just with the scarf but with makeup, as well. But I could still see them and wondered what had caused them, a struggle with Vivianne, perhaps? I already knew Harriet was violent. Did Vivianne fight back and put those scratches on her neck?

CHAPTER 9

"You look awfully familiar and it's certainly not from working here," Harriet said, ignoring Cliff and turning back to me. "Now, I want to know who you are and what you're doing here."

The room had grown silent as everyone turned to look at me. Ticia was looking panicky as though her Rollins-induced trance had finally been broken and she'd suddenly realized I shouldn't be there. I felt a firm hand on my elbow and a smelled a familiar whiff of cologne.

"I'll take care of this, Harriet," said Rollins smoothly. "No need for you to get yourself all worked up. I'm sure this young lady was just leaving," he said, guiding me out of the nearby door and pulling it shut behind us. I jerked angrily out of his grasp.

"What the hell are you doing?" I hissed.

"Calm down, Kendra. You should be thanking me. This is the second time I saved you this evening. She was about to remember who you really are. Then what were you going to do?" he asked, walking ahead of me out of the funeral home. I silently followed him to his car. He was right, of course, though I was hoping he wasn't going to make me cook him two dinners.

"I saw you talking to the Prestons and their son. Surely you had time to find out something useful."

"Oh, I found out plenty, especially about your buddy, Harriet Randall."

"Harriet? What about her?" I could tell I was amusing him. I briefly told him what Stephanie Preston had told me, hoping to wipe the smirk off his face, but he didn't appear at all surprised.

"That's ancient history, Kendra. What would that have to do with Vivianne's murder?"

"Maybe Harriet found out and killed her."

"I know Harriet Randall a whole lot better than you do. I know she can be abrasive, but she's no murderer. I knew her husband Elgin, too."

"What do you know about Elgin Randall?" I asked, unable to contain my excitement. Rollins grinned widely and I knew I was in trouble.

It was almost eight o'clock when I finally got home. Rollins wouldn't tell me what he knew about Elgin Randall until I made him the dinner I owed him, which was now scheduled for tomorrow night. I'd barely made it through my front door when my phone rang. It was Donald Cabot, finally.

"He's coming tonight," Cabot said, foregoing any kind of greeting.

"Your buyer?" I cradled the phone against my shoulder

as I sat down on my couch, kicked off my pumps and massaged my barking dogs.

"Who the hell else would I be calling you about?" he replied irritably.

"No need to get pissy. I just wanted to make sure," I said, getting testy myself.

"Can you meet me at the shop at eight-thirty? He doesn't have much time."

"I'm on my way," I said, hanging up. I quickly changed into a warm-up suit and my runners and headed out.

Downtown Springfield was pretty empty most of the time, but at night it really looked like a ghost town. I pulled into the parking lot of the marketplace and didn't have to worry about finding a space. I parked next to Cabot's beat-up white VW van. I didn't see the green Honda that I'd seen Noelle and Kurt sucking face in and knew Kurt must not have arrived. I wondered if he'd bring Noelle with him and what they would say when they saw me. I walked up to the main entrance and tugged on the doors. They were locked. I walked around to the side entrance by the elevator and bakery. Thankfully, I found it unlocked and I walked inside. All the businesses were closed but it wasn't completely dark. The stillness unnerved me, and I quickly walked over and buzzed for the elevator. I got out on the second floor. I could hear the faint strains of music coming from the shop as I walked down the narrow hallway. The door was ajar and I pushed it open, walked into the shop and stopped dead in my tracks.

The shop had been trashed. The display cases were

smashed, their contents spilled out onto the floor. The posters had been torn off the walls, racks had been knocked over. I crept a little farther into the shop and saw a figure dressed in black, wearing a ski mask and clutching a hammer, leaning over Donald Cabot, who lay on the floor on his back. Cabot's glasses were smashed and his eyes were wide open and vacant, staring at nothing. He was dead. I ran.

I raced down the narrow hallway, crashing into a ladder that was propped against the wall and falling flat on my face. I heard footsteps behind me as I half crawled, half ran for the elevator. I pressed the button and the doors slid open. I dived in.

I turned to see Mr. Ski Mask running down the hall after me, the hammer still clutched in his hand. The doors started to slide shut. He sped up and made it to the elevator and stuck the hammer between the doors before they closed all the way. I screamed.

He tried to wedge the doors open. I looked around frantically for some kind of weapon. He succeeded in prying the doors open wide enough for him to get through but I kicked him hard in the crotch. His eyes widened in shock and surprise and he let go, doubling over in pain. The elevator doors slid shut to the sound of his screams.

Once outside, I got in my car and tore out of the lot. I drove across the train tracks heading south and parked on a dark side street. I pulled out my cell phone and dialed 911 to report what had happened. Afterwards, I laid my head back against my seat and took deep breaths to try and calm down. This had to be the same person I'd seen at Mama's house the other night. I knew I wasn't crazy. I hadn't been sleepwalking. But what had he wanted and why had he killed Donald Cabot? Poor Donald Cabot. Did I get him killed? Was it Kurt in the ski mask? I was in too much shock to cry. I heard sirens in the distance and started my car up to head back to the marketplace.

When I pulled into the parking lot at the marketplace, there was not only a police car but Kurt Preston's rented green Honda. The police cruiser's lights were flashing, lighting up the night and turning the brown brick exterior of the building a gaudy red. Kurt was standing by the Honda with a petite, curly-headed, female police officer and gesturing at the building. I parked next to his car and got out.

"I'm the one who called, officer," I said as I approached them.

"Why the hell are you here?" Kurt asked, looking truly bewildered. He was still dressed in the same rumpled-looking suit he'd had on at the memorial service. I explained what had happened, leaving out the part about Kurt selling his mother's things, and the officer told us to stay put while she and her partner, a muscular brother built like a haystack, went to check it out.

"I guess it's better to show up late than never, huh, Kurt?" I said, leaning against his car.

"Okay, I'm confused. Who are you and why were you meeting Cabot?"

"Think, Kurt. Why are you here? Weren't you supposed to be meeting a buyer for some of your mother's memorabilia?" I watched him closely and saw by the way his face went slack that he'd finally put it together.

"You? You're the buyer Cabot was going on about?"

"Yep. See, I know you and Noelle sold off some of your mother's things to Cabot the other day. He told me he had a private seller and I figured it had to be you."

"So what! What goddamned business is it of yours what I do with my own mother's shit? I could burn it all in a bonfire and it still wouldn't be any of your business."

"I'm Allegra Clayton's sister. And the police seem to think she may have had something to do with Vivianne's murder. She had absolutely no motive for killing Vivianne. But you sure do."

"What the hell are you talking about?" he demanded throwing his hands in the air.

"Tell me, Kurt. Did you murder Vivianne so you could make a fortune when you found out the value of her memorabilia would increase after her death? Did you kill Cabot to cut out the middle man?" He looked as though he'd been punched.

"Are you insane!" he yelled. "I hated Vivianne, but I sure as hell didn't kill her, and Cabot owed me more money, which I'm probably never going to get now. So, that blows that little theory out of the water. I oughta sue your ass for slander for even saying that shit."

Ah, the lawsuit. Hollywood's way of handling everything. Kurt's hands were balled into fists and he took a step forward as if he wanted to take a swing at me. One of the officers, the female, emerged from the building and rushed over to her cruiser. We listened as she got on her radio and called in a suspicious death of a white male at the marketplace and requested the coroner and evidence techs. Then she came over and joined me and Kurt.

"Looks like the poor guy surprised a burglar," she said, eyeing me and Kurt closely.

"The man that chased me had a hammer. He must have just killed poor Mr. Cabot with it when I walked in," I said, but the officer shook her head.

"Ma'am, I'm not sure who or what you saw, but the deceased didn't have a mark on him that we could see. There was no blood, either. It'll be up to the coroner to determine cause of death. In the meantime, I'll need you both to stay and go over what you were doing here this evening when the homicide detective gets here."

"Stay! Officer, I just got here less than five minutes ago. I didn't even step foot inside the building before you guys showed up. And I didn't see any man with a hammer, either. For all we know, she made that shit up because she's the one who broke into the shop and hurt Mr. Cabot," he said, sneering at me and making me wish I had a hammer myself.

"Me! Why would I call the police and then come back here if I was the one who did it?" I said, stabbing a finger in the direction of his chest while he stood there and smirked. The officer stepped between us.

"That's enough," she said. "Richards?" she called to

her partner, who'd just emerged from the building. "You two stay right here and don't move." We watched her rejoin her partner at the cruiser. She whispered something to him and they both turned and looked at us. Great!

"Thanks a lot," I said.

"It's no fun being accused of shit you didn't do, is it?" he asked, pulling out a pair of black sunglasses from inside his suit jacket that looked suspiciously like the ones his character Jabari wore on *Ninja Dudes*. Could he even see out of those things at night? I rolled my eyes.

"So, where's Noelle this evening? I'm surprised you didn't bring your little girlfriend with you."

"Sorry. I don't know anyone named Noelle," he said, his eyes hidden from me now.

What were they hiding?

After talking to a Springfield homicide detective for almost two hours, it was nearly eleven when I got home. To my surprise, Allegra was asleep on the couch in her underwear, snoring lightly with one arm flung over her head and a long leg hanging off the side. I was tempted to wake her up and tell her what had happened. But I wasn't up for it and tiptoed past her into my bedroom. I sure hoped she'd appreciate what I was trying to do for her when this crazy mess was over.

"As far as I know, there's no crime in selling movie memorabilia, Miss Clayton. Nor does someone having scratches on their neck make them a murderer," said Detective Trish Harmon. I'd come to the station to see her first thing that morning to tell her what I'd found out about Kurt Preston and Harriet Randall. Not that it made a bit of difference. As usual, Harmon couldn't see the forest for the trees.

"Then I guess Vivianne having had an affair with Harriet's husband and her memorabilia increasing in value since her death and the fact that Kurt is desperate for money makes no never mind to you," I said drily.

"You've told me nothing but gossip, Miss Clayton. Of the two people who can verify that Harriet Randall's husband had an affair with Vivianne DeArmond, one is dead and the other one has been on the run from the law for over twenty years and could be dead, as well. As for Kurt Preston needing money," she said with an irritated sigh, "he's an unemployed actor, therefore it only stands to reason that he needs money."

"You're not even going to look into it?" I'd figured she wouldn't believe me. Trying to get Trish Harmon to think outside the box is like trying to get Allegra to shop at K-Mart.

"Miss Clayton, I understand your concern for your sister, really I do. But I think your efforts would be better spent convincing your sister to cooperate fully with us during this investigation and come clean about what she may be holding back. Instead—" she tossed a copy of the *Springfield News-Sun* in front of me "—of playing detective."

I looked at the paper with the front-page headline blaring, Shop Owner Found Dead in Shop. May Have

Surprised Vandal. My name was mentioned in the article. I shoved the paper back across the desk at her and changed the subject.

"Allegra has been cooperating. Why would you think she's holding something back?" I suddenly felt uneasy. Had something else come up?

"Your sister stated in a television news interview last night that Vivianne DeArmond told her she had exciting news to announce to her fans. In all the interviews we've done with your sister, she never once mentioned this to us. Now, if she's held that back from us, I'm wondering what else she hasn't told us. That is, if what she said on the news is even the truth."

I got up to leave. Not because Harmon had pissed me off, but because I was beginning to wonder if she could be right. I knew my sister wasn't a murderer, but could she be lying about something?

"I can see I'm wasting my time, Detective. The person who murdered Vivianne is still out there, probably thinking they've gotten away with murder, while you look for ways to pin this on my sister. I guess this is my tax dollars at work," I said and stalked off.

I called Allegra on my cell when I got to my car, but she wasn't answering her phone. Then I called Carl at work and was told he was in a meeting. As I drove to the store to pick up groceries for the dinner I had to cook for Rollins that night, I drove past the Holiday Inn and saw Kurt Preston heading to his car. Impulsively, I pulled in the lot, parked and called out to Kurt. He acted like he didn't hear me and started walking faster.

"Hey, Kurt," I said, catching up to him as he unlocked the driver's-side door.

"What do you want?" I noticed he had his *Ninja Dude* sunglasses on again.

"I've been thinking. Do you think it's possible that Noelle, you know, that woman you don't know, could have gotten desperate for cash to pay off a gambling debt and killed Vivianne herself to increase the value of her memorabilia? I think the police might be interested in Noelle's little problem, don't you think?" Harmon had dismissed the memorabilia angle but Kurt didn't know that. I expected him to try and hit me, but he sagged against the car instead.

"How do you know about... She's no murderer. She's got a serious problem but she's never hurt anyone to get money." He took off his sunglasses and wiped his eyes. He was crying.

"Where is Noelle, Kurt?"

"I don't know. She got her hands on that money Cabot gave us the other day and I haven't seen her since. I think she may be off gambling someplace."

"I didn't realize it had gotten so bad."

"She was doing really good for a long time. But she's been under a lot of pressure at work. That whole mess with *Hollywood Vibe* and Ross Abbott is the reason we can't go public with our relationship. Ross Abbott is my best friend."

"My sister told me people think Noelle had something to do with her predecessor getting fired." Kurt shifted uncomfortably from foot to foot and looked off into the distance.

"She did have something to do with it, didn't she?"

"No! Look, Noelle and I met in rehab. I fell in love with her. When we met she was just an assistant producer at *Hollywood Vibe*. I think she thought with my father being who he is that I could help her with her career. I'm just a has-been with a drug problem. My father and I don't even like each other. One day when I was hanging at Ross's crib, I got an idea of a way I could help Noelle get ahead at *Hollywood Vibe*. So we got one of Ross's exes, who was sleeping with *Hollywood Vibe*'s executive producer, Bob McLean, to feed him that info about Ross being bald, short and not having any teeth. They took that story and ran with it. Then Ross sued and got a big settlement, Noelle's boss was made a scapegoat and got fired, Noelle got her boss's job, and I got Noelle. Everyone made out like a bandit, but—" he said, shaking his head.

"But the job turned out to be more than she could handle, and she relapsed and started gambling again?"

"Noelle is superambitious but that job of hers is really running her into the ground."

"And you felt guilty about putting her in that position and sold Vivianne's stuff to get money to help pay off Noelle's debts."

"Yeah, but I didn't kill Vivianne. I've been taking stuff from her for years. When I was kid, my dad made me spend two weeks every summer with her. She never took me anywhere. We never did anything fun. She wouldn't even give me any money to do stuff on my own. I started stealing stuff from her and selling it. Back then it wasn't worth much except some pocket change. Now, her stuff's worth a mint. Seems ole Vivi has built up quite the cult following over the years."

"Stephanie was telling me about Vivianne having an affair with Harriet's husband. Do you know if Harriet knew about it?"

"If she didn't, she sure as hell knows now." Kurt laughed.

"You told her?" I asked, trying hard to contain my excitement.

"Dad dragged me here for that recognition program in order to help him butter Vivianne up so she'd take that part in *The Wiz*. I went to her house to ask if she'd loan me some money. She told me no as usual and we got into an argument. Then Harriet jumps in it and starts calling me a horrible son and saying how I should have a job. I just snapped. I told her she shouldn't be taking up for a woman who fucked her husband."

"What did she say?"

"Vivianne just stood there with her mouth hanging open. Harriet called me a filthy liar and told me to get out and never come back. I left."

I wondered what Harmon would say about that. I tried calling her but she was out, of course.

I pulled into the grocery store parking lot and was about to get out of my car when someone pounded on my driver's-side window. I almost wet my pants. It was Lynette's mother, Justine, and she didn't look happy.

"Hey, Ms. Martin. What's wrong?" I asked cautiously. But I knew by the way she was eyeing me, like she was trying to figure out where it would hurt the most if she hit me, that she'd found out about Lynette.

"Well, let's see, Kendra. My daughter is supposed to be getting married in three days and she's up and run away. You and Greg didn't even bother to tell me. I'm her mother. I would have liked to have known. We have people arriving from out of town on Friday, not to mention the rehearsal dinner, the caterer, photographer and the DJ to deal with. We've got a deposit on the reception hall that's nonrefundable. I have no idea what to do. No one's heard from her. Why the devil wasn't I told about this!" She tossed her long, manelike weave over her shoulder. The harsh morning sunlight was not doing Justine any favors. I could see wrinkles fanning out from the corners of her eyes and her foundation was caked in the creases of her neck.

"I'm so sorry, Justine. Greg and I thought she'd be back by now," I offered weakly.

"Y'all thought wrong. I knew that silly gal was going to mess this up. I kept telling her ass she wouldn't be able to hold on to a good man like Greg."

Lord forgive me. I just couldn't hold my tongue. "What's wrong with you? Why would you tell her that? She's under enough stress over this wedding. Why would you put more pressure on her by saying things like that?

Sounds like you don't *want* her marriage to work out. No wonder she ran off." I though Justine's head might start spinning around.

"Now, hold up. Who are you talking to like that? I know you're not trying to jump bad with me, young lady. Not *you* of all people," she said, shaking a ring-laden finger at me. What in the world was she talking about?

"Me of all people? Is that supposed mean something to me?" I said, jumping out of the seat and slamming my car door behind me. Justine took a step back on her too-small high-heeled mules.

"It should. You're the last person who should be talking. The whole town knows about what you've been up to. Running around on that nice lawyer. You should be ashamed of yourself."

"Ashamed of what?"

"You were seen, Kendra. You and Morris Rollins were seen coming out of the Heritage Arms together. Everyone knows. It's all over town."

"We were looking for Lynette!" I screamed.

"How dare you drag my daughter into your dirt, you little liar." She turned on her heel and started to tip across the parking lot into the store then stopped and turned to yell at me. "And if you hear from Lynette, tell her if she's not back by Friday morning I'm canceling that wedding of hers, and she can get the hell out of my house since I'm causing her so much stress."

I was aware that people were staring at me and whispering. I got in my car and got the hell out of Dodge.

I was tempted to go home and hide but thought better of it. After all, I hadn't done a damned thing with Morris Rollins. I was going to kill Lynette when I finally caught up with her. I knew Mama was ready to kill *me,* since she was firmly plugged into the Willow gossip network and had probably caught wind of the rumor. I decided to steer clear of her. Thank goodness, Carl, although he spent a lot of his time in Willow, actually lived in Columbus and was pretty oblivious to town gossip. I wondered what people would say if they knew I was having dinner with Rollins that night. I wondered what Carl would say. Would he even care?

I headed to Perkins and had a big breakfast of pancakes, sausage and eggs and finally read the issue of the *Springfield News-Sun* that Harmon had waved under my nose at the station that morning.

SHOP OWNER FOUND DEAD IN HIS SHOP.
MAY HAVE SURPRISED VANDAL.

Forty-eight-year-old Donald Cabot, owner and proprietor of Cabot's Cave, a store specializing in movie memorabilia and collectibles, located downtown in the marketplace, was found dead in his shop Tuesday evening. Officers were called to the scene by Kendra Clayton of Willow after she arrived at the shop for an appointment with Donald Cabot and found Cabot's body on the floor. Police theorize that Cabot may have surprised vandals in the process of wrecking his shop. Cause of death is not immediately known and, though the autopsy results are not expected until tomorrow, Cabot's mother, Viola Cabot, has told police that her son suffered from a serious heart condition.

I couldn't believe it. Not one mention about the masked man that chased me or about Kurt Preston being present at the scene. Did they think I'd just made the whole thing up? I also didn't think the store had been broken into by vandals. I only saw one person—the masked man—who must have been looking for something. But what? I slammed the paper down on the table, knocking over my orange juice in the process and splashing it on my white shirt. I tried to mop up the spill, only succeeding in making a sticky mess. I'd have to go home and change.

I pulled in front of my apartment at the same time as Allegra, who was carrying a McDonald's bag. She was wearing a white denim pantsuit, trimmed in gold studs, and gold sandals. The girl even dressed to the nines to go get a Big Mac. Unbelievable.

"Mama just called me looking for you. She wants you to call her. She sounded pissed off about something. Did you puke on yourself?" she asked, wrinkling her nose at my stained shirt as we climbed the steps to my front door.

I mumbled a terse, "No." I was relieved I'd left my cell phone at home. I wasn't looking forward to talking to Mama. I wondered if it was about Rollins or if Justine Martin had called and blabbed about our argument in the parking lot. Either way, the call would have to wait.

I started to unlock the door, but it was already unlocked and ajar, which didn't fully register until Allegra pushed past and walked in ahead of me. I followed, ran smack into her and started to angrily shove her out of my way, when I saw what had stopped her in her tracks. My apartment was a wreck. It looked like a bomb had gone off. There were clothes everywhere, even hanging off my ceiling fan. Allegra dropped her bag.

"What the hell!" I yelled. I kicked my way through the pile of clothes on the floor to the center of the room and ran around the apartment. Allegra was rooted to the spot. My bedroom was a mess, as well. The closet door was wide open and clothes and boxes had been pulled out. The kitchen had a few cabinets opened and some plastic containers were scattered on the counters. The bathroom was untouched. As far as I could tell, nothing had been taken. At least, nothing of mine.

I walked back into the living room to find my sister silently picking up her designer duds from the floor. Her Louis Vuitton suitcases, which she never fully unpacked since she was constantly running back and forth between my place and Mama's, had been emptied and lay in front of the couch. I noticed every single flap and pocket had been unzipped and unsnapped. Allegra remained strangely silent.

"Are you missing anything?" I asked absently as I searched the mess for my phone. I figured her silence was due to the theft of one of her precious high-end possessions. She remained silent, avoiding eye contact. Then it hit me, and I whirled around to face her.

"It's you, isn't it? Whoever broke in here was looking for something you had! Answer me, Allie!" I screamed when she still wouldn't say anything.

She sighed, threw down the shoe she been clutching and sat down in my rocker. "All right! Yes! Are you happy?"

"What do you have that someone would break in here to get?"

"Had, Kendra. Whoever broke in took it. It was a check. It was in my suitcase," she said sullenly.

"A check?" I cleared a space on my couch and sat down.

"Yeah. When I walked into Vivianne's dressing room and tripped over her purse, I picked the purse up, and something fell out of it. It was a check. Then I found Vivianne's body and the fire alarm went off. I dropped the purse and I ran. When I got outside I realized I still had the check with me. I wasn't about to go put it back. I was too scared to tell the police. I knew they'd think I stole it." She had good reason to be scared. I'd inadvertently walked off with something from a crime scene once and Harmon had threatened to arrest me.

"What was the check for?"

"It was a check for five thousand dollars from a Diamond Publishing Company in Columbus for an advance against royalties for a book Vivianne had written."

"Do you think this was the exciting news Vivianne had for her fans?" I asked. Allegra just shrugged.

"Any idea what kind of book she wrote?"

"No. But the check referred to the title—*The Onyx*

Man." Allegra jumped out of the rocker and started pacing nervously. "What if the police find out about that stupid check? They'll arrest me for sure. I don't want to go to jail," she wailed.

"Calm down, Allie, I won't say anything." I knew I wasn't doing the right thing but figured since the check was now gone, there was no real reason to tell the police. And if I kept telling myself that, maybe I'd actually start believing it.

"Not even Carl, Kendra. You can't tell him, either. Promise me you won't. He was really mad about me not telling him about touching Vivianne's purse. If he finds out about the check, he'll freak."

"I promise not to tell Carl. You didn't tell anyone else about the check, did you?"

"Just Noelle. She got all excited and wanted me to hand it over but I wouldn't. She probably wants to get an exclusive story out of it for herself for *Hollywood Vibe.*"

Noelle. Of course! She had to be the one who broke in here to steal the check. She must have been the one on Mama's back porch that night. Allie had been staying with Mama that night and had all her stuff with her. Noelle must have taken the check to try and cash it to cover her gambling debts. She must really be getting desperate. Allegra had mentioned that she thought Noelle had resorted to stealing to feed her habit. I didn't let Allegra in on my little theory. Instead, I called the police, who came and took a brief statement and suggested I get my locks changed, and Allegra and I cleaned up my apartment.

CHAPTER 10

A couple of hours later, Allegra left for Mama's, but not before I made her promise to say she hadn't seen me and didn't know where I was. I got on the phone to information and got the number for Diamond Publishing Company in Columbus. As I dialed, I wondered how I was going to get them to tell me what I wanted to know.

"Diamond Publishing. This is Alison. How may I help you?" said the cheerful voice on the other end on the line.

"This is Harriet Randall, Vivianne DeArmond's assistant," I said in my haughtiest voice. "In light of her recent death, I need information regarding Ms. DeArmond's book." When I heard an exasperated sigh on the other end of the line, I knew it wasn't going to be good.

"Please hold, Ms. Randall, while I put you through to our editor." I heard ringing which was promptly answered by another irritated female voice.

"Ms. Randall, this is Margo Diamond. I told you when you called yesterday that I couldn't give you any information about Ms. DeArmond's book over the phone. When you can provide legal documentation proving that you are the executor of Ms. DeArmond's estate, then I will gladly provide you with the information. Until then, I'm sorry, but our hands are tied."

I said a quick, "Thank you," and hung up.

Someone had already called about Vivianne's book. Was it really Harriet or was it Noelle? Why would Noelle call about the book? If, as I suspected, she was the one who stole the check, then why bother about the book? Unless Allegra was right and she was trying to get info about the book for some kind of story for *Hollywood Vibe*. For that matter, knowing how ambitious Allegra is, she could have been the one who called. But if it was actually Harriet who called then that could mean she didn't know what Vivianne's book was about. That could also be the reason Vivianne hadn't told her assistant about her interview with Allegra. She didn't want Harriet to know about the book. I couldn't help but wonder what in the world *The Onyx Man* was about. And was there something in that book that Harriet Randall would have killed Vivianne over? I decided to find out.

I hopped in my car and headed out to Troyer Road where I knew Vivianne's farm was. Harriet Randall, as far as I knew, had lived with Vivianne for years. It was hot out and my air-conditioning was on the fritz. I had all the windows in my Nova rolled down but was still sweating like a pig and knew I'd have to shower and change yet again before heading over to Rollins's house for dinner. I was at a four-way stop about to make a left-hand turn when a silver Cadillac came flying past me headed in the opposite direction. Even though the person driving looked as though they could barely see over the steering wheel, I could tell it was Harriet by the two-toned hair. I made an abrupt illegal U-turn and started following her. Harriet drove like a bat out of hell and I had a hard time keeping up as she weaved in and out of traffic. After about ten minutes and a few near misses involving two cars and a motorcycle, she finally pulled into the parking lot of Woodlawn Nursing Home on a residential street of Park Hurst that I didn't think I'd ever had the pleasure of driving down before. Most of the homes in Park Hurst were modest single-storied homes on slabs with tiny front yards and carports instead of attached garages.

Woodlawn Nursing Home consisted of two nondescript, white, single-storied buildings parallel to each other and joined together by another brick building in an almost U-shaped formation, kind of reminding me of army barracks. While the buildings weren't much to write home about, a lot of attention and money had gone into the landscaping. The bushes that flanked either side of the front entrance were neatly trimmed and the lawn was the lush green that only comes from professional lawn treatments. There was a concrete walkway leading to a large, circular, stone-paved area in the center of the front lawn with some wooden benches arranged around a small fountain.

Harriet parked her Cadillac, taking up two spaces, and got out and walked in. I pulled in several spaces down from her to wait. After about fifteen minutes, Harriet emerged pushing a wheelchair occupied by an elderly black woman with silvery-white hair that hung to her shoulders. An oxygen tank was attached to the side of the chair and I could see the tube snaking from it had been looped around the woman's ears so as to keep it positioned in her nose. Harriet pushed the chair out to the fountain, parked the wheelchair next to one of the benches and sat down. I watched her for the next forty-five minutes as she chatted to the woman, occasionally reaching out to stroke her face or long hair, surprising me with her tenderness. The woman in the wheelchair didn't seem to have much to say and mainly stared vacantly at Harriet, who didn't seem at all bothered by the lack of response, or she wheezed so loudly I could hear it from where I was sitting. I wondered who the woman was—Harriet's mother, perhaps?

I kept checking my watch. It was getting late and I still had to change and buy groceries for my evening with Reverend Rollins. I knew there were women who'd cut off an ear to spend an evening with Morris Rollins. If I didn't have to get some much-needed info on Harriet Randall, I'd have probably told him no thanks. When it appeared that Harriet wasn't about to wrap up her visit any time soon, I reluctantly started up my car and left.

I arrived at Morris Rollins's house around seven that evening. He had recently sold his castlelike mansion in the Briar Creek area of Willow and moved to a more modest brick ranch about a ten-minute drive outside of Willow.

I couldn't blame him. His old house held too many bad memories. His new house sat back from the road up on a hill. I turned into the long winding driveway, noting that Rollins's gold Mercedes was parked in front of a large detached garage in the same red brick as the house. The garage had two stories and the windows on the top floor indicated that there must be an apartment up there. I knew Rollins's daughter Inez now lived with him and wondered if she stayed over the garage. I parked behind his car and got out. Rollins must have heard my car because he emerged from the backyard dressed in faded jeans and a blue short-sleeved T-shirt. He grinned his high-beam smile when he saw me and I couldn't help but smile back.

"You didn't have any trouble finding the house, did you?" he asked, walking up to the car.

"I only got lost once," I replied truthfully, handing him two grocery bags. I grabbed a cake box from my front seat and he led the way into a large backyard with a deck that ran almost the entire length of the house. I followed him through a set of sliding glass doors into a bright and airy kitchen.

I set the cake box on the brown-, black- and gold-flecked granite counter top and looked around. The kitchen was huge with a dining area at one end and an island cook top in the center. It opened up into a large family room inhabited by an armoire on the back wall that was opened revealing a TV and CD/ DVD player. A large, square, glass coffee table sat in the middle of the room in front of a brown leather sectional. The walls were painted a soft yellow. A set of built-in shelves against one wall held family pictures, pieces of wooden sculpture and multicolored ceramic bowls and vases. The opposite wall housed a brick fireplace. The overall effect was warm and inviting.

"I think I like this house better than your old one."

Rollins laughed and said softly, "Thank you, Kendra. I like it, too." He was staring at me strangely and I suddenly wondered if I'd made a mistake wearing the skirt, lacy camisole and blouse. But the look he was giving me wasn't exactly lustful, just curious.

"So, what's for dinner?" He walked back into the kitchen and started looking in the grocery bags.

"You like spaghetti, don't you? It seemed like a safe bet."

"I love spaghetti. Is there anything I can do to help?"

"Can you put a pot of water on to boil?"

After Rollins rounded up the necessary utensils, I got to work chopping onions and garlic for the sauce, and decided now would be as good at time as any to bring up the real reason I'd agreed to come over.

"How long have you known Harriet Randall?"

"Ah, yes, Harriet. No one can accuse you of beating around the bush, Kendra," he said drily. I stopped chopping and stared at him until he answered me.

"I've known Harriet Randall since I was a kid. Her family lived next door to mine and sometimes she'd babysit me and my brother. I knew her husband Blackie for longer than that."

"Blackie?"

"Elgin 'Blackie' Randall. He was quite a character," Rollins said, chuckling.

"Why'd they call him Blackie?" I asked, thinking about the title to Vivianne's book, *The Onyx Man*. Could *The Onyx Man* refer to Vivianne's old love, Blackie Randall?

"Well, it wasn't because he was a dark-skinned man. In fact, he sort of put you in mind of Ron O'Neil, that actor who played Super Fly, even had that pretty hair women seem to love so much. He was one of the flashiest cats I've ever known. He got his nickname 'Blackie' because he was addicted to black and mild cigarettes. I don't think I ever saw him without one pinched between those long fingers of his."

"Was he a friend of the family?"

Rollins chuckled again. "Let's just say my mother, like a lot of women, had a thing for Blackie Randall, even though she was a good twenty years older than him."

"Was the feeling mutual?" I asked, handing him a can of tomato paste to open.

"No. I think he thought of my mother as the big sister he never had. Blackie would show up at our place whenever he wanted a home-cooked meal, or when he needed a little bit of pocket change to buy cigarettes and liquor. But the only woman I've ever known him to be head over heels in love with was Annie Burns."

"Annie Burns? Oh, you mean Vivianne." I suddenly remembered that was her birth name.

"They were supposed to get married, but Vivianne went off to Los Angeles about a week before the wedding.

Told everybody she was visiting relatives. Turns out she'd hooked up with a talent agent—"

"Cliff Preston?" I asked, interrupting him. He nodded in agreement and continued.

"She never came back. Blackie even borrowed money from my mother to fly out to California to beg her to come back to Willow. No such luck. She convinced him to stay out there with her for a while but they never did get married."

"Why?"

"Two reasons, the main one being that Vivianne was running around on him with Cliff Preston. And secondly, men like Blackie don't do well in big cities. As long as he was a big fish in a little pond like Willow he was fine. But in a city like L.A.," Rollins said, shaking his head, "he was a hick from the sticks."

"How'd he end up with Harriet?" The short, squat, sour-faced woman was a far cry from Vivianne and her stunning beauty.

"Blackie lost his step after he came back from California. Started drinking heavily. Getting into bar fights. Harriet Perkins was Vivianne's best friend. But she'd been in love with Blackie herself all along. I think she was the one who encouraged Vivianne to go out to California to seek her fame and fortune. Once Blackie came home alone, Harriet saw her chance. She became Blackie's rock. Got him clean and sober. Even got him into church. Blackie ended up marrying Harriet, though I don't think he loved her the way he loved Vivianne."

"When did Vivianne come back into the picture?"

"Late seventies. She was in her midforties and by then her career and marriage were over. Her parents were long dead and had left her the family farm. I don't think Harriet was very happy when her ex-best friend moved back home. She kept her distance at first, but Vivianne was determined to be friends with Harriet and Blackie again, especially Blackie. Then things got bad for the Randalls."

"You mean the bank robbery?"

"Exactly. Blackie never had a real job in his life. He used to tend bar at an after-hours bootleg joint but that couldn't have paid much. Besides that, I can only imagine where he got the rest of his money from."

"I bet it wasn't from anything legal," I added, stirring the spaghetti sauce. Rollins laughed.

"Once he married Harriet, she wouldn't let him run the streets anymore. Eventually he got a job as an orderly at Willow Memorial making minimum wage. Harriet was mainly supporting them on her salary from her job at Bank Ohio. But Blackie had the streets in his blood. After years of being married to Harriet and never having much money, he hooked up with some of his old running buddies. He was a middle-aged man when the still-beautiful Vivianne, who he probably never stopped loving, moved back to town. I think hooking back up with his old friends made him feel young again, like when he and Vivianne were still together."

"Were they the ones he robbed the bank with?"

"Blackie was definitely there when that bank got robbed. But his involvement has always been open to debate."

"How so?"

"I have a hard time imagining Blackie willingly being a part of robbing the bank his wife worked at. I've always wondered if he even knew what was going down that day. I think he drove his friends to the bank not knowing they were going to rob it. A whole lot of people say they saw him sitting in his car in front of the bank that day looking like he didn't have a care in the world."

"No one actually saw him in the bank?"

"It didn't matter whether he was in the bank or not. He still drove the getaway car. That made him an accomplice."

"I know he got away, but did they catch the others?"

"Eventually. It took them a while to track them all down. But they never found Blackie, just his abandoned car with some blood smears that matched his blood type. People think he may have been killed by the others to keep him quiet."

"What happened to Harriet after that?"

"Poor Harriet. Life got really hard for her. First she kept getting dragged down to the police station and questioned for hours on end because they thought she was in on the robbery. She was absent from work that day and that looked really bad for her. Then the bank fired her. She couldn't get another job and couldn't pay her bills. She lost the little house she and Blackie owned. And to make matters worse, some people in the community shunned her. She changed after that. She wasn't always the hard, aggressive woman she is today. Luckily, Vivianne offered her a job as her assistant, though to be honest, since she was no longer acting, I have no idea what exactly Harriet assisted her with and where Vivianne got the money to pay her."

"And no one ever saw Blackie Randall again?"

"Nope. There were rumors that he had been spotted as far away as Canada. The three friends of his who actually robbed the bank never admitted to killing him and would never say why his blood was in the car. They served their time for the robbery and got out of prison. Two have since died and the third one killed some guy up in Cleveland and is back in prison for life this time. I don't think Harriet ever gave up hope that Blackie would come home one day."

I drained the spaghetti and wondered if Vivianne's book, *The Onyx Man*, was about Blackie Randall and the bank robbery. Did Vivianne find out Blackie was alive and reveal in her book where he'd been hiding for the past twenty years? Could Harriet have killed her friend for being about to reveal her husband's hiding place? Or could Blackie Randall have found out about the book and emerged from hiding to kill Vivianne himself?

I put Rollins to work chopping vegetables for the salad. Our fingers touched as I handed him a head of lettuce. The warmth of his fingers made me feel flustered and I quickly turned back to the stove where my sauce was bubbling away, filling the kitchen with its aroma.

He walked up behind me and looked over my shoulder into the sauce pot. I could feel his hot breath on my neck. "I don't know which smells better—you or the sauce," he said in a low voice that sent a delicious shiver down my spine. I wiped a trickle of sweat from my brow. I was suddenly hot and it wasn't from the heat of the stove.

"Is Inez home? Will she be joining us for dinner?" I asked hopefully.

He gave my neck a quick feather-light kiss before answering. "Inez is so busy since her new beauty shop opened that I barely see her." He poured us each a glass of wine. I took a big gulp.

"You can relax, Kendra. I don't bite. We're just two friends enjoying each other's company. Nothing wrong in that, is there?"

Yeah, right. He sounded sincere enough, but there was definitely something in his eyes that said otherwise.

"Not everyone would agree with that assessment," I said, and filled him in on the rumor that was currently floating around town about us, at which point Rollins threw back his head and howled with laughter. In fact, I don't think I'd ever seen him laugh so hard. I was starting to get a little offended.

"That sure explains a lot," he said, after he'd calmed down. "Some of the church sisters were giving me mighty strange looks when I ran into them today. I couldn't figure out why. Guess I know now." He chuckled, taking a sip of wine.

"I sure hope your lady friend doesn't believe it. Maybe you should call her and explain," I said drily.

"What lady friend?" he asked, looked genuinely confused.

"Winette Barlow. I heard the two of you are an item now." I fixed two heaping plates of spaghetti and followed him to the kitchen table.

"You heard this from the same people who are currently spreading the rumor about us, right?" I felt foolish and didn't answer. He started laughing again. "Kendra Clayton, what am I going to do with you?" I still didn't answer. But I could fantasize.

Two hours later, after we'd eaten the spaghetti, salad and big slices of the chocolate cake I'd brought and had done the dinner dishes together, Rollins walked me to my car and managed to turn an innocent kiss on the forehead into an erotic experience by letting his warm mouth linger seconds longer than was necessary. It was definitely time for me to go. But I had one last question.

"What do you think happened to Blackie Randall? Do you think he's dead?" I asked. Rollins thought for a moment before answering.

"I have no idea what happened to him. But there is one interesting fact that points to him being alive," he said, holding my car door open for me.

"And that would be?"

"There were four men involved in that robbery. The police only recovered three-fourths of the money that got stolen. There's still a fourth of that money that's never been found or accounted for."

* * *

"Calm down, Greg. It's going to be okay," I told my best friend's fiancé. Greg had shown up at my front door first thing that morning babbling about Justine threatening to cancel the wedding. He hadn't shaved and was dressed in a wrinkled tank top and sweatpants. I hadn't slept well the night before and couldn't fully focus on what he was saying. I was trying hard to get him to talk quietly because Allegra had gotten in late and was still sound asleep on the couch. But he was much too upset to care about waking up Sleeping Beauty. I finally led him past Allegra's slumbering form back to my kitchen and made us a strong pot of coffee.

"Can she do that?" he said angrily. "Cancel our wedding, I mean? Lynette and I paid for most of the wedding. How can Justine cancel it?" He looked so lost and upset that I wasn't sure who I was madder at: Justine, for making a bad situation worse, or Lynette for running away in the first place.

"She's just blowing smoke out her ass, Greg. Don't worry about Justine. We need to focus on finding Lynette. Have you heard from her at all since that first call?"

"No. Not a word and I'm really getting worried. You don't think something has happened to her, do you?"

"I don't know, Greg. I would have thought she'd have been home by now." I took another bracing sip of coffee and tried to shake the cobwebs from my mind.

"You think we should call the police?"

"I'd say if she's not back by the end of the day then, yes, we should call the police." He sighed heavily and buried his face in his hands. Then something must have occurred to him because his hands fell away from his face and he looked panic-stricken.

"Kendra, if I ask you something will you tell me the truth?"

"Of course." I had a feeling I knew what he was going to ask.

"There's not another man is there? When you saw her at the Heritage Arms she was alone, wasn't she?"

"Of course she was alone, Greg. There is no one but you. Lynette loves you." Finally—a question I could answer truthfully.

After Greg left, I got dressed, and headed out to run errands and, at Greg's request, pick up things for a wedding that might not even happen. Allegra was still asleep when I left, making me wonder where she'd been last night and if it was with Carl. Not that I had a right to be too upset since I'd spent my evening with another man. Carl and I hadn't been spending much time together lately, and for some reason it wasn't bothering me nearly as much as it should have.

By the time I arrived at Garrison's Print and Copy Shop it had started to drizzle. I dodged raindrops as I headed inside to pick up Greg and Lynette's wedding programs. I walked up to the counter and had to wait a few minutes while the skinny woman with frizzy gray hair manning the counter finished a phone conversation before coming to the counter to greet me.

"I've come to pick up the order for Lynette Martin-Gaines. It's for wedding programs."

"Yes. I was wondering if someone was going to pick up that order. It's been ready since Monday," she said mildly and then turned to the wall of shelving behind her. The shelves were filled with boxes of printing to be picked up. She scanned the boxes until she came upon a white one and brought it to the counter. She told me the price and I handed her the cash without asking to see the programs first. Big mistake.

"Here you go," she said and slid the box across the counter. "Have a nice day." The phone rang again and she hurried off to answer it.

I opened the lid of the box to look at the programs. Greg and Lynette smiled up at me from their engagement picture printed on the cover of the cream-colored program. Gold lettering beneath the picture listed the date of the wedding and underneath that larger gold lettering declared, Grog & Lynette Forever. Huh? I flipped though the stack of programs and sure enough, Grog & Lynette Forever was printed on each and every one. Oh, no.

"Excuse me," I said loudly to the woman behind the counter, who was still on the phone. I could tell by the way she was smiling and laughing that it wasn't business-related. She turned and looked at me as though she'd never seen me before and I waved a program at her.

"There's a typo on these," I said, pointing at the offending O in Greg's name. This should be *Greg* not *Grog*," I said, as she approached the counter. She pulled a pair of spectacles from her pants pocket, perched them on the end of her nose, and squinted at the programs.

"Yeah, that's a mistake all right." She checked the copy of the order form taped to the top of the box, which indeed confirmed that it should be *Greg* and not *Grog*. "Sorry about the mistake ma'am. I'll redo these personally and you can pick them up next Monday."

"Next Monday? The wedding is *this* Saturday," I said, my voice rising to a high-pitched shriek. I gestured to the date on the front of the program. "I need these redone today."

"Today? Nope. Not possible," she said shaking her head vigorously. "If you'd have come in on Monday when they were ready then maybe I could have redone them this week. But I'm the only one here today and I'm swamped."

"But it's *your* mistake and it's not my fault you're swamped. Is the manager in?" I asked. looking past her.

"I'm the manager and *owner,* young lady," she said, gesturing to the name tag that read Patsy Garrison/Owner pinned to the front of her denim smock, "and I don't appreciate your tone." She leaned forward menacingly against the counter and I caught a whiff of her onion-and-coffee-scented breath. I took a step back before it melted my face and she smirked.

"And I don't appreciate the fact that these programs have been paid for and there's a typo in them. I demand they be redone today or I'll—"

"Or you'll what?" she said, straightening up and crossing her arms over her bony chest. "What can you possibly do?"

"Picket! I'll stand in front of this shop all day if I have to and make sure everyone who comes in here today knows you do shoddy work."

"Go ahead. If you want to stand outside in the rain like a fool, you go right ahead. That still don't change the fact that I don't have time to redo these programs today." She turned her back on me.

I turned and looked outside to see that the light drizzle had turned into pouring rain. Standing outside in that downpour was not my idea of a good time.

"Look, ma'am, isn't there any way you could redo these programs today? It's really important," I pleaded. I even tried to wring out a few tears but they wouldn't come. Not that she'd have noticed anyway as she continued to ignored me, instead giving me a view of her flat polyester-encased ass as she bent over a box on the floor.

"I'll pay extra," I said finally. That got her attention and she turned to smirk at me.

"No need, young lady. I have something else in mind."

Instead of paying extra for a rush job on the corrected programs, I ended up spending the next two hours dressed in a denim smock helping Patsy Garrison work through her backlog of printing jobs. Before she got busy redoing the programs, she showed me how to run two of the large, complicated-looking copiers and left me several boxes of résumés, flyers and brochures to copy on various types and textures of colored paper.

The résumés and flyers were easy enough and I got

them copied and out of the way in no time flat. But the brochures were giving me fits. The copier that did two-sided copying was out of order, which meant I had to manually flip the copies over to the other side in the paper tray once one side had been finished. The first time I did it the print on the flipside of the brochures was upside down. I was in such a hurry to get done that I failed to test one to makes sure it came out right side up. I ended up ruining two hundred and fifty brochures for the Venus De Milo Day Spa and discreetly pitched them in the re-cycling bin before Patsy could see what I'd done and punish me by breathing her dragon breath in my face. By the time I finally got them to come out right, which took three tries, I was highly annoyed and almost in tears. Wedding jitters or not, Lynette had now moved to the top of my shit list.

I heard the door to the shop open and ignored it since I figured Patsy was taking care of the customers. A minute later I heard an impatient, "Excuse me, miss." I turned around and was greeted by the sight of Winette Barlow. Great! She was dressed to perfection as usual with a tan trench coat over a coral-colored suit that flattered her still-youthful figure. Her thick glossy gray-streaked black hair was loose around her shoulders and bright red lipstick ac-centuated a wide unsmiling mouth. Her dripping black umbrella was making a large puddle at her feet. She didn't seem to care. Her laserlike stare was unwavering and un-nerving.

Had she heard the rumors about Rollins and me? Were

the rumors about her and Rollins true? Now that I thought about it, he'd never quite denied it. And more importantly, why did I care? We stared at each other uncomfortably for a few seconds before Winette finally spoke.

"Cat got your tongue, sweetie?" she asked in her soft Southern drawl. Winette is originally from Virginia and usually polite and gracious to a fault. Today, I couldn't gauge her mood by the tone of her voice. Instead, I smiled at her. She didn't smile back. Ouch. I guess I had my answer about whether she'd heard the rumors.

"Hi. Winette. What brings you in here?" I asked coolly.

"I'm here to pick up the flyers for the annual Holy Cross car wash this Friday. Morris asked me at breakfast this morning if I'd pick them up for him," she said and finally smiled. But the smile didn't reach her eyes and was more a flashing of teeth than a symbol of friendliness.

Dinner with me and breakfast with Winette Barlow. Rollins was sure keeping his social calendar filled. I wondered who got him for lunch? Not that I gave a damn. I turned wordlessly to the shelving unit behind me and located the order for Holy Cross. I handed her the box and she snatched it from me so fast I got a paper cut on the invoice.

"Damn! Was that necessary?" I asked, sticking my finger in my mouth to staunch the flow of blood.

"Oh, that little bit of blood is nothing, honey, compared to what you got coming if you don't stay the hell away from my man. He's old enough to be your daddy, little girl," she practically spat at me, managing to make the word *girl* sound like an insult.

"You need to tell *him* to stay away from *me*. I've got a man!"

"Then act like you got one and you can put this," she said, tapping the top of the box in her hand with a red-tipped fingernail, "on the church's account." She flounced out of the shop and I heard a low whistle to my left. I turned to see Patsy Garrison grinning at me.

"Boy, you sure know how to piss people off."

CHAPTER 11

I finished up my stint at Garrison's and left with the corrected programs practically hot off the press. I tossed them in the backseat of my car and headed off in search of chocolate therapy, or more accurately, hot fudge cake. It was almost noon and I really needed a fix. Just the thought of cold vanilla ice cream sandwiched between layers of chocolate cake and covered in hot fudge and whipped cream had a very calming effect on my nerves. The rain had finally stopped, leaving it cool outside. I pulled into the parking lot of Frishes Big Boy and headed inside. As I was being seated, I noticed a familiar couple sitting in the back of the restaurant in the corner. It was Cliff and Stephanie Preston. I was surprised they were still in town. From their body language I could tell they were not having a good time. I headed back to say hello. Before I reached their table, Cliff abruptly stood up. He was angry and red in the face and headed out the nearest exit without even noticing me. Stephanie remained seated, staring after him with tear-filled eyes.

"Excuse me, Mrs. Preston. Remember me from the funeral the other day?" Stephanie looked a little startled then gave me a weak smile.

"Of course. But I'm sorry. I don't remember your name," she said looking embarrassed.

"Nola Morgan," I said, lapsing back into my lie. Apparently, her stepson hadn't blown my cover.

"I remember now. You did Vivianne's hair for the funeral. Won't you have a seat? My husband's gone to get some fresh air."

I slid into the opposite side of the booth that Cliff had just vacated. Stephanie was staring out the window. "Are you okay, Mrs. Preston?"

"Tell me," she said, turning to me—her tears had caused her mascara to run in black streaks down her cheeks, "why in the world a man would still be in love with a woman who mistreated their son and cheated on him throughout their entire marriage?"

"You're talking about your husband and Vivianne?"

"Who else?" She took a sip of her coffee.

"What makes you think he's still in love with Vivianne?"

"I don't think he ever stopped loving her. I mean, I know he loves me in his own way. But he can't stand to hear a word against her. Even after everything she put him and Kurt through. How can he still be in love with her?"

"Why did Vivianne lose custody of Kurt?" I asked, since she was being so open about her family business.

"Because she was a lousy mother. Cliff told me about a time when she took Kurt to the set of one of her movies. She forgot about him and left him in her trailer all day long. He got into some of her sleeping pills and had to have his stomach pumped. He was only two years old. He almost died," she choked back a sob. I waited for her to compose herself and couldn't help but admire her love for Kurt.

"Another time, after Cliff and Vivianne had separated, one of Vivianne's boyfriends beat Kurt because he wet the bed. She stood by and let that man beat her child. Cliff said he had welts all over him." She shook her head in disgust.

"That's horrible," I said. Vivianne apparently had a laundry list of people she'd done wrong to who hated her enough to kill her, starting with her own son. I was amazed that my sister was the only one the police could find evidence against.

"How'd you get along with her?"

"I made sure I never had to deal with her. I think I only ever talked to her once or twice when she'd call to bitch about something to Cliff. Even after she stopped acting she always found a reason to call. It was usually over money."

"Money? Was your husband paying her support?"

"No, nothing like that. She'd see some old movie of hers on late-night TV or an episode of some show she did a guest spot on and start calling Cliff bugging him about where her residual check was."

"Vivianne sounds like she had some major problems. I can see why you'd be upset thinking your husband might still have feelings for her." She nodded like she'd finally found an understanding soul.

"How'd you and your husband meet?" The question brought a smile to her face.

"I was a showgirl in Vegas," she said, straightening her back and thrusting her double D's out proudly.

"Really. That's sounds exciting. Which casino did you work at?"

"Ah, well, it was one of the smaller casinos off the strip called the Kontiki. It's been closed for years now." She turned to stare out the window again.

The Kontiki? Hmm. Sounded more like a strip club to me. I wouldn't be at all surprised if Stephanie's stint as a dancer in Vegas involved a pole, a G-string and grinding nightly on the laps of strange men. Cliff Preston certainly wouldn't be the first man who'd fallen for a stripper.

"Did you meet Cliff at one of your shows?"

"No. Actually, we met after I auditioned for a role in a movie. I didn't get the part and someone suggested I get an agent and recommended Cliff, who had an office in Vegas. But instead of signing me to his agency, he asked me out. I said no at first. I mean, he's old enough to be my father—"

I blanked out for a few seconds thinking back to what Winette Barlow had said to me and could feel myself getting pissed all over again.

"Eventually, he wore me down," Stephanie continued, unaware that I hadn't quite been paying attention. "He's so sweet. No man has ever treated me the way Cliff has. We ended up getting married six months later."

"And you didn't mind being a stepmother to Kurt?" She looked shocked at the question.

"No, not at all. Kurt was such a cutie pie and he was starved for a mother's love, which is what I gave him. All

Vivianne cared about was her career. After Cliff married me, we fought for sole custody of Kurt. We won, of course. Vivianne didn't put up much of a fight, not with so many witnesses testifying in court about her neglect."

"Wasn't it around that time that she stopped acting?"

"What? You think she stopped acting because she was upset over losing custody of Kurt?"

"No. No. It was just a question," I said quickly when her eyes narrowed and her face turned bright pink under her heavy makeup.

"Sorry," she said flashing me one of those showbiz smiles. "I just get so mad when people assume Vivianne was so destroyed over losing custody of her child that she couldn't act anymore. It's just such bullshit, you know. Viviane stopped acting because she couldn't get any good parts anymore. The last gig Cliff was able to get her was as the spokeswoman for an all-natural vitamin supplement for menopausal women called Vitipause." Stephanie started laughing and it took a minute for her to continue.

"Vivianne was supposed to do a series of infomercials and travel the country doing speaking engagements about the wonders of Vitipause. They had a whole advertising campaign planned around her. They were going to call it *Vivi for Vitipause*. But she pulled out of the contract and left Cliff in a big legal mess."

"Why?" I asked. But was I really surprised Vivianne didn't want to be the face of Vitipause? It sounded like a brand of doggy treats.

"She said she was way too young to be shilling for a menopausal supplement. That no one in their right mind would believe she was old enough to be going through menopause. She agreed to do it long enough to cash the big fat check they gave her then refused to go through with it."

"Why was Mr. Preston still representing her? I'd have thought after the divorce and the custody case they'd have severed their working relationship."

"I think Cliff felt guilty about taking Kurt away from her, though I can't for the life of me understand why. Plus, by then, no one else was interested in being Vivianne DeArmond's agent. She was a has-been and what's worse than representing a has-been is representing a has-been with delusions of grandeur. Cliff felt sorry for her."

In my opinion guilt and pity were what Stephanie was mistaking for Cliff's so-called love for Vivianne. But why would Cliff feel guilty about acting in the best interest of his son by gaining custody from Vivianne?

"Do you and Mr. Preston have any other children?" She shook her head and gave a harsh little laugh.

"That's been the other sore spot in our relationship. Cliff never wanted more children. He even went and got a vasectomy behind my back about ten years ago. The only reason I found out about it was because he blurted it out during one of our fights about having a baby. We almost split up over that one. He ruined my second chance. But like I said, no man has ever treated me the way Cliff does," she said drily. The tight smile on her face made me wonder if she even believed what she'd just said, because getting a vasectomy without his wife's knowledge didn't exactly make Cliff Preston sound like a prince to me.

A waitress had appeared to refresh Stephanie's coffee. I put in an order for some hot fudge cake to go. After the waitress left, Cliff returned to the table and stared down at me. His frown was a silent command for me to remove myself from his seat. I complied immediately.

"Cliff, don't be so rude. It's Nola Morgan, the nice young woman from the funeral home."

"Here's the thing," Cliff said, sliding into the booth. "I spoke to one of the owners of the funeral home after the service and you know what he told me?" I knew but I pretended not to anyway.

"He told me that he's the one who did Vivianne's hair and makeup. He's never even heard of a Nola Morgan. Now what do you think about that?" he said, looking at Stephanie.

"Oh my God! Are you a reporter?" Stephanie looked horrified. Her hands flew to her mouth like she was trying to keep anything else incriminating from escaping. Too late.

"What the hell have you been telling her, Stephanie!" Cliff's hands were curled into fists.

"Just a bunch of girl talk, Mr. Preston. Nothing you'd be interested in," I said mildly and took a step backwards and out of pummeling range of Cliff Preston's fists.

"I don't know who you are. But you'd better stay the

hell away from my wife, lady, or I'm calling the cops," Cliff said menacingly.

I started to leave and could feel the eyes of Cliff, Stephanie and a few other diners on me. Then a thought came to me and I marched back to the Prestons' table. Cliff slammed his coffee cup down, sloshing coffee on the table and making Stephanie flinch.

"That's it! I'm calling the cops," he said, pulling a cell phone from inside his sport coat.

"Did either of you know Vivianne had written a book?" I said quickly before he could press a button. He froze and the color drained from his face. I took that as a no.

Stephanie was staring at her husband strangely. Then Cliff regained his composure and scowled at me. He held up his phone and deliberately pressed a button. I hurried away from their table, only stopping long enough to pick up my order of hot fudge cake, and beat a hasty retreat.

I sat in my car in the parking lot of Cartwright Auditorium finishing up the last of my hot fudge cake. After placing the final spoonful of ice cream and chocolate cake in my mouth, I licked the fudge from my fingers and, feeling quite fortified, got out of my car and entered the building.

It had long since stopped raining, but it was cold, dark and overcast outside. The chill was seeping through my thin shirt and I wished I'd worn a sweater. The building was unlocked but seemed deserted, and I heard my footsteps echoing in the empty lobby. Besides Vivianne's recognition program, which now felt as though it had happened a million years ago, the last time I'd been in Cartwright Auditorium had been eleven years ago for my high-school graduation. I remembered lining up in my cap and gown with my fellow graduates in the same lobby I was now standing in, which had seemed bigger back then, waiting to march into the auditorium and take our seats. We were all so happy and filled with hope for the future. I sure didn't envision myself standing in the same spot more than a decade later trying to prove my sister didn't kill a washed-up actress. Funny how life works out.

I heard someone humming and followed the sound into the main auditorium. There was a middle-aged black man in a gray uniform sweeping the stage. I called out to him, but he didn't answer or look up. As I got closer, I could see he had a Walkman on with the music blaring so loudly that I could hear Al Green singing about love and happiness. When I reached the edge of the stage he finally looked up, noticed me standing there and almost jumped out of his skin.

"Girl, you gave me a heart attack," he said, chuckling. He pulled his headphones off and let them hang around his neck.

"Sorry, sir. I'm hoping you can help me. I was here for that recognition program last weekend and I lost an expensive bracelet. I can't find it anywhere and think I may have lost it here. Were you working that day?" I was hoping he had so I could grill him about who he may have seen going into Vivianne's dressing room.

"No, sweetheart, I was off last weekend. But Joyce worked that day. Maybe she found it."

"Is she here today?" I asked hopefully.

"She's eatin' lunch in her office. Just go back out there to the lobby and it's the first door on the right." I thanked him and headed back out to the way I came.

I knocked on the first wooden door on my right that I came to. The door had a mail slot in the center of it. A brass nameplate mounted at eyelevel on the wall next to the door read J. Clark, Manager. I knocked again and heard a distinct sigh and what sounded like exasperated muttering. I was interrupting Joyce Clark's lunch and she was none too pleased about it. I could hear movement behind the closed door and seconds later it swung open and the smell of food, pizza to be precise, wafted out. The doorway was filled with a large, irritated, light-skinned black woman in a denim jumper whose expression told me there wasn't a whole lot that made her happy. Lucky me.

"I'm so sorry to bother you, ma'am. But I was told you might be able to help me."

"With what?" she asked bluntly, not budging an inch from the doorway. I could see a smear of pizza sauce in the corner of her mouth. I looked her in the eye and rubbed the corner of my own mouth figuring she'd get the hint and wipe her mouth. Instead, she looked at me like I was crazy and then peered over my head out into the lobby as though she expected to see men in white coats coming to claim me.

"I was here for the recognition program last weekend and I lost a very expensive bracelet. Did anyone turn in a bracelet last weekend?"

"Nope. Sorry," she said, not impressing me one bit with her customer service skills, and started to swing the door shut.

"There's a reward," I called out before the door completely shut. The door opened again and this time Joyce Clark's entire attitude had changed and a smile was spread across her round face. Ah, the power of money. She stepped aside and gestured for me to come into the office.

"Must be a pretty expensive bracelet," she said, pulling a chair from against the wall of the tiny cluttered office and motioning for me to sit down. She closed the office door and sat back down behind her desk. There was two-thirds of a large pizza with the works sitting in a box in the middle of her desk. It was still hot and I could see steam rising from it. My mouth watered. She noticed me looking longingly at the pizza, closed the lid and pushed the box aside.

"It's a diamond tennis bracelet. My boyfriend gave it to me. If he finds out I lost it he's going to kill me."

"Well, we do have a lost and found but it's mostly junk that gets turned in. I doubt anybody would be honest enough to turn in an expensive piece of jewelry. But I could post some signs. What kinda reward are you talking about?" her eyes glittered greedily.

"Two hundred dollars." She sat back in her chair and I could almost see her mentally calculating how many pizzas she could buy with two hundred dollars.

She leaned down and pulled a drawer in her desk open, withdrew a yellow form and handed it to me across her desk. It was a claim form to report lost property. I grabbed a pen from her desk and started to fill it out, using bogus information, of course.

"I bet you got to meet Vivianne DeArmond last weekend. What was she like?" I asked.

"She was all right," replied Joyce Clark, shrugging. "Kinda stuck up. But I guess that's normal for somebody who used to be in movies. That little assistant of hers worked my last nerve though."

"Really?" I said, my ears perking up.

"She chewed out a member of my custodial staff. Accused him of stealing a necklace of Ms. DeArmond's. My people don't steal. None of them even went into that dressing room once Ms. DeArmond and her assistant arrived. I was the only one who kept checking with them to make sure everything was okay and I sure as hell don't steal. She probably just misplaced it or forgot to put it on, period. Ms. DeArmond was real upset about it but we never found any necklace. Who knows, maybe the same person who found your bracelet has Ms. DeArmond's necklace."

"Wow. Did you or any of your staff see anybody strange lurking around her dressing room?"

"You ask me, all them show-business people are strange. Ms. DeArmond's assistant was doing a good job of keeping people away. I personally saw her turn away about two dozen fans. Only one I saw go in that dressing room was an older, light-skinned black man. Then I had to go make sure the film festival committee members had everything they needed for the presentation. I was running around all morning long. My feet still hurt."

"You're right, you know. My bracelet's probably long gone by now," I said, handing her the form. "Things got so crazy after that fire alarm went off. I didn't even realize it was gone until later that night."

"Girl, crazy is right. We get the auditorium all emptied out after that alarm went off. Then next thing I know Ms. DeArmond's assistant comes running up to me screamin' for me to help Vivianne. I thought maybe she had a heart attack or somethin'. I go runnin' down there like a fool ready to perform CPR and there was blood everywhere. I didn't know somebody had killed her. Lord Jesus, if I never see a sight like that again it will be too soon." She pulled a piece of pizza from the box and started eating it to calm her nerves. Apparently, I wasn't the only one using food for therapy.

So Harriet had been the one to discover Vivianne's body after the dust cleared. I wondered where she'd been up until that time? What was she doing when the alarm went off? Cleaning blood from her clothes perhaps? Or maybe tossing Vivianne's purse in the Dumpster. Donald Cabot had said she stuck to Vivianne's side like glue that morning. Could Vivianne have sent her on some fake errand to get her out of the way so she could do her interview with Allegra? Or is Harriet the one who killed her then pulled the fire alarm to distract everyone?

"Did you ever find out who pulled the alarm?"

"No one pulled the alarm. Someone was smoking in the men's room and set off the alarm. We found some cigarettes in the trash can."

"What kind of cigarettes? Were they black and milds?" I asked. I felt a little lightheaded. Had Blackie Randall come out of hiding to silence Vivianne? Could he have been the older black man seen going into Vivianne's dressing room? Joyce Clark just shrugged.

"No idea," she said. She looked over my form and set it on top of the pizza box. "I'll have my staff look around for your bracelet, but like I said, mostly we just find junk. We post it on that lost and found board behind you and after a month we pitch it."

I thanked her and got up to leave and saw the lost and found board propped against the wall by the door. There was an assortment of objects tacked to it: two sets of keys, nail clippers, a tarnished hoop earring, dog tags, a watch with a broken strap, a man's tie. She was right. Just a bunch of junk but something else caught my eye. There was a framed painting hanging on the wall by the door. The picture showed a group of cowboys gathered around a campfire at night. The skill of the painter was nothing remarkable. It was the subject matter that had gotten my attention. Camping! I suddenly realized I knew where Lynette was.

John Bryan State Park was in Yellow Springs, home of Antioch College, Glen Helen Nature Preserve and children's author Virginia Hamilton. It was also a mere fifteen-minute drive from Willow. When Lynette and I were Girl Scouts we'd gone camping several times with our troop in John Bryan Park. Lynette used to love it. I didn't. I remembered her staring at the picture of us as Girl Scouts when I'd gone to her house on the morning of Vivianne's murder and talking about how our lives had been so uncomplicated back then. I was banking that she was trying to relive that time by going camping again, though she'd have to really be in love with camping—or just plain crazy—to be out in the cold, dreary weather we were currently experiencing.

I arrived at the park. Not surprisingly the parking lot was empty save for two cars, a brown Buick Regal and a familiar black Nissan Altima. Lynette's car. Hallelujah! I parked next to her car and got out. It was raining again and I rooted around in my trunk, finally finding an old, raggedy umbrella that wasn't going to offer much protection from the rain but was better than nothing. I also found a lint-covered blue sweater and pulled it on. It smelled moldy, and there was a rust stain on the sleeve from where my tire iron had been lying on top of it, but I didn't care. It was warm.

I headed back to the campgrounds. It had been years since I'd been to the park, but everything still looked much the same as it had long ago. The rain seemed to make everything look more lush and green, but I could hardly appreciate my surroundings under the circumstances. I squelched through mud in some spots, staining my running shoes, and twice I almost slipped on the wet grass in my haste to find Lynette. The campground was, not surprisingly, empty. No tents were pitched and no one appeared to be in any of the cabins. I walked on, eventually giving up on the useless umbrella and tossed it in a nearby trash can. I clutched my sweater close around me and wiped the rain dripping through the tree branches hanging overhead from my face with the sleeve. Finally, I saw a canvas teepee pitched on a wooden platform in the distance. I hurried toward it and called out Lynette's name. Nothing. I called out again, louder this time, and finally the flap of the teepee opened and Lynette stuck her head out.

"How'd you find me?" she said when I reached her. She held open the flap and stood aside so I could enter. She was dressed warmly in a gray sweat suit and a jean jacket. The teepee wasn't exactly toasty, but it was sure better than being out in the rain. I saw a pot of coffee and a pan of what smelled like beef stew warming on top of a propane stove. Lynette actually looked not only happy to see me, but a lot happier than when I'd seen her last. I, on the other hand, was cold, wet, miserable and in no mood for any mess.

"That's all you have to say to me? How'd I find you? How about saying you're sorry you ran away and made me, Greg and your mother worry? And that you're sorry me and your mother almost got into a fistfight in the grocery parking lot? Or that you're sorry that I went looking for you at the Heritage Arms with Morris Rollins and now everyone in town thinks I'm screwing him, including his girlfriend, Winette Barlow, who tried to kill me with a paper cut!" I snapped indignantly. Lynette's eyes got big.

"Morris Rollins is kicking it with Winette Barlow?"

"Lynette!" I bellowed.

"Okay. Okay. I'm so sorry, Kendra. I truly am. I just had to get away for a few days, that's all."

"Well, your vacation is over. Pack this mess up and let's get going. Your mother is threatening to cancel your wedding if you're not back home tonight."

Lynette laughed. I could see no humor in the situation at all.

"Yeah, right. She can't cancel anything. She was just bluffing."

"She sure seemed to think that she could."

"Kendra, you know how my mother is. She can't stand it when she's not in charge. I let her help me make all the wedding arrangements, but my name is on all the reservations that were made. She can't cancel anything without my consent."

"So you do plan to marry Greg on Saturday?" I asked cautiously.

"Does he still want to marry me? Because I love Greg. Being away from him for the last few days made me realize just how much I do love him. I just hope I haven't ruined it," she said looking at her feet.

"Of course he still wants to marry you, fool," I said and grabbed her hand. "And what about that other issue? You know, the sex thing—"

"I think it's going to be okay, Kendra. I was under so much pressure and my mother wasn't making it any better constantly throwing my marriage to Lamont in my face every time I turned around. I started second-guessing myself. I really needed a break to think without the kids and my mother breathing down my neck. But now I know things with Greg will be different. I didn't mean to make you all worry. I'm sorry. Can you forgive me?"

I hugged her to show that all was forgiven.

"You need me to help you pack up?" I asked, reaching for a nearby cooler.

"I'm not going back tonight," she said simply.

"Huh? I thought you just said—"

"I already paid for this teepee for the night. I'll go home first thing in the morning." She looked like an excited little girl and I had a hard time not smiling.

"You look hungry, Kendra. Let's have some stew. And then for dessert, guess what I have?"

"I can't begin to imagine," I said sarcastically. Like I said before, I hate camping. I watched Lynette as she rummaged through a grocery bag. She turned to me beaming and waving a bag of marshmallows, a box of graham crackers and a giant Hershey Bar.

"S'mores!" We both said in unison

A couple of hours, a bowl of stew and a half dozen s'mores later, I headed home. I called Greg from my cell on the way and told him his runaway fiancée would be home first thing in the morning. I'd leave it up to him to inform Justine. After I hung up with Greg, my cell phone rang and I saw that it was Mama's number. I didn't answer. I just wasn't up to getting a singed eardrum from her ranting and raving over me and Morris Rollins. My cell phone beeped, indicating that she'd left me a voice mail message that I was in no hurry to listen to, either. Instead, I headed home so I could get out of my still slightly damp clothes and take a hot bubble bath. But when I turned onto my street, all thoughts of a bath flew right out of my mind. There was a group of neighbors on the front lawn of my duplex. My landlady, Mrs. Carson, was smack in the middle of the crowd talking and gesturing wildly. I parked and got out. Mrs. Carson came rushing up to me.

"Where you been, missy? Everybody's lookin' for you." I felt the bottom drop out of my stomach.

"What's wrong?"

"What's wrong is they just arrested your sister for murdering Vivianne DeArmond. They carted her off in handcuffs 'bout half and hour ago."

Great!

CHAPTER 12

When I arrived at the Willow police station I had to fight my way through the crush of media crowded into the lobby. Two officers were keeping the press at bay, preventing them from proceeding beyond the lobby. I tried to explain I was a relative of Allegra Clayton's, but they wouldn't let me through. News reporter Tracy Ripkey spotted me trying to shove my way past the officers and decided to get a statement. Bad idea.

"Miss Clayton, how do you feel about your sister being arrested for the murder of Vivianne DeArmond?" She shoved a microphone in my face. Another reporter, a large sweaty man in a tight suit, caught wind that I was a relative of the accused and brutally shoved Ripkey out of the way, practically sending her flying, and stuck his microphone in my face. It was too crowded for me to see where Ripkey had landed, but I was sure her big hair had probably cushioned her fall.

"Has your sister confessed to murdering Ms. DeArmond? What was her motive?" The sweaty man asked. Then a third reporter jumped in my face.

"What evidence do the police have against your sister,

Miss Clayton?" I was surrounded by reporters and could barely move.

Tracy Ripkey, not at all pleased about being shoved out of the way, rushed up to the sweaty male reporter and stomped on his foot. His face went white with pain and he angrily elbowed her in the shoulder causing her to drop her microphone on another reporter's foot. Soon it was a free-for-all with the lobby full of reporters punching and kicking each other like bikers in a bar fight. I ducked several punches as I eased my way out of the crowd and clung to a nearby wall. The two officers plunged into the brawling crowd in an attempt to restore some kind of order, leaving me free to rush past them into the main part of the building. I headed around the corner and down a long hallway until I spotted my family: Mama, Alex, Gwen and Carl. Alex and Gwen looked away as I approached but Mama and Carl greeted me with tight angry expressions. I hadn't done anything. Why were they mad at me?

"Did you know?" Carl spat out at me. Mama was standing rigidly by his side with her arms crossed.

"That Allie's been arrested? Yeah, Mrs. Carson told me. Where is she?" I asked looking around.

"No, Kendra. Did you know about that check Allegra took from Vivianne DeArmond's purse? That they found the check in Allegra's rental car?"

In her rental? That meant that Allegra had lied to me about the check being stolen. She'd had the check all along. I was too stunned to be angry, but my shock at being lied to didn't keep me from feeling hurt and betrayed. I felt like I'd been kicked in the stomach.

"How'd they find out about the check?" I asked meekly.

"They found out about Vivianne DeArmond's book. They also found out that she'd been issued a check for an advance against royalties that they didn't find among her possessions and that hadn't been cashed. So they had the post office put a trace on it. It had arrived at her house the morning of her murder. Harriet Randall said Vivianne got the mail that morning and she saw her putting some mail in her purse. But no letter was found when they dug the purse out of the Dumpster. They got search warrants for every place Allegra had been staying, including your grandmother's house and your apartment, plus they impounded Allegra's second rental car. They found the check in the glove box of Allegra's rental."

"Where is she now?" I asked again.

"She's being processed like a common criminal, having her mug shot taken and being fingerprinted," Mama said stiffly. I reached out to touch her but she shook my hand off.

I told them everything that had happened after we'd found my apartment broken into and tossed and about Allegra confiding in me about the check. It was too little too late. They were all furious with me.

"Good Lord, Kendra, why in the world didn't you at least tell Carl about that check? Do you know how this makes your sister look? She doesn't have the good sense that God gave a goat, but I thought you'd have known better than this. Now, I'm going to have to try and track down your parents in Europe and tell them their daughter has been arrested," Mama said, sounding close to tears.

She walked away from me, shaking her head, and went to join Alex and Gwen. Gwen put a comforting arm around her. Alex usually stays pretty neutral, but even he was looking at me like I was an idiot.

"I made a mistake. I'm sorry. But I swear Allie told me that check had been stolen during the break-in," I said to Carl.

Since we'd been dating, I'd never had an occasion to see Carl truly angry, especially not at me. It was not a pretty sight. It looked like it was taking everything in him not to scream, which I would have preferred to him starring daggers at me and not speaking. Had I made a mistake in not telling Carl about the check? Yes. But, hell, I'm not the one who took the damn check in the first place, and I didn't appreciate being made the scapegoat.

"You know, Carl, I'm really surprised Allie didn't tell you about the check herself. I mean, you've probably seen more of her this past week than I have. In fact, the two of you have gotten quite cozy lately." I could tell by the way his eyelid started twitching that it had been the wrong thing to say but I didn't care. Being picked on tends to bring out the worst in me.

"I don't believe this shit. I'm trying to keep your sister from spending the rest of her life in prison, so, yeah, we've been spending time together. She's my client. At least you know who I've been with and why. But from what I've been hearing, you haven't exactly been missing me, have you?" He was practically vibrating with hostility.

He'd heard the rumor about me and Rollins. Boy, this just kept getting better and better by the second.

"I haven't been doing anything that you haven't been doing," I said, rolling my eyes.

"You need to grow up, Kendra. And while you're at it, go home. You've upset your family enough and I don't have time for your petty insecurities," he said. He turned to rejoin my family, who were gathered around my visibly upset grandmother. No one looked at me.

They didn't want me there? Fine. I was leaving. I headed out to the lobby and barreled my way back through the now calm and strangely subdued flock of reporters. A couple of the braver ones started to follow me until I whirled around and screamed at the top of my lungs, "No! Comment!" They fell back, looking at me fearfully, like whipped dogs. But one of the photographers snapped my picture midscream. I had a good idea who was going to be on the front page of tomorrow's *Willow News Gazette*.

I headed for my car, hot tears of frustration and hurt feelings blurring my vision, and ran smack into a very tall man. I looked up. It was Morris Rollins. I clung to him and bawled like a baby while he held me and stroked my hair.

Rollins insisted on following me home even though I told him I was okay. Once at my place, I felt obligated to invite him in for coffee, and of course, he accepted. I just hoped Winette Barlow wasn't lurking around in my bushes waiting to administer a *Steel Magnolia*-style beat down on me.

"Why'd you come down to the station?" I asked and handed him a mug of freshly brewed coffee. He was sitting at my kitchen table with his long legs stretched out underneath.

"I saw the report of your sister's arrest on TV. I came to lend my support to you and your family. I knew you had to be very upset." He didn't know the half of it. I filled him in. He let out a low whistle.

"I wouldn't take this too personally, Kendra. Your family is just upset and since your sister wasn't around right then they were taking their frustrations out on you."

"Maybe. But you have to admit I did make a big mistake in not at least persuading Allie to tell Carl about that check." I joined him at the table.

"Why didn't you?"

"You've never met my sister, have you? Her talent for getting her own way is only rivaled by her talent for flirting. She has my whole family wrapped around her finger. All she has to do is start whining and everyone bends over backwards to make her happy. I thought I was immune to it, but I guess not."

"Are you jealous of your sister?" he asked bluntly. Was I jealous of Allegra? Now there was a loaded question. I thought about it for a few seconds before answering.

Jealousy implied that I resented my sister for all of her accomplishments and begrudged her her success, and that certainly wasn't the case. On the other hand, I *was* envious of Allegra's effortless charm, her model looks and her fearlessness in pursuing her career goals even though her choices haven't always been to my taste.

"I'm very proud of my sister's accomplishments. I only want to see her happy," I said simply, avoiding Rollins's eyes. He let out his infectious laugh.

"Spoken like a true diplomat."

I saw Rollins to the door about half an hour later. We stood in the doorway awkwardly. Finally, he bent down and gave me kiss on the lips. It started out a nice simple kiss. But it quickly changed into something else. Something deep and warm. An invitation to someplace we knew we shouldn't be going. At least not yet. But as I thought back on Carl's angry face and harsh words I found myself wrapping my arms around Rollins's waist and pulling him closer, inhaling his wonderful scent. His hands were massaging my lower back, pressing me tightly against him. I started sucking on his tongue and heard a low groan escape from the back of his throat. His hands found their way underneath my shirt and felt hot against my skin. I could feel his erection pressing against my stomach and was mere seconds away from pulling him back inside my apartment and tearing his clothes off when we were hit by a bright blast of the car's headlights.

A car was stopped at the corner across the street. The high beams were on us, blinding us momentarily. We pulled apart just in time to see the car make a turn in front of my duplex and speed off down the street, tires squealing. I caught a glimpse of an angry woman's face. Her eyes were shooting me the dirtiest look I think I'd ever been given. It was Winette Barlow. Had she been out here the whole time? Well, I sure couldn't say I hadn't been warned. Winette had told me to stay away from Rollins, and what did I turn around and do? Had myself wrapped around him like Saran Wrap on a tuna casserole. Talk about more drama I didn't need.

"I think we just pissed off your girlfriend," I said sarcastically, putting some distance between us. Rollins sighed heavily.

"Winette and I have been out a few times. But it's not serious. She's looking for a husband. It's been less than a year since I buried Nicole. I'm not looking to get married again just yet. Looks like I'm going to have to have a little talk with her," he said sheepishly.

"Make it soon," I said sincerely. But I knew it was only a matter of time before Winette made good on her threat.

Later that evening I was lounging in hot lilac-scented bath water, hoping my phone would ring and one of my family members would be on the other end telling me what the heck was going on with Allegra. But I knew it wasn't going to ring. I wondered what in the world my sister could have been thinking, holding on to that check, and why lie to me about it? Then I realized if she had lied to me about the check being stolen, had she also lied about having told Noelle about the check? I hadn't seen Noelle since the day I saw her and Kurt with Donald Cabot.

Where had she been all this time? Gambling? She wasn't at the station when Allegra got arrested. Did she even know?

I called the Holiday Inn and had them connect me to Noelle's room. There was no answer. Why did I have such a bad feeling? Did someone Noelle owed a gambling debt to show up to collect? Had she been beaten up, or worse, killed? I reluctantly left my hot tub and threw on sweatpants and a long-sleeved T-shirt. When I got to the hotel I asked which room Noelle was staying in and, of course, they wouldn't tell me. Our Holiday Inn is nice but very small. Only one story and about fifty rooms. The front half of the building was the oldest. An addition of about twenty luxury suites had been added off the back. The new rooms were bigger and much nicer, complete with Jacuzzi tubs and big-screen TVs. They were also more expensive. I couldn't imagine a producer for a Hollywood news program staying on the cheap.

I had an idea of a way to find Noelle's room, but I had to get back to the area where the suites were in order to pull it off. Unfortunately, the door that led back to the rooms was located near the front desk and, for security reasons, was locked. Hotel guests used their room key-cards to open the door. I sat in the lobby as though I was waiting for someone. The hotel clerk, a snotty-looking woman whose features were crowded into the middle of her face, making it look permanently pinched, kept eyeing me suspiciously. It was after ten at night on a Thursday. It wasn't as if there was much else for her to do except watch me. But what did she think I was going do—make off with the ashtrays? Every once in a while the phone would ring and she'd answer it, but she still kept one eye on me.

I was half-asleep in one of the lobby's comfortable leather chairs when a party of six men entered the hotel laughing, singing and talking loudly. It was apparent they were very drunk as one of the men was playing matador and had taken off his suit jacket to use as a cape while one of his companions was doing an impersonation of a bull with his index fingers held up next to his head as horns. The bull stumbled around, chasing the matador in front of the desk. The other men roared with laughter. The hotel clerk did not look pleased and had come out from behind the desk to chastise the men. She was addressing the matador, shaking a bony finger in his face, when the bull rushed up behind her and gored her in the butt with his horns, sending her almost sprawling to her knees. Maybe if she'd been nicer to me I wouldn't have giggled my ass off. Predictably, she didn't see any humor in it at all. She lost it.

"If you gentlemen do not settle down this instant. I'm calling the police," she hollered.

The men laughed and the matador threw his cape/ jacket on her head and twirled her around in a circle. I got up to go help her when she suddenly threw off the jacket, spun around, and landed a roundhouse kick in the middle of the matador's chest. He let out a surprised, "Oof," similar to the sounds let out by villains on the old

Batman series who were getting their asses kicked, and went toppling backwards over a couch in the lobby, knocking the couch over in the process. The men fell silent and looked from their fallen friend to the smug-looking clerk.

"I've got more if you want it," said the clerk with her hands up in a karate stance. The men didn't want any more and rushed over to pick up their friend. They helped him to his feet and headed to the door leading back to their rooms. I fell in line behind them as the clerk went to pick up the couch that had gotten knocked over. It took a long minute for the man with the keycard to negotiate the slot. Once they got the door opened, they all lurched through it, muttering angrily that the "bitch of a clerk just needed to get laid," assuring the matador, who'd just got punked, that he could have taken her if he'd really wanted to and asking who among them still had some beer in their room. I silently crept in behind the group, until they were all through the door, then walked quickly past the inebriated men, ignoring their invitations to party with them, and headed back to the new section.

I could tell by the newness of the carpet when I'd reached the addition. I walked down the hall until I figured I was about in the middle and pulled out my cell phone. I dialed the front desk and asked the Karate Clerk to connect me to Noelle's room again. I listened closely until I heard the phone ringing in a room three doors down from where I was standing. I pressed my ear to the door. The phone rang and rang but no one answered it and I could hear no movement behind the door. As I pressed myself closer to the door, it swung open abruptly and I went sprawling onto the carpeted floor of Noelle's room, which apparently was also Kurt's room, as he was the one who'd opened the door and was now frowning down at me.

"What the hell are you doing?" he asked. Kurt was dressed only in a white towel that was almost slipping off his slim hips. His skin looked damp and there were beads of water in his hair. His eyes were glazed and bloodshot. I wondered which he was: drunk, high or both.

"I was looking for Noelle," I said, averting my eyes when Kurt's towel slipped south of the border. He grabbed it just in time and secured it more tightly.

"You the one that just called?"

"Yeah. Why didn't you answer the phone? Where's Noelle?" I asked suspiciously.

"Your guess is as good as mine. I got here about an hour ago and crashed. I just got up a few minutes ago and hopped in the shower. What do you want with Noelle?"

"I have something important to tell her about my sister." Obviously Kurt had no idea an arrest had been made in his mother's murder. Would he even care?

"Like I told you before, I haven't seen Noelle since we got that money from Cabot." He rubbed his eyes and looked at me bleary eyed. He must have really had a rough night.

"Aren't you worried about Noelle?" If my man disappeared I'd sure be worried. That is, if I even still had a man.

"She's done this before. She'll take off and get in on some private card or dice games. She'll be back when she runs out of money."

"I'm surprised you and your family are even still in town."

"Ole Vivi's will gets read tomorrow morning. My pops seems to think she left him something. I think he's a fool."

"Maybe she left you something," I said. He considered it for a moment. I could see the conflicting emotions flitting across his freckled face.

"Naw. I don't think so. The woman barely gave me the time of day when she was alive. Why would she leave me anything in her will? And even if she did, I don't want it," he said unconvincingly.

"You sure about that? You've been stealing stuff from her to sell for years. Least if she left you something you'd have come by it legitimately."

"I only took junk. Stuff that she wouldn't miss. It wasn't like I was ripping off expensive jewelry and shit. What do you care anyway?" He took a step toward me and I realized being alone in a room with a man who could have killed his mother wasn't a good place to be.

"Can I leave Noelle a note in case she comes back?" I asked quickly.

"Knock yourself out, and make sure you pull the door shut behind you," he said and headed back to the bathroom where I could hear the water in the shower running.

I grabbed a notepad from beside the bed and jotted down my name and phone number with a brief message to please call. As I was tucking my pen back in my purse,

I spied a brown stain on the beige carpet by the bed. It was about the size of a dime. I got on my hands and knees and ran my index finger over the spot. It was stiff and dry. I couldn't be sure, but it looked very much like dried blood to me. Was it Noelle's? I wondered how Kurt could have not noticed the stain. I could hear him humming tunelessly in the shower and decided to look around. The king-size bed was unmade and Kurt's clothes, a pair of white dress slacks and a gray-and-red patterned silk shirt had been tossed on the floor at the foot of the bed. I checked the clothes but besides reeking of marijuana, they were blood-free. No wonder he hadn't noticed the stain and didn't seem worried about Noelle. He was too busy having fun with Mary Jane. I crossed the room to the closet by the door and opened it slowly, half expecting Noelle's dead body to fall out. But all that was in the closet were a few articles of men's and women's clothing.

I looked around on the floor for more bloodstains. Nothing. There were more dirty clothes piled in a chair in the small sitting area in front of the TV. I picked through the clothes and discovered they weren't stained with blood, just in need of washing. But as I turned to leave, I saw a torn piece of white paper lying in front of the big-screen TV. I picked it up. It was the top section of a sheet of typing paper that read: Onyx Man/DeArmond. It was a piece of Vivianne's manuscript. Allegra hadn't lied about telling Noelle about the check and Vivianne's book after all. How had Noelle got a hold of the manuscript? And more importantly, where was Noelle now?

I was still holding the scrap of paper when Kurt emerged from the shower again, naked this time. We stared at each other, and Kurt put his hands on his hips and smiled widely at me before I stuffed the scrap of paper in my pocket and quickly left.

I was at the Willow County Courthouse bright and early the next morning for my sister's arraignment. I saw my family file into the courtroom and sit in the seats behind the table where Carl and Allegra were seated. I was sitting in the back of the courtroom. I didn't want to be a distraction, plus I was still feeling hurt and sulky about last night. I'd talk to Carl afterwards about what I'd found. I watched my sister. Even though I was mad at her I was still worried sick about the possibility of her going to jail for murder. I was amused to notice that Allegra had even managed to make her jail-issue orange jumpsuit and slip-on tennis shoes look good. Her honey-highlighted hair hung in a long glossy ponytail down her back and her lack of makeup only made her look younger and more vulnerable. I watched as Carl leaned over and whispered something in her ear, and she turned to the back of the courtroom and gave me a solemn wave. I returned it and gave her a smile and a thumbs-up. Carl and I nodded to each other like strangers. Mama didn't turn around at all. And Gwen and Alex appeared to be doing what they did best—arguing. I saw Gwen shaking her finger in my uncle's face and Alex turning his back on her.

The judge entered the courtroom and the bailiff commanded us all to rise for the Honorable Judge Peter Franklin, a dapper little man with white hair and a thick salt-and-pepper mustache. When Judge Franklin asked Allegra how she pleaded, she dramatically replied, with hands on heart and head held high no less, "I am innocent, Your Honor." A few people in the packed courtroom giggled.

"Glad to hear it, Miss Clayton," Judge Franklin replied drily. "And to the matter of bail?" he continued, looking both at Carl and the prosecuting attorney on the other side of the room, a pleasant enough looking middle-aged woman in a plaid skirt and ruffled blouse. She looked more like an accountant than a lawyer.

"Your Honor, this was a particularly vicious crime. We ask that the defendant be denied bail and remanded to jail pending the outcome of the trial."

"Nonsense, Your Honor," Carl piped up. "My client has strong ties to this community and poses no flight risk. May I also add that my client has never been in trouble with the law before and is a popular television personality easily recognized all over the country, which would severely hamper any attempts to flee the area. She looks forward to defending herself against these charges."

Judge Franklin set bail at two hundred and fifty thousand dollars. Yikes. I knew Mama would probably have to put up her house to raise bail. Allegra was led away and I reluctantly made my way to the front of the courtroom. Alex whispered something in Gwen's ear and they both turned to look at me. I waited until the prosecuting attorney had left the room before speaking.

"I'm sorry about not telling anyone that Allegra had that check. I don't know what I was thinking," I began before Alex cut me off.

"Don't sweat it, kiddo," he said, squeezing my shoulder. I was doing good to get that bit of affection from Alex. He's not big on public displays of affection, but Gwen is.

"Yeah. Everyone was upset last night. We were all trippin'," said Gwen, putting her arm around my shoulders and pulling me tightly to her side. Gwen's five-ten, in heels, over six feet. I felt dwarfed by her embrace but grateful for it all the same.

Two down, two to go. I peered over at Mama who was talking to Carl, probably about arranging bail for Allegra. She turned to look at me and gave me a neutral look. Not mad, but not exactly welcoming, either.

"Soon as I bail Allie out, I'm having a cookout," Mama announced. "No need for any of us to be hanging our heads. I have faith that this foolishness will all be resolved soon enough and we can all put this behind us." She breezed past me without speaking and then turned back.

"Kendra, you're going to help me get everything ready." It wasn't a question at all. It was a command to be obeyed.

"Of course," I said, quickly bringing a satisfied smile to her face. Work was apparently going to be my penance for stupidity. And if that was the case, I wondered what she had in store for Allegra.

Mama, Alex and Gwen left, leaving me alone with Carl, who was shoving papers into his briefcase with his back to me.

"I have some information that might help Allegra's case," I said timidly. He turned around. He looked tired. I wanted to give him a hug, but I didn't know if he'd let me.

"Well, I need all the help I can get because, to be honest, Kendra, this isn't looking too good for your sister," he said quietly.

I told him about Noelle and finding a piece of the manuscript and my theory that the title *The Onyx Man* could be referring to Harriet's husband, Blackie, who could have had something to do with Vivianne's murder. I was happy to see he looked somewhat pleased.

"Allegra told me she told Noelle about the check and Vivianne's book. I'll see if I can subpoena the publisher into handing over a copy, but right now I need to make bail arrangements." He snapped his briefcase shut.

"Carl, we need to talk," I said, when he still wouldn't look at me.

"I know, Kendra. It's just that now's not the right time." He walked away, leaving me standing in the empty courtroom.

I was headed to my car and a nice big pancake breakfast when my cell phone rang. It was Greg and he wasn't happy.

"So, where is she?" he asked, sounding highly fed up.

"Who?" I was still feeling a little off balance from my conversation with Carl, and not really thinking.

"Lynette. Who else? Is she with you?" he asked. I'd forgotten all about Lynette returning from her camping trip that morning. I looked at my watch. It was only nine-thirty.

"No. I haven't talked to her since last night. But it's still early, Greg. She's probably on her way home now." I'd reached my car and noticed someone had placed a flyer under my windshield wiper. I reached across and grabbed it, intending to throw away.

"She'd better be. I've tried to be patient and give her her space but I don't know how much more she expects me to put up with."

"Why don't I ride out there and hurry her up? Will that make you feel better?" I said to appease him.

"I'd appreciate it, Kendra. I'd do it myself but my parents are here and I don't want them to know anything is wrong."

I hung up with Greg and was looking around for a trash can to the throw away the flyer, when I finally looked at what I was holding. It wasn't a flyer at all. It was one of Greg and Lynette's wedding programs. Except Lynette's face had a big red X through it. I frantically looked in the back of my car and, sure enough, the box was open and the programs were strewn across my backseat. Someone had been in my car. Not only was the box of programs open but my glove box was hanging open, the contents spilling out onto the floorboard. I turned the program I was holding over and on the back, written in the same red ink, was a message: You have something that I want and

I have your friend. Go home. I'll call at noon. Tell no one or she's dead! The word *dead* was underlined so heavily it had almost broken through the paper.

Oh my God!

CHAPTER 13

I felt like I was going to be sick. I had something someone wanted? What could I possibly have that someone would kidnap Lynette to get? This couldn't be happening. And after I took a few deep breaths to calm myself down, I'd pretty much convinced myself that it wasn't. This had to be joke, right? I'd just head on out to the John Bryan Park and check on my friend and hurry her on her way to her fiancé's waiting arms. Yep. That's just what I'd do. My hands were shaking so badly it took me three tries to get my key in the ignition and start my car.

I flew down the highway, making it to the park in just under ten minutes and wondering how I hadn't gotten a speeding ticket. Today the parking lot had a few more cars than yesterday. By the end of the day it would most likely be packed since it was the start of the weekend. Lynette's car was still parked in the same spot and I didn't know whether to be relieved or not. I looked through the driver's-side window. Lynette kept her car spotless and nothing looked amiss. No bloodstains and nothing indicating the car had been searched. All the doors were locked. I headed on back to the campground and spotted the teepee Lynette had rented in the distance. I approached it slowly. I called out her name tentatively.

"Lynette, are you in there?" My voice was hoarse from my dry throat. No sound was coming from inside the teepee.

In one quick fluid motion I lifted the flap and peered inside. It took a few seconds for my eyes to adjust to the darkness. The teepee was empty. No Lynette. No sign of a struggle. But Lynette's sleeping bag and grocery sacks were sitting neatly inside the teepee's entrance as though she'd been just about to go. I went back outside on the off chance she was somewhere outside.

"Lynette!" I screamed so loudly she could have heard me back in Willow. No response. Just the sound of birds chirping and a squirrel scrambling up the side of nearby tree. No Lynette. Shit! I walked a few feet from the teepee and called again. Still nothing. I leaned against a tree and buried my face in my hands as tears threatened to spill. What was I going to do? Then I noticed something at my feet. I bent down for a closer look. It was two black and mild cigarette butts. Blackie Randall. Had he been here? Did he have Lynette?

I hurried back to my car and pulled my cell phone out of my purse. I started to call 911 but stopped. The message had said to tell no one or Lynette was dead. The memory of the word *dead*, underlined in red ink, burned itself into my brain. I quickly put down my phone. I looked at my watch. It was ten o'clock, two hours before whoever had Lynette was going to call me. I started up my car and headed for the home of the one person I knew could tell me where Blackie Randall was: His wife... Harriet.

I headed down Troyer Road until I came upon a lone farmhouse with a large barn in back. Vivianne's farm was the only one around for several miles. I turned into the gravel driveway that led up to the plain, white, two-story, Shaker-style house with green shutters. I didn't see Harriet's silver Cadillac. I got out anyway and walked up on the porch and rang the doorbell. I heard it chime through the house. No one came to the door. I got back in my car, intending to wait for her when I remembered what Kurt had said about Vivianne's will being read that morning. I figured that's where Harriet was. At the lawyer's office. If I knew where the office was I could go there and wait for her. Willow had dozens of lawyers. The office could be anywhere, even out of town. I looked at my watch. It was almost twenty after ten. I still had time to track Harriet down. Then I remembered the old woman Harriet visited the nursing home in Park Hurst. Maybe she could help me.

My cell phone rang as I headed to Woodlawn Nursing Home. It was Greg's number. I didn't dare answer it. What could I tell him? Sorry Greg, I got your bride-to-be kidnapped because someone thinks I have something they want. And just what was it I was supposed to have anyway? I hope this person didn't want money. Anyone with eyes could take one look at my raggedy Nova and thrift-store wardrobe and tell I barely had two sticks to rub together. The cell phone stopped ringing and I turned it off.

Woodlawn Nursing Home may have had a beautiful lawn but the inside smelled just like every other nursing home I'd been in. A mixture of disinfectant, food and urine. They must bottle this scent and sell it to nursing homes all over the country to mask the odor of decay and sadness. I walked up to the front desk and stood in front of the surly-looking nurse's aide, who was filing her nails while watching a small color TV, and who I'm not sure I'd trust a pet with, let alone a family member. She finally looked up at me, annoyed, like I was interrupting something important.

"Can I help you?" she asked, as her eyes reverted to something more interesting on the TV screen.

"I'm Harriet Randall's niece. I'm her to see my grandma, um, Perkins," I said quickly thinking back to Rollins's mention of Harriet's maiden name. "Can you tell me which room she's in?"

The woman's face frowned up like she smelled something bad, though there wasn't much that smelled worse than parfum de Nursing Home.

"Who?" she asked.

"Mrs. Perkins? Her daughter, my aunt, Harriet Randall, is here all the time visiting."

"Oh, Mrs. Randall," she said, finally recognizing the name. "She is here all the time but it's not to see her mother. And if you're really her niece you'd have known that wouldn't you? What are you, a reporter?"

Great. I watched her reach under the counter and press a button. A big, black, burly, bald male nurse's aide rounded the corner. His white uniform strained to contain his muscles and he looked as if he was allergic to smiling.

"You got a problem here, Candy?" he asked, giving me the once-over.

"No big deal," I said backing away. I already had enough problems. I didn't need to add broken bones to the mix. "I just got my nursing homes mixed up that's all. Grandma must be in Sunnyvale across town. Y'all have a nice day."

I beat it out the door just in time to see Harriet Randall's Cadillac pull into a parking space. Talk about perfect timing. I marched right up to her as she was slamming her car door shut.

"I want to know where Blackie Randall is hiding, Harriet. I know you know where he is." I caught her off guard. She looked startled and jerked back like I'd hit her. Her mouth was hanging open and I could tell she was scared. It was the only time I'd seen her at a loss for words.

"Everything okay, Ms. Randall?" yelled the bald nurse's aide from the doorway.

"Just fine, Cookie," Harriet replied giving him a friendly wave. Cookie and Candy? I'd rarely seen two less sweet people in all my life.

"Blackie has my friend Lynette and is holding her for ransom. If you don't tell me where he is I'm calling the police." I pulled out my cell phone. Harriet looked at me and her eyes narrowed.

"I remember you now. You're that Clayton woman's sister. You crashed Vivianne's funeral. I knew I'd seen you before. If anyone needs to call the police it's me."

"Go ahead and call them. Then you can tell them how you killed Vivianne because she wrote a book revealing where your bank-robbing husband has been hiding all these years. Or maybe you killed her because she and Blackie had an affair. Is that how you got those scratches on your neck? Did she fight back?"

Harriet looked dumbfounded. Her fingers flew to her neck. Then she started laughing so hard she had to lean against the hood of her car for support. Somehow I'd imagined this going much differently. I glanced at my watch. It was eleven o'clock.

"Please," I pleaded. "I really need to know where Blackie is. He has my friend."

Harriet wiped her streaming eyes. "Oh, my. You're serious aren't you?"

I nodded instead of speaking, afraid I'd start crying. She was eyeing me strangely, as though she was trying to make up her mind about something, then let out a heavy sigh.

"Go wait for me over by the fountain. I'll be right back."

I watched her walk into the nursing home. I walked across the grass and took a seat on one of the wooden benches by the fountain to wait for her. Minutes later, she emerged pushing the same elderly woman with long white hair she'd been visiting before only this time, as she got closer, I could see it wasn't a woman at all. It was a man.

She parked the wheelchair right in front of me and the elderly man looked at me with blank eyes. He was breathing heavily through the oxygen tube wrapped around his head. Harriet looked around to make sure we were alone. Then made the introduction.

"I'd like to introduce you to my husband, Elgin Randall. Blackie to his friends," she said in a low whisper.

My mouth fell open, and it was a several long seconds before I could speak. "But, how?" I asked, looking at the frail man in the chair.

"He showed up at the farm five years ago when he found out he was dying. He has emphysema. He'd been homeless and on the streets for fifteen years and didn't want to die alone. Vivianne and I did the best we could to take care of him, but it got to be too much for us. We weren't young women anymore," she said, stroking Blackie's long hair.

Rollins had said that Blackie Randall resembled actor Ron O'Neal and had pretty hair that women loved. Even though the man in the wheelchair was old and sick, I could still see that he'd once been a very handsome man until all those black and mild cigarettes finally caught up with him.

"Does the nursing home know who he is?" I asked, looking over at the entrance to see Cookie's large form still standing in the doorway watching us.

"No," Harriet said sharply. "He's registered under my late brother's name, George Perkins. George died when he was three from influenza."

"So, did he really help rob that bank?" I couldn't help

it. I wanted to know. Harriet's head jerked up and she glared at me.

"He had no idea what those losers he called his friends were up to that day. They told him to sit in the car and wait while they went in to make a withdrawal. Then they came running out and stuck a gun to his head and told him to drive." Blackie let out a loud phlegm-filled cough that made his thin frame shudder violently. Harriet rubbed his back until it was over then wiped spittle from his lips.

"I heard they found his blood in the getaway car."

"Nosebleed. Blackie has high blood pressure and he often gets nosebleeds."

"What about the money? What did he do with the money?"

"He told me he buried it in the woods. He was too afraid to spend it because he thought the serial numbers would be traced. That's how they caught those other three idiots."

"But I thought Vivianne and your husband had an affair. Weren't you angry with her?"

Harriet shrugged. "They had a lot of history. Vivianne was Blackie's first love. She broke his heart when she married Cliff Preston. When she came back to Willow to live I could see he hadn't gotten her out of his system. I thought there might be something going on between them, but I never knew for sure. But I knew he loved me and more importantly he trusted me. After what she did to him, he never trusted Vivianne again."

"Weren't you shocked when Kurt told you about them?"

"How'd you know about—"

"Kurt told me," I said, cutting her off. I glanced at my watch again. It was almost eleven-twenty.

Obviously, Blackie Randall didn't have Lynette. I'd have to be going soon if I was going to be home in time to get that phone call.

"It was a long time ago. My husband is dying. I wasn't about to rake that ancient history up because of something Kurt said." It sounded all well and good but the grim expression on Harriet's face said otherwise.

"So you didn't kill her?" I persisted. Harriet stood up and towered over me. I shrank back against the bench.

"Despite all of her flaws, I loved Vivianne. She was the closest thing I ever had to a sister. She could be very kind and compassionate. She never purposefully set out to hurt anyone. She was a passionate and impulsive person and that always got her into trouble, especially with men."

"I think her son would disagree. If she was so wonderful, then why did she lose custody of Kurt?" Harriet made a disgusted noise and sat down next to me.

"Vivianne lost custody of Kurt because Cliff Preston is a monster. He's not the person everyone thinks he is." I waited for her to elaborate but she wouldn't, just sat stone-faced and staring straight ahead.

It was time for me to go, but I had more questions. "Where were you when Vivianne was murdered? I heard you stuck to her like glue at the auditorium."

"I was in the ladies' room when I heard the alarm go off. I suffer from irritable bowel syndrome. It was particularly bad that morning." She rubbed her stomach. I didn't have time to dwell on the irony of her ailment and pressed on.

"Did you know about Vivianne's book?" I asked.

"I knew she had some scheme up her sleeve to try and earn some money for Blackie's nursing-home fees but I didn't know she'd written a book until after she died."

"Why didn't she just start acting again?"

"Because she knew how badly Cliff wanted her to and it was the only way she could think of to get back at him." Once again I waited for her to elaborate. Once again she wouldn't.

"Any idea what her book was about?"

Harriet was thoughtful for a moment then replied, "I'm betting it's a love story. Vivianne always was a sucker for a good love story," she said and let out a harsh, humorless laugh.

"Did Vivianne have a computer that could have a copy of her manuscript on it?"

"Are you kidding? Vivianne barely knew how to turn on the TV without a remote, let alone how to use a computer."

Blackie started coughing again and I took it as my signal to leave.

"You won't tell anyone, will you?" I heard her call out to me as I walked away. I looked back and she gestured toward the still coughing Blackie.

"Your secret's safe," I said. And I mostly meant that.

* * *

Lunchtime traffic was heavy and by the time I pulled up in front of my duplex it was 11:51 a.m. I raced up my steps and heard my phone ringing as I hurried to unlock the door. I flew across the room and grabbed my cordless phone from its stand.

"Hello." I was so out of breath I could barely get the words out.

"Kendra, what's wrong with you?" It was Mama. Crap!

"I just walked in. I'm expecting an important call, Mama. Can I call you back?"

"And I'm expecting you to help me with the cookout. Everybody's here, including your sister, who really needs cheering up."

Damn. I'd forgotten all about the cookout. If I told her I couldn't come she'd want to know why. My only resort was to lie. "I'll be over in a few minutes." I walked into the kitchen and grabbed a bottle of water from the fridge.

"Whose call are you waiting for? And you better not say Morris Rollins. Mattie Lyons told me some mess about the two of you coming out of the Heritage Arms together. I told her she didn't hear any such thing 'cause my granddaughter has better sense than that and—"

I listened to her rant, keeping a sharp eye on the digital clock on my microwave. It was 11:59 a.m. "Mama, we'll talk about this when I get over there, okay? Love you. Gotta go. Bye."

I pressed the off button just as clock flashed 12:00. The

phone rang in my hand and I was so startled I almost dropped it.

"Hello?" All I heard was silence on the other end. "Hello? Is anybody there?"

I heard a muffled voice speak a single word, "Mailbox."

"Mailbox? What are you talking about? Is Lynette okay? What do you want from me?" But I was talking to the dial tone. The person had hung up. I couldn't even tell if it had been a man or a woman.

I was standing in the middle of the kitchen still holding the phone when I realized I was being instructed to *look* in my mailbox. I dropped the phone and raced out my front door. I had a brass mailbox just outside my door instead of a mail slot. I ripped open the lid so hard I almost torn it off its hinges. Inside was a manila envelope. I felt the hair on the back of my neck stand up. Was someone watching me? I looked around, but all I saw were some neighborhood kids on bikes and a teenage boy cutting grass across the street. I took the envelope back inside and opened it. It was a typed letter that read:

Be at cabin four at John Bryan Park at 8:00 p.m. Bring Vivianne's computer disk. Don't be late. Come alone or your friend is dead. No tricks. I'll be watching you.

Vivianne's computer disk? I thought Vivianne didn't know how to use a computer. I didn't have Vivianne's computer disk, and why would anyone think I did? It didn't take a rocket scientist to figure out that Vivianne's manuscript must be on the disk Lynette's kidnapper was so hot to get his—or hers—hands on. And there must be something incriminating in her book that someone was willing to kill to keep from being revealed. The disk must have been what the person who broke into my apartment had really been looking for. But why did they think I had the damned disk? I needed to find out what Vivianne's book was about and the only other place I knew to look was Diamond Publishing Company in Columbus. I had a little less than eight hours to save Lynette.

Diamond Publishing Company was a small independent publisher that had been in business for about twenty years. They were mainly known for their non-fiction titles about Ohio historical figures, and for coffee-table books of photography. They'd recently started publishing fiction. At least that's what I was told when I called the reference desk of the Willow Public Library to get some info on the company that was publishing Vivianne's book.

I navigated my way through the streets of downtown Columbus in search of the eighteen-hundred block of East Broad Street. I always love coming to Columbus, as long as I don't have to drive. The only significant time I'd spent in the capital city of Ohio was when I'd attended college at Ohio State and even then I rarely ventured away from campus. And even though Carl lives in Columbus, he does all the driving whenever I hang out with him in his hometown. I drove past the Columbus Museum of Art, regretting the fact that I couldn't go inside, and kept an eye on the addresses of the buildings.

It wasn't long before I came upon a nondescript one-story brick building with smoked-glass windows that kind of reminded me of a doctor's office. I pulled into the parking lot and noticed a group of people wearing green pants and white short-sleeved shirts with the words Haley's Industrial Cleaners emblazoned in black letters on the back. There was even a large black van with the same lettering on the side parked in front of the entrance to the building. I got out and was immediately hit with the acrid stench of smoke. As I got closer to the building, I could see that the windows were not smoked glass at all. The windows were actually black with soot. I felt my stomach knot up.

"What happened?" I asked one of the cleaners who was unloading supplies from the back of the van.

"They had a fire last night." The man replied simply and turned back to what he was doing.

No shit, Sherlock, I wanted to say. "Anybody get hurt?"

"Not that I know of. It happened after everyone had gone home for the day."

"How much damage is there?" I persisted.

"Most of the fire damage was to the reception area, but the rest of the offices got heavy smoke damage."

"Do you know what caused it?"

The man finally turned to give me a curious look then shook his head slowly. "You'd have to ask one of the people who work here. But I could have sworn I heard one of them saying something about a lit cigarette in a trash can."

A cigarette. The same person who'd killed Vivianne and caused the alarm to go off at Cartwright Auditorium had apparently been here, too. The killer must have decided to light the place on fire for good measure to destroy any other trace of Vivianne's manuscript. Now I knew I was doing the right thing by not going to the police. I was dealing with a murderer and an arsonist who wouldn't hesitate to kill Lynette. Lucky me.

I heard the click of high heels on concrete and turned to see a stylishly dressed white woman in her late forties hurrying across the parking lot. She was dressed in a soft green-and-white pinstriped pantsuit over a white silk shell. Her dark brown hair was shoulder-length and her eyes were red-rimmed. She rushed right past us into the building without speaking and I followed her inside.

I found her standing in what must have been the reception area. The smoke smell was ten times stronger here. The walls were blackened, the plastic frames of the pictures hanging on them were melted together with the prints they held, and the carpet was badly scorched. The receptionist's metal desk had large burn marks on the top and sides. The glass that covered the top of the desk was cracked and black. What ever had been sitting on top of the desk that wasn't burned beyond recognition was covered in a thick layer of greasy soot.

The woman in the pinstriped suit was staring at the

damage as if she was in a trance. She didn't notice me standing behind her and let out a loud gasp when she turned around and saw me.

"Who are you?" she asked, pulling herself together.

"I'm Kendra Clayton," I said, holding out my hand. She didn't take it and I pressed on. "I'm really sorry about the fire. Is it possible for me to talk to someone in charge?"

"I'm Margo Diamond," she replied impatiently. "I'm the senior editor, as well as the owner of Diamond Publishing, such as it is," she said drily, looking around at the ruins of her business. "So, I guess that makes me in charge. How can I help you?"

She must have been the Margo I'd spoken to when I'd called about Vivianne's manuscript the other day. I had a feeling I was going to be wasting my time with her.

"I'm here about Vivianne DeArmond's book. I'd really appreciate it if you could tell me anything at all about it."

Margo Diamond threw her hands in the air in exasperation. "I'm so sick of being asked about that damned book!"

"How many people have been asking?"

"I haven't exactly been keeping a running tally but someone has either been calling or coming by on a daily basis since the woman died asking about that book. I just don't get it." She absentmindedly leaned back against the desk, cursed as she realized she'd got soot on her pantsuit, and unsuccessfully wiped at it with her hand.

"Well, she *was* a famous actress who grew up about a half hour from here. I imagine a lot of her fans will be interested in her memoirs," I said casually. I hoped Margo

Diamond was too upset about her suit to realize I was fishing.

"That's just it," she said, looking around for something to wipe her hands on. I handed her a tissue from my purse. "The book wasn't a memoir. It was a novel."

"What was it about?" Memoir or not, something was in that book that someone had been killed over.

"It was about a small-town girl who runs away from home to try and make it big on Broadway and all the heartache she encounters along the way."

"What kind of heartache?"

"She becomes a prostitute addicted to drugs, has a kid out of wedlock that dies as a result of her neglect, marries a talent agent who makes her a star but he's got a big secret of his own."

Hmm. So far it sure sounded sort of semiautobiographical, but my ears really perked up at that last part. "What kind of a secret?" The eagerness of my expression must have startled her because she took a small step backwards.

"He's passing," she said.

"Passing?"

"You know. He's a very fair-skinned black man passing for white."

I had to practically catch my jaw to keep it from hitting the floor. Cliff Preston was passing? That would certainly explain the title *The Onyx Man*. Harriet had told me that Cliff wasn't the person everyone thought he was. Was this what she meant?

"Do you still have a copy of the manuscript?" I asked eagerly.

"It was sent out to be copyedited. There was another copy on my office computer but as you can see—" she said, making a sweeping gesture around the room "—my computer is out of commission."

"Who else did you tell about Ms. DeArmond's book?"

"Until today, I haven't discussed that book with anyone and I'm beginning to regret that I've done so with you. Who did you say you were again?" I ignored the question.

"Did a young woman with red spiky hair named Noelle Delaney ever come here or call asking about the book?" She opened her mouth to say something that probably wasn't going to be very nice when we were interrupted.

"Margo," said a timid voice from the doorway that led back to the offices of Diamond Publishing.

We both turned to see a slightly overweight young woman with glasses, limp blond hair and a mild case of acne dotting her chubby cheeks. Wearing an ankle-length khaki skirt, denim blouse and flat sandals, she wasn't exactly dressed for success.

"What is it Alison? I'm in the middle of something," replied Margo Diamond as though it was taking every-thing in her not to scream at the poor girl.

"They told us not to touch anything. What do you want me to do?" She was staring at Margo like someone afraid of getting punched.

"Just go home, Alison. I'll call you later and let you know what's going on." Alison hesitated, then hurried past us, giving me a curious look on her way out the door.

"I've done about all the talking I plan to do regarding Vivianne DeArmond's book. Now, if you'll excuse me, I have a business to salvage." Margo Diamond headed off in the direction that Alison had emerged from and I left.

The cleaners were still in the lot taking a break, though I didn't know what from since it appeared that they hadn't even started working yet. I was unlocking my car when there was a light tap on my shoulder. It was Alison.

"Can I help you?" I asked the girl, who upon closer inspection looked to be about nineteen.

"Do you know Noelle?"

"Delaney?"

"Yeah, do you know her?" She kept glancing over her shoulder at the building as if she was afraid Margo would come out.

"I know Noelle, why?" Alison was clenching and unclenching her hands together nervously.

"I gave her something the other day and she promised she'd bring it back but she never did. I really need to get it back or I'll get fired." Her eyes filled with tears.

"What did you give her?" Allison looked over her shoulder again before answering.

"That actress's manuscript. See, I was supposed to send it to our copy editor but Noelle came in that day to try and see Margo about the book. But Margo was in New York. She started telling me about how she was this big TV producer on *Hollywood Vibe* and she could get me a job on the show as a correspondent if I could just help her out. I gave her the manuscript and she swore she'd bring it back. But she never did."

That answered my question about how Noelle had gotten hold of Vivianne's manuscript. But where was Noelle now? I thought back to the dried blood on the carpet of her hotel room and the mental images that popped into my head were grim.

"Do you know how I can get in touch with her? She has the only copy of that manuscript and I really, really need it back."

I told Alison to write down her number and promised her I'd try and track down Noelle for her, though in truth I knew that the manuscript had probably been destroyed by now.

"Do you know if the job at *Hollywood Vibe* is still open?" she asked hopefully. I looked at her lank hair, round face and drab clothing and wondered how Noelle had had the heart to lie to the poor girl.

"I'll have to check with Noelle." It was all the lie I could manage while staring into her eager face.

I drove past the cleaning crew who were finishing up their breaks and watched as one man put out a cigarette with his foot. One of his coworkers teased him.

"Man, you need to give up that filthy little habit of yours. I bet your lungs are as black as these windows we're about to clean." The smoking man grinned and flipped his coworker the finger.

A filthy habit. Something clicked in my memory.

Hadn't I overheard Stephanie scolding Cliff about criticizing Kurt's addictions when he had a filthy habit of his own? Did she mean smoking? If so, then Cliff could easily have been the one to set off the alarm at Cartwright Auditorium just as he could have set Diamond Publishing on fire and left those cigarette butts outside Lynette's teepee. Was he the person I'd seen on Mama's back porch and who had chased me with the hammer at Cabot's Cave?

CHAPTER 14

I barely remembered the drive home. All I could think about was Cliff Preston. If he was actually a black man passing for white, then what lengths would he go to keep his secret? He must have started passing in order to have the kind of career in Hollywood that wasn't available to a black man at the time. I sure couldn't imagine his high-profile white clients putting their careers in the hands of a black man back in the fifties and sixties. Cliff's talent agency used to be very prestigious and was now not doing so well. What would happen to his agency if his lie was revealed? At Vivianne's funeral he'd mentioned how he had to fight tooth and nail for every part he got Vivianne. How successful would he have been as a black man in getting her those parts?

Cliff had also told me that Hollywood was the land of illusion where nothing and no one were what they seemed. Boy, had he been right. No one wonder he didn't want any more children and had gotten a vasectomy behind Stephanie's back. No one would question him having a child that looked black with Vivianne because she was black. But the truth might have come out if he'd had a child who looked black with his white second wife, Stephanie. I'd reached the Welcome to Willow sign when I remember the manager at Cartwright Auditorium mentioning seeing an older light-skinned black man going into Vivianne's dressing room. I now knew it couldn't have been Blackie Randall. But was it Cliff? Only one way to find out.

It was going on two o'clock when I walked into the auditorium. This time the door to Joyce Clark's office was open. She looked up as I walked in.

"We haven't found that bracelet of yours," she said by way of greeting. I noticed an empty pizza box folded up and stuffed in the trash can by her desk.

"I figured you wouldn't find it. I hope whoever has it is enjoying it."

"If it was that expensive your boyfriend might have had it insured. Then you can get yourself another one."

"I'll ask him when I get up enough nerve to tell him I lost it." We both laughed.

"I was just wondering," I said, taking a seat in the chair in front of her desk without being invited. "Do you remember telling me about an older light-skinned black man you saw going into Vivianne DeArmond's dressing room the morning she was killed?"

Joyce gave me a strange look and shrugged her shoulders. "Yeah. What about it?"

"I know this is going to sound weird but was he really a black man? Could he have been white?"

Joyce shook her head vigorously. "Nope, that man was

black. But I could tell that brother was passing. He couldn't look me in the eye, probably 'cause he knew I could tell what he really was. I got a sister that's light enough to pass and that's just what she does. Ran away from home when she as a teenager and married a white man. Has to sneak home to Willow to visit her own family so her husband won't find out her secret. I can't see how she lives with herself." She shook her head in disgust. I thanked her and left.

When I got home, I poured myself a glass of wine and tried to figure out what to do. If Cliff was the one who had Lynette and had killed Vivianne to keep his secret from getting out in her book, then why in the hell did he think I had Vivianne's computer disk? Maybe it was because I had been the one to tell him about Vivianne's book the last time I'd seen him. According to Harriet, Vivianne didn't own a computer let alone know how to use one. So who typed her manuscript? I grabbed my phone book, from the top of my fridge and flipped through the Yellow Pages in search of listings for typing services, which referred me to secretarial services, which only showed a listing for office temp agencies. Frustrated, I threw the phone book across the room, knocking my spice rack from the wall. Then I saw the newspaper wadded up in my trash can.

I'd immediately pitched the paper that morning after seeing the hideous image of me caught in midscream at the police station last night splashed across the front page, complete with the caption, "Sister of Murder Suspect Rages At The Press." I wouldn't be exaggerating one bit to say my mouth was opened so wide you could see the fillings in my back teeth. I looked like a lunatic.

I grabbed the paper, which was stained from coffee grounds and a banana peel, and quickly located the classifieds where people advertised services for hire. I found five listings for people who did word-processing. I immediately started dialing. I struck out with the first three but got lucky with the Tippy Tap Typing Service—I kid you not—owned and operated by Betty McKee. I called and inquired about Vivianne's manuscript, pretending to be Harriet Randall and informing Ms. McKee that she'd failed to include the computer disk with the completed order. Betty did not sound pleased.

"What do you mean you didn't receive the computer disk? I put it in the box along with the typed manuscript, Ms. Randall. I shredded all of Ms. DeArmond's notes just like you asked and handed you that box myself. You checked it before you paid me, remember?"

"Sorry, Ms. McKee. I must have misplaced it," I said and quickly hung up.

Harriet had picked up the typed manuscript yet she claimed not to have known about the book until after Vivianne's death and didn't know what the book was about. Yeah, right. It was high time I found out just what else Harriet Randall knew.

I grabbed my purse and headed back to Troyer Road.

"Harriet, you got some 'splainin' to do," I said, attempting Ricky Ricardo but sounding more like Pee Wee

Herman. Harriet frowned at me from behind the screen door of Vivianne's farmhouse.

"What do you want now?" She didn't bother to hide the look of distaste on her face, but hey, the feeling was very much mutual.

It was two forty-five. Eight o'clock wasn't far off and I didn't have time to waste. I pulled open the screen door and pushed past her into the house. The house, what I could see of it from in the foyer, was sparsely furnished but neat, and the furniture I could see had seen better days but must have been very expensive back in the day.

"How dare you barge in here. This is private property." Harriet was wearing a cotton house dress decorated with large sunflowers. Her feet were bare and so hard and crusty-looking I'd have bet a sandblaster wouldn't improve them much. The hairpiece on the back of her head was crooked, like she'd stuck it on in a hurry when she'd heard the knock on the door. I wondered if she'd have bothered if she'd have known it was me.

"You lied to me, Harriet. You lied about not knowing Vivianne had written a book until after she died, and you're lying about not knowing what the book is about, aren't you?"

"Okay, I lied. So what! Now get out of my house!" She held the door open for me.

"You knew that book was about Cliff Preston passing for white. You had to know he would kill to keep his secret. Yet you said nothing to the police. You let them arrest my sister! How could you stand by and let my sister take the blame?"

Harriet's shoulders slumped. She sighed heavily and sagged against the wall. "Don't you understand? I couldn't say anything," she said. Tears rolled down her cheeks. It was 2:53 p.m. I didn't have time for tears or sympathy.

"Oh, this oughta be interesting. I can't wait to hear how you can justify letting an innocent woman go to jail."

"He knows about Blackie. Cliff knows."

"How?" I asked.

"Blackie had been back here for about a year when Cliff showed up unexpectedly. We never get visitors, being out here in the country with no neighbors for miles around. We hardly ever locked the door. Vivianne, Blackie and I were having supper one night and in walked Cliff, big as you please. Cliff recognized Blackie right away. He threatened to call the police."

"So why didn't he?"

"Because Vivianne told him she knew about him passing. She'd known for years, but he didn't know she knew."

"And how did she find out?"

"When she and Cliff were married she found out he was sending money to a woman in Indiana. Vivianne thought he had a mistress. She hired a private investigator and found out that Cliff was sending money to a black woman who turned out to be his mother. Cliff Preston isn't even his real name. He's living under a stolen identity. But Vivianne was so afraid of him she never confronted him about it."

"If the two of you were so afraid of Cliff turning Blackie in, then why did she write that book?"

Harriet wiped her face with the back of her hand. "Revenge," she said simply. She walked into the living room and I followed her. The furniture was rust-colored silk brocade, faded from the sunlight that streamed in through a large picture window. We sat down and she continued.

"Everyone thinks that Vivianne was a bad mother. That she lost custody of Kurt because she was unfit. But it's all lies. Vivianne loved that boy, but when she left Cliff he vowed to get even with her and he did. He ruined her relationship with her only child."

"How? Stephanie said that Vivianne neglected Kurt and—" She cut me off angrily.

"The only things Stephanie knows about Vivianne are what Cliff told her and they're all lies. All lies! Vivianne left Cliff because he was abusive. Her face was her claim to fame so he only hit her where it wouldn't show. Why do you think Stephanie wears such heavy makeup? I bet he's using her as a punching bag, too."

"How was Cliff able to make Vivianne look like a bad mother?"

"Once, after they'd split and she'd made it clear she wasn't coming back, Cliff had Kurt for the weekend. Vivianne was on location filming a movie. Cliff showed up on the set and just left Kurt in Vivianne's trailer without bothering to tell her. He was only two or three. He was there for hours alone. Vivianne suffered from occasional bouts of insomnia and took sleeping pills. Kurt got into her pills and almost died. Everyone blamed Vivianne, but she had no idea he was there. Another time, Cliff beat Kurt black and blue because he wet the bed, then he told everybody Vivianne's new boy-friend had done it and she'd stood by and let him. When she finally took Cliff to court to get sole custody, he paid people to lie about her on the witness stand. Most of them were extras on her movie sets whom Cliff promised to make stars. Vivianne lost custody of Kurt."

"If all of this is true then why did Kurt hate Vivianne so much if Cliff is the one who mistreated him?"

"Kurt didn't hate Vivianne because of anything she did to him. He hated her for not saving him from Cliff. Why do you think he got so mixed up in drugs? It was all Cliff's fault. He was abusing him."

"I'm surprised Vivianne didn't threaten to tell his secret during the custody case to keep him from taking her child."

"She was too terrified that Cliff would make sure she'd never see Kurt if she confronted him about his real identity. He only let her see Kurt for a couple of weeks every summer. She thought she might not even get that if she told what she knew. Not that it mattered."

"Meaning?"

"Meaning it's hard to be a mother to a child you only see once a year. She tried and tried to maintain a close re-lationship with him. She wrote him letters, sent him presents, tried to call. But Cliff was always in the way messing things up. Telling him his mother didn't care. Throwing away her cards and letters when they arrived. Then Cliff married Stephanie and Kurt started calling her Mom. Vivianne told me that broke her heart. By the time Kurt was a teenager their relationship was beyond repair."

"Stephanie seems to think Cliff was still in love with Viviannne. Was he?"

Harriet made a disgusted noise. "That's the biggest joke of all."

"How so?"

"In his own warped way Cliff loved Vivianne very much. He still tried to find work for her until she decided to retire. I think on some level he felt guilty about what he'd done to her. Cliff's the type of man who'd rather be respected and feared than loved. And Vivianne feared him all right."

"Well, something must have changed if she had the courage to write that book," I said watching her closely.

"Something did change. But all Vivianne would tell me is that she had something to keep Cliff off her back. I swear she never told me what it was."

I hoped I wasn't being a fool, since Harriet had already lied to me once, but something in her expression and the way she was looking me in the eye made me think she was telling the truth.

"I really need to get my hands on the computer disk with a copy of the book. I called the typing service Vivianne used and I know the disk was in the box with the typed manuscript you picked up. Cliff has my friend and he's threatening to kill her if I don't bring him the disk tonight." I checked my watch. It was three-thirty.

"Then we should call the police." She jumped up and headed for a phone perched on a nearby end table.

"Touch that phone and I'll call the police myself and

tell them where to find Blackie Randall." Harriet froze and stared at me fearfully. "I was told not to involve the police or my friend will be killed. Look, all I need is the disk. Do you have any idea where it could be now?"

Harriet thought for a moment. "Follow me."

She headed up a flight of stairs just off the foyer and I was hot on her heels. I didn't even stop to admire the photos of Vivianne that lined the walls up the stairway. She stopped at a door at the top of the landing and pulled a key ring from the pocket of her house dress. Before she unlocked the door, she turned to me.

"You know, I really had no idea Vivianne had set up that interview with your sister. She was an impulsive woman. I never knew what she was up to half the time."

I nodded absently and followed her into a room that looked like a cotton-candy machine had exploded all over it. Pink as far as the eye could see. Pink walls, pale-pink velvet curtains hanging in the two large windows framing a round bed with pink satin bedding and covered in big fluffy pillows made of pink fur. The carpet was plush and hot pink. The only things in the room that weren't pink were the white vanity table and chair that were trimmed in pink, and the two white nightstands on either side of the bed. An ornate crystal chandelier hung from the ceiling, It wasn't pink, either, but it might as well have been as the profusion of pink reflected in the crystals gave it a pink glow. It looked like a teenager's room.

"Wow," I said taking it all in.

"I loved her dearly, but Vivianne's taste was always just

a little bit on the vulgar side," Harriet said. "I remember mailing the manuscript to the publishing company weeks ago. If the disk is still here than I bet Vivianne hid it somewhere."

She opened the double doors of a walk-in closet almost the size of my kitchen. I came over and stood beside her. The closet was filled to the gills with clothing. One whole wall was rack after rack of shoes. Purses, belts and scarves hung in plastic garment bags. The top shelves held boxes with names of various old-school designers such as Oleg Cassini, Bob Mackey and Halston. Harriet looked at the boxes and frowned, then got on her hands and knees and hunted around on the floor of the closet.

"What are you looking for?"

"There was a box of junk in here that Vivianne had been bugging me for months to take up to the attic. I don't see it. Huh. Maybe she took it up herself."

"What was in it?"

"Like I said, junk. Old stuff she didn't wear anymore. Shoes, purses, some hats."

Junk. Kurt had recently sold a box of Vivianne's stuff to Donald Cabot. He told me he only took old stuff she wouldn't notice was gone. Hadn't Donald Cabot told me that the purse of Vivianne's that I'd bought had just come in, which must have meant it was in the box he'd bought from Kurt. The purse! I gasped out loud and Harriet looked at me like I was crazy. But I didn't care. I knew where the disk was. I thanked Harriet, whose mouth was hanging open in dumbfounded confusion, and raced back to my apartment. Mrs. Carson was sitting on her porch and trying to say something to me about Mama looking for me, but I tossed her a breathless hello and breezed past her up the steps and into my apartment.

Once inside I had to calm down and stop to think about where I'd put the little black evening bag of Vivianne's that I'd bought from Cabot's Cave. I finally remembered and pulled a large suitcase from under my bed. Since my apartment was so small, I had to find creative ways to use my space. I stored all of my purses in a suitcase under my bed. I popped the lock and rooted through it until I found the purse. Really looking at it for the first time since I'd bought it, I again noticed the purse's hard bottom that I'd originally thought must be cardboard. I turned the purse inside out and noticed a tear in the lining along one side. Something hard and blue was poking out and I pulled it free. It was a three-and-a-half-inch floppy disk. Thank God.

Vivianne must have hidden the disk in that box of junk not thinking that Kurt would steal it. I'd had the purse with me at Vivianne's memorial service and Cliff must have recognized it as having been hers. That was the only thing I could think of that made sense as to how he'd have known I had the disk, though it didn't explain everything. But who cared how Cliff knew? I had the disk and that's all that mattered. It was four-fifteen. I still had time to kill and was dying to read Vivianne's book and wanted to make a copy of the disk for the police. Only, I didn't own a computer. I headed out, and as I passed by my landlady's porch, she called out to me.

"Kendra, your grandma is boilin' mad. You better be on your way over there. She done called me three times already askin' if I've seen you."

"If she calls again, tell her I'm on my way over there now," I lied. I hopped in my car and took off. Lynette's life and clearing Allegra's name were much more important than barbecue at the moment. When all was said and done, Mama would understand. Until then she'd just have to get over it.

Since everyone else I knew who had a computer would ask entirely too many questions, I ended up at the Willow Public Library. The library had recently installed ten new computers for patrons to surf the Internet and do word processing. Much to my disappointment, all ten computers were in use when I arrived. I added my name to the sign-up sheet at the reference desk and waited impatiently for a computer to become available. The computer disk was burning a hole in my pocket and I didn't know how much longer I could wait. Twenty long minutes later, I was finally able to sit down in front of a computer. Before I could insert the disk in the drive, a large hand reached over and covered the slot.

"My friend wants this computer," said a belligerent voice next to me. I turned and found myself face to face with an overweight teenaged boy with long hair that hung in his eyes like a sheep dog's and wearing a tight yellow T-shirt that showed off his love handles, man boobs, and sporting Kiss My Fuzzy Logic! in big green letters.

I looked over my shoulder and saw another boy, who

could have been Fuzzy's twin, shifting from foot to foot impatiently like a toddler doing the pee-pee dance. How precious.

"I was here first," I said and once again tried to insert the disk. Once again Fuzzy covered the slot.

"There's another computer behind you, lady. My friend and I want to sit together." His voice had taken on a whiny quality that to someone like me, who hates whiners, was equal to nails on a blackboard.

"Look, I was here first and I'm in a hurry. I'm sure it won't kill you and your friend to be apart this one time. Hey, it's a beautiful day out. Why don't you two go outside and get some fresh air and maybe some exercise," I said eyeing their bulk. At the mere mention of fresh air and even worse—exercise—both boys made gagging noises as though I'd just suggested they eat maggots.

"We don't have to take this, Wayne," said the boy behind me in a high-pitched nasal twang.

"Are you gonna let my friend sit here or not?" asked Fuzzy aka Wayne.

"Not," I said, holding my ground but I didn't like the sly look that passed between the two boys one little bit.

"You asked for it, lady," said Fuzzy, reaching over and clicking the mouse on my computer. The Internet browser, which had been minimized and out of sight when I sat down, instantly popped up and was filled with vulgar pornographic images of people in sexual positions that could only be achieved by contortionists. My mouth fell open in shock.

"Porn! Porn! She's looking at porn!" yelled Fuzzy and his friend, pointing at me and the screen.

I frantically started pushing buttons on the keyboard and clicking the mouse trying to clear the images from the screen to no avail. New windows of filth kept opening up one on top of the other. Everyone turned to stare at me and a librarian rushed over to see what all the fuss was about. My hands were covering the screen but she could still see that what was underneath wasn't anything G-rated. Her face turned bright red, or at least what I could see of her face underneath her long thick bangs.

"Ma'am, we do not allow this kind of…of…perversion in the library. We have impressionable young children here!" She pointed to a large sign hanging from the ceiling between the two rows of computers. It read: Absolutely no Pornography! Anyone caught viewing pornography will be banned from the library for thirty days. No exceptions!

"But this was on the screen when I got here," I tried to explain.

"No, it wasn't. I watched her pull it up," said Fuzzy Wayne smugly with his fat arms crossed over his boobs. His friend was nodding his head and looking equally smug.

"You little liar!" I said, indignantly abruptly standing up and towering over the still-seated teen.

"My son does not lie," exclaimed the librarian. I looked at her and instantly noticed the resemblance between them. Wayne had his mother's sheep-dog hair and cup size.

"I'm telling you, this was on the screen when I got

here. I really need to use this computer. I don't have a lot of time," I pleaded.

"She was mean to us, Mom, make her go away, please." Wayne's bottom lip was trembling, but when his mother looked away, he grinned at me. Unbelievable.

"Ma'am, I must insist that you leave the library this instant before I call security."

"All right. Fine. I'm going," I said through gritted teeth. I'd barely stepped away from the computer when Fuzzy's friend practically knocked me over in his rush to get his round hiney in the chair.

A vision of Wayne in about ten years shoving Twinkies in his face while watching Internet porn and being supported for the rest of his life by his mother flashed in my mind as I walked away, making me realize I should probably be afraid of the little sociopath in the making. I walked out of the library with visions of tearing Fuzzy away from the computer and forcing him and his friend to run laps around the block until they puked. Now what was I going to do? Where else could I get access to a computer? Then it hit me. Rollins. Didn't he have a computer in his office at Holy Cross? Yes, he did.

The Holy Cross Church parking lot was filled up with cars. I'd completely forgotten that today was the church's annual car wash. About a dozen teenagers and several adults, including Morris Rollins, were up to their elbows in sudsy water washing cars. I had to park across the street. I was debating whether I should try and sneak into Rollins's office and use his computer while he was busy washing cars when he spotted me across the crowded parking lot. He grinned as I approached and playfully flipped a wet towel in my direction spraying me with water. I laughed and looked around on the sly for Winette Barlow.

"Have you come to help or do you need your car washed?"

"Neither. I need a favor," I said. Honesty was going to save me time in this instance. Rollins looked intrigued.

"I really need to use your computer."

"Sure, no problem. My office's is unlocked. Is everything okay?" he asked, squeezing my shoulder. Our eyes met and I could tell he was thinking about our kiss last night. I broke eye contact first.

"It will be," I said and headed into the church.

I sat behind Rollins's round, islandlike oak desk, and situated myself in his leather chair before inserting the disk in the drive of his large computer. There was only one file on the disk and it was labeled Onyx. I opened it and for over an hour skimmed through Vivianne's book. I was surprised to discover that Vivianne wasn't a half-bad writer, though she was prone to exclamation points and flowery, unrealistic dialogue. And there was another thing that was also very obvious: she wasn't at all sympathetic to her two main characters, Roxanne Gayle, who fled from her small town to try and make it big on Broadway, and Elwood Smalls, a black man who starts passing for white after going off to fight in the Korean War and stealing the identity of a white officer in his unit named Warren Duke.

The book was divided into three parts: Roxanne's story, Elwood's story and the last part telling how their paths crossed and the fiery, tumultuous relationship that followed. Even though Vivianne had made Roxanne Gayle a prescription-drug-addicted whore who had resorted to prostitution to make ends meet before getting her big break, there were a lot of parallels to Vivianne's actual life: She and Roxanne were both from small towns and eventually made it in show business, she and Roxanne both married their agents, and, like Vivianne, Roxanne had a child, a daughter, though her child had been born out of wedlock fathered by one of her johns. There was even a scene reminiscent of what had happened to Kurt, where Roxanne's child gets into one of her prescriptions while she's strung out on painkillers. But unlike Kurt, Roxanne's daughter dies.

As for Elwood Smalls, besides the fact that he was passing for white using a stolen identity, I had no idea what else he had in common with Cliff Preston that wasn't a fictional embellishment of Vivianne's. The character of Elwood Smalls had dreamed since he was a child of being in show business. He was born into a poor black farm family, who, despite looking white, were very proud of their black ancestry, except for Elwood, who felt trapped by the restrictions of his race. In order to escape a life of farming, Elwood joins the army just as the Korean War breaks out and is assigned to an all-black combat unit. He becomes friends with Warren Duke, a white officer in charge of his unit. During a combat mission Warren goes missing in action and Elwood is gravely injured and gets an honorable discharge. Instead of going back to the family farm, Elwood uses the name of Warren Duke to build a new life for himself as a white man in New York City. He goes on to become a sought-after talent agent who represents some of the biggest names on Broadway, eventually moving on to represent movie stars.

It all sounded like a simple case of stolen identity *until* I got to the part where the real Warren Duke turns up alive and well and tracks down Elwood Smalls, threatening to expose him, which results in Elwood killing him. I sat up straight in the chair. Was that part true? If it was then, Cliff Preston had a lot more to worry about than having his true race exposed. Had he killed the real Cliff Preston? Was this the info Vivianne claimed, as Harriet had put it, would keep Cliff off her back? Did she somehow find proof that Cliff was a murderer, as well as an identity thief? I rummaged around in Rollins's desk drawer and found a box of blank floppy disks and, figuring he wouldn't mind, took a disk and copied the manuscript to it. By the time I closed out the file and shut down the computer it was well after six o'clock. The car wash was still in full swing. I didn't want to interrupt Rollins again. So I stuck a note thanking him on his computer screen and headed out a side door so he wouldn't see me.

When I got to my car I turned my cell phone back on and saw that I had twelve voice mails. Four of them were from Mama, furiously wanting to know where I was. Seven were from Greg wanting to know what was going on with Lynette. His messages started out angry, gave way to desperate, and his last message was downright pitiful. The final voice mail was from a contrite-sounding Allegra apologizing for lying to me about the check and wanting to know if she was the reason I was refusing to come to the cookout. Leave it to Allegra to make it all about her. I didn't return any of their calls. Instead, I put the disk I had copied into my glove compartment, along with a note telling anyone who found it to give it to Detective Trish Harmon, just in case anything happened to me at the park that night. I put the original in my pocket.

I was about to start up my car when I looked over and saw Winette Barlow talking to Rollins while he was washing a car. Winette was dressed in neatly creased and pressed designer jeans, a red shirt, white blazer, pumps and a long multi-strand beaded necklace that kept catching on her belt. Not exactly an outfit to wash cars in. I watched in amusement as she kept jumping back every time a stream of soapy water approached her leather pumps. She tried unsuccessfully to flirt with Rollins who was busy and looked a little annoyed. When she finally gave up and walked away, I could clearly see how upset she was. But it wasn't until she angrily flung her long necklace over her shoulder that I remembered something Joyce Clark had told me. Vivianne had had a necklace that went missing at Cartwright Auditorium. Harriet Randall had accused one the custodial staff of stealing it. Joyce Clark had said the necklace was never found. But thinking back to what I'd seen pinned to the lost and found board in Joyce's office, I realized they had found it and just didn't realize it.

I was so lost in thought I didn't see Winette Barlow charging toward my car with blood in her eyes. Her mouth was set in a hard angry line. Her hands were curled into fists. I frantically looked over at Rollins, who had his back to us, oblivious to everything except the dirty car in front of him. I quickly started up my car and pulled away from the curb just as Winette Barlow's well-aimed kick grazed my driver's-side door. Crazy bitch. She was yelling something at me that I didn't catch. I had no time for her drama. I had a best friend to save. I wasn't sure Cartwright Auditorium was still open. It was going on seven o'clock. But I had to try and get into Joyce Clark's office.

I was about three blocks from the auditorium when a car pulled up behind me and started frantically honking. I looked in my rearview mirror. It was Winette Barlow. Crap! She was gesturing for me to pull over, probably so she could lodge one of her expensive leather pumps in my ass. This was not good. I ignored her and kept on driving. To my relief, I lost her at a red light and kept driving until I got to the auditorium. My heart sank when I saw that the parking lot was empty, indicating that everyone had gone home for the day. I parked, got out and tried the front doors. They were locked. Great. I headed around to the side of the building and my heart sank even further when I saw Winette pull into the parking lot and jump out of her car.

"I don't know what your problem is, Winette, but I'm not arguing with you," I said as she came charging over to me.

"Who said anything about arguing? I told you to stay away from my man. Now, you're gonna to pay the piper, sweetie." I watched as she kicked off her pumps. This heifer wanted to fight me.

"You want to fight me over some man? I thought you were classier than this, Winette." Out of the corner of my eye I saw someone emerging from the side door of the auditorium. I turned to see that it was the custodian emptying a trash can into the Dumpster. He had his Walkman on and didn't notice us. He went back inside and I could see the door hadn't shut completely behind him. I had to get in there. I made a run for the door. Winette was hot on my heels.

"You come back here and get what you got comin' to you," she screamed.

Fortunately for me, Winette couldn't run very fast in her bare feet across a parking lot strewn with tiny rocks and debris. I heard her curse when I reached the side door and turned to see her picking what looked like glass out of her foot. She threw it at me and I ducked inside the door and pulled it shut behind me.

CHAPTER 15

I found myself in what I thought was a dimly lit hallway. I started walking, noting the heavy curtains along the way, and realized I must be behind the curtains on the stage. I could hear someone, probably the custodian, whistling softly somewhere on the other side of the curtains. I came upon a set of about six steps that led down to an open doorway. I headed down the steps and out the doorway, listening to hear if the custodian's whistling sounded like it was getting any closer. To my relief, I ended up in the lobby. Joyce Clark's office was dark. The door was closed and—surprise, surprise—locked. The clock in the lobby told me it was five past seven. I debated whether to leave and head for the park, but I needed all the leverage I could get for my meeting with Cliff. I needed that necklace in case he tried to get cute.

The door to Joyce's office looked like the type that opened with a key but locked when she left each night and pulled it shut, meaning that it could be opened from the inside. There was a large mail slot in the middle of the door. I pushed it open and stuck my hand through the slot. I was able to reach up to the doorknob on the other side but grabbing the knob and turning it was something else entirely. I pulled my hand out and had almost made up my mind to break the glass in the door when I noticed there was a gap of about an inch between the bottom of the door and the floor. I lay on my stomach and looked under the door. Light was streaming in from the office's window and I could see the edge of the lost and found board propped up against the inner wall right by the door. If I could reach it, then I'd be able to pull it out from under the door.

I couldn't fit my arm under the door to reach the board. I looked around the lobby and saw a broom, the nylon kind with plastic bristles, propped against the far wall. I ran over and grabbed it then stopped to listen for the custodian. He was still whistling in the auditorium. I slid the broom under the door until the bristles touched the board then shoved gently until the board slid down the wall and landed flat on the floor. Then I lifted the broom slightly and put it on top of the board and pulled hard. The board slid across the floor and wedged under the door. Once I pulled the broom out, I was able to pull the board from under the door. Feeling entirely too pleased with myself, I started to take a look at the board when I heard the custodian's whistling getting louder. He was headed my way. I ran across the lobby into the women's restroom. The noisy clack of the items pinned to the board echoed loudly in the empty lobby.

I let out a breath and took a look at the board. Nestled amongst two sets of keys, a comb, a tarnished hoop earring, a man's tie and a watch with a broken strap was the set of dog tags that I'd noticed when I'd been in Joyce Clark's office the first time. They were army dog tags. This had to be the necklace Vivianne had lost. The chain was broken. The name on the tags was Jasper Hairston, which must be Cliff's real name. This must be what Vivianne had told Harriet she had that would keep Cliff off her back. She must have been frantic when she lost the tags.

I had to hand it to Vivianne. She'd thought it all out. She knew what would happen once her book was published. Anybody who knew anything at all about her would read the book and notice all the parallels to her life. People would wonder what was true and what was fiction. Anyone curious enough to do a little research would look up Cliff Preston and find out it wasn't his real name. Vivianne wouldn't have had to say a thing. The reading public and the scandal-loving media would expose Cliff for her. Cliff wouldn't dare sue her for slander, either. It was brilliant.

I stuffed the tags in my pocket and put my ear to the door. I couldn't hear anything. I pushed the bathroom door open and peeked out. The custodian was mopping the lobby and there was no way he wouldn't see me if I left the bathroom. My watch read 7:18 p.m. One of the bathroom's two large windows over the row of sinks was open a crack. I climbed up onto one of the sinks, pushed the window open all the way, and with great effort, hoisted myself up and climbed out. One foot caught on the ledge and I fell right into the bushes a few feet below, scratching up my arms and knocking the wind out of me. But at least I was out and nothing was broken. I dusted myself off and ran across the parking lot to my car—and stopped cold. Since she hadn't been able to get her hands on me, Winette had settled for my car. It was trashed. The windows were all busted out, the word *Bitch* had been keyed into the paint on the hood, but that wasn't the worst part. All four of my tires had been punctured and were flat as pancakes. It was 7:27 p.m.

I had about thirty minutes to get to a park that was fifteen minutes away and now I had no car. I pulled my cell phone out of my pocket to call a cab but hung up when I realized I had exactly five dollars to my name. It would cost more than five dollars to take a cab to Yellow Springs. I had more money in my bank account. All I needed to do was find an ATM machine. I spotted a Dairy Mart a half block up the street and took off running. My heart rejoiced when I saw the sign indicating they had an ATM machine. I rushed inside. I had my card out of my purse and swiped before I read the message on the screen: Temporarily Out of Order. Wonderful.

"Do you know if there's another ATM around here?" I frantically asked the woman behind the counter. She shook her head without even looking up from her *Cosmo* magazine with Cindy Crawford pouting sexily on the cover.

"*No*, there isn't another ATM around here, or *no*, you don't know if there's another ATM machine around?"

"Only other ATM I know of is about six blocks from here," she replied, still not looking up.

I left and took off walking. It was 7:32 p.m. Six blocks would put me downtown. I could go to my own bank. I spotted a city bus headed downtown and flagged it down at the nearest corner. I got on and handed the driver my five-dollar bill.

"One way, please," I said breathlessly.

"I need seventy-five cents. I can't change a five," said the driver, a squinty-eyed skinny man with slicked-back hair. He pointed a bony finger at a sign taped to the corner of the windshield: Must Have Exact Fare. Driver Can't Make Change. Great! I didn't have any other change.

"You can't make an exception this one time? I'm really in a hurry. It's an emergency."

"And I'm on a schedule, lady. Either give me seventy-five cents or get off my bus."

"No need to get nasty," I said turning to the other passengers on the bus. "Is there anyone here who can loan me seventy-five cents?" I pleaded.

No one spoke up and few turned away to stare out the window. It was 7:38 p.m. I didn't have time to argue or plead any further. I scowled at the driver and got off the bus. He left me in a cloud of exhaust that made me nauseous. I started walking and about a block later, spotted a yard sale down a quiet tree-lined side street. As much as I love yard sales, garage sales, tag sales and estate sales, now was not the time to indulge in my love for second-hand treasure. But then I spied something propped up against a tree in the yard and made a quick detour.

Once I got to the house in question, I could see that my eyes hadn't deceived me. There was a ten-speed bike propped against the tree. The tag said twenty dollars. If there was one thing that my appreciation of second-hand goods had taught me, it was how to bargain.

"Would you take five for the bike?" I asked the pleasant-looking man rocking on the front porch. He got up from his rocker, opened the screen door of the house and yelled inside.

"Son, someone's interested in your bike." Seconds later, the screen door banged open with a thud and out walked Fuzzy Wayne, my library nemesis. This could not be happening. I rubbed my eyes and looked again. It was him all right, in all his glory, still wearing the same tight T-shirt. Now that he was actually upright, I could see his love handles spilling out over the top of his equally tight jeans. He tugged the shirt down but it didn't do much good.

It wasn't until he got closer that he recognized me from the library, though I was surprised he could see anything with all that hair falling in his face. He gave me a nasty look.

"Bet you're sorry you weren't nicer to me, huh? The price just went up to fifty dollars."

"The tag says twenty," I said patiently.

"It's my bike. I can change my mind if I want." Actually, I was surprised he wasn't selling it for a lot more. It didn't look like it had ever been ridden. Looking at Fuzzy's less than buff physique, I knew there was no way his wide behind had ever even sat on the seat.

I turned to walk away. "Hey, wait," he said stopping me. "How much ya got?"

"Five dollars," I replied. He burst out laughing.

"No way I'm selling my bike for five dollars. But I got another bike for you. You interested?"

"Does it work?" I asked walking into the yard. Beggars can't be choosers and it was now 7:45 p.m.

"'Course it works. I'll let you have it for ten dollars and not a penny less," he said smirking. I wanted to wipe up the pavement with his face. But I needed that bike so I decided to appeal to his appetite, instead.

"Look, I work at Estelle's restaurant. How about I give you the five plus a week's worth of free dinners?"

"Deal," he said, snatching the five-dollar bill out of my hand. He disappeared into the house and emerged with a purple kid's bike complete with a white banana seat and sparkly streamers trailing from the handles. My mouth fell open. Oh, hell, no.

Fuzzy could barely contain his laughter. "Here it is. And I'll be in tonight for my first free meal."

Lesson learned: Never piss off a nerd.

I took off on the bike, trying to ignore the stares and laughter. My face was burning and my legs, which were too long for a bike that size, soon started to cramp up. I kept on pedaling. There was a bike path that led from Willow to Yellow Springs. So at least I was spared the indignity of being on the road with cars. Instead, I endured the curious and amused looks of my fellow bike-path riders.

"What a pretty bike," said one woman, pedaling past me on an expensive mountain bike.

"Yeah, I think I had one just like that when I was ten," said the woman's companion. They laughed and pedaled away and were soon specks on the path.

To keep my mind off the pain in my legs, I started thinking about Vivianne's book. There was something about the book that didn't quite make sense to me. I could completely understand why Vivianne had painted the character of Elwood Smalls with such contempt. But why had she made Roxanne Gayle, the character based on her own life, so unsavory, as well? In fact, the character of Roxanne Gayle was in many ways worse than Elwood Smalls'. Her drug abuse and neglect had caused the death of her own child, and she was a prostitute. Vivianne had played a prostitute in her most famous role in *Asphalt City*, which had to be where the prostitute angle came from, but I'd never heard anything about her being on drugs except for, according to Harriet, the occasional sleeping pill. With everything she'd gone through with Cliff, it seemed like Vivianne would have made Roxanne a more sympathetic character. Why hadn't she?

I was so lost in thought that I wasn't paying attention to where I was riding. The front tire of my bike hit a big rock that was lying in the middle of the path. I went flying over the handlebars of the bike and landed hard on my back. I was paralyzed for a few minutes as pain coursed through my body. I rolled over onto my stomach and caught a glimpse of my watch. It was eight o'clock.

It was also starting to get dark. Tears pricked my eyes as I painfully got to my feet. I went over to inspect the bike. The front end was bent to hell. There was no way I'd be riding it to the park. I started walking, or limping to be more precise. My back hurt, my head hurt and my legs felt like jelly. It was completely dark by the time I reached the park. I was twenty minutes late. I prayed Lynette was still alive as I made my way back to the campground.

The park was full of campers. No one paid much attention to me. I finally came upon a row of six log cabins. All the cabins appeared occupied except cabin number four, the one the note said for me to go to. That cabin was dark. My heart jumped into my stomach. Was Lynette in there dead? I approached the cabin and knocked softly on the door. Nothing. After knocking again with no response, I turned the knob. It was unlocked. I opened the door.

"Hello? I'm here and I have the disk." I walked into the dark cabin. I hadn't taken five steps inside when someone grabbed me from behind. A cold, ammonia-soaked rag covered my face. Chloroform. Panic welled up in me. I struggled, but the arms around me were too strong. Then everything went black.

I was dreaming. I dreamt I was Pearly Monroe standing on a corner under a streetlamp and swinging the little black purse I'd bought from Cabot's Cave. Men kept driving by trying to get me in their cars. Each one of them waved something in my face trying to entice me. Carl had a fist full of money. I turned my back on him. Cliff Preston had a diamond ring. I stuck my tongue out at him. Fuzzy Wayne offered me a new bike. I spat on him. It wasn't until Morris Rollins, dressed like Super Fly, walked up and offered me a hot fudge cake that was concealed under his fur coat, that I left my corner and got into his car. He pulled out a knife to cut the cake. But instead plunged it right into my heart. Ouch! I woke with a start.

It took a while for me to get my bearings and remember what had happened. But once I did, I soon realized my hands and ankles were tied with plastic ties, my mouth was taped and I was lying on the floor. I was in a cabin but it couldn't have been cabin number four, which had been dark and empty when I arrived; I must have been one of the other cabins. The floor beneath me was hard wood. I rolled over and saw Lynette, also tied up and gagged, lying in the bottom bunk of a set of bunk beds against the wall. Her whole body was shaking and her eyes were opened wide. She started blinking frantically and rolling her eyes upwards. At first I thought she might be having a seizure. Then I realized she was wanting me to look up. I did and wished I hadn't. On the top bunk was another person covered up with a sky-blue blanket and not moving. I could see spiky red hair peeking out from beneath the blanket. The blanket was stained with dried blood. Noelle was no longer missing. I could think of nothing I wanted as badly as I wanted out of that cabin.

I rolled across the floor to Lynette. The bunk bed was metal and bolted to the floor. I scraped my face against one of the bolts until the tape over my mouth came away. I managed to sit up and leaned over Lynette like I was about to kiss her. It took me a couple of tries, and I inadvertently gave her face a faint hickey, but I was able to pull the tape off her mouth with my teeth.

"You okay?" I asked Lynette.

"What's going on, Kendra? How did you know where I was?" she asked. A single tear rolled down her cheek.

"First we've got to get out of here. There are campers out there. If we make enough noise, we might be able to attract some attention."

"We'll have to hurry. That crazy person is coming back soon," she said, sounding slightly hysterical.

"It's Cliff Preston, isn't it?" I asked. She shook her head in confusion.

"I don't know. I was grabbed from behind when I was about to leave this morning. Someone put chloroform over my face and I woke up here. The person wears a ski mask and hasn't spoken a word to me."

The door to the cabin opened and Lynette and I both jumped. A figure dressed in black walked in. It wasn't Cliff Preston. When I saw who it was, I realized just how wrong I'd been and why. Something in the back of my mind hadn't quite been able to understand how Cliff Preston would figure out that Vivianne's computer disk was in the purse I bought from Cabot's Cave. Men don't notice things like purses. Women did.

"Hello, Stephanie," I said. I swung my legs around and twisted my body so I was facing her.

Her face was pale and devoid of its usual thick layer of makeup. She looked even harder and older and her bleached hair was frizzy and wild. I could see a vivid bruise on her left cheek. A gift from her husband, most likely. She was carrying a gas can, which she set on the rolltop desk by the door. I tried hard not to stare at the can. But knowing she'd set Diamond Publishing on fire wasn't making me feel very hopeful that Lynette and I would be getting out of this situation unsinged.

"Hi, yourself, Kendra. And just in case you thought you were being slick, I knew all along who you were at Vivianne's memorial service. I think you missed your calling as an actress. And by the way," she said waving a square of blue plastic, "thanks for bringing the disk."

"I made a copy, Stephanie."

She shrugged her shoulders. "So, what?"

"So what? You killed Vivianne and you kidnapped my friend to get your hands on that disk. When the other disk surfaces, Cliff's secret will be out. Everyone will know he's been passing for white all these years and wonder what happened to the man whose identity he stole."

"Whatever happens to Cliff he more than deserves," Stephanie said. She sat down at the desk and pulled a pack of cigarettes and a lighter out of her pocket and lit one up. She took a long drag and blew smoke in our direction.

"Why, because he's black?" I asked. She looked genuinely offended.

"I don't give a damn what color he is. All I wanted was

a child. I love Kurt but I wanted a child of my very own and he took that away from me. I haven't loved Cliff since the day I found out he got that vasectomy behind my back. He ruined my second chance to be a mother," she said, bitterly wiping a tear from her eye.

"Your second chance?" Then I knew. "You're Roxanne Gayle, aren't you?"

"Roxanne who?" she asked, frowning. Deep wrinkles popped out on her forehead.

"In Viviane's book. There's a character named Roxanne. A Broadway actress whose child dies when she gets into her stash of drugs. You're Roxanne." Stephanie quickly stubbed out the cigarette.

"All I know is that bitch was about to rake everything back up again in that damned book of hers. She said everyone was going to know what kind of a mother I really was, especially Kurt."

And all this time I'd thought it was Cliff who was the main focus of Vivianne's revenge. It had been Stephanie all along. Stephanie, the woman who stole the love of her only child, Kurt. Stephanie who hadn't been the mother she should have been to her own daughter while Vivianne's reputation had been falsely tainted. Cliff's secret being revealed in the process was just icing on the cake.

"What happened to your daughter?" I had to keep her talking so she wouldn't notice I was rubbing the plastic tie around my wrists against the edge of the bunk bed's frame.

"I tried to be a good mother. I really did try. But a kid just wasn't in the plan. I wanted to be a showgirl on the

Vegas strip. I wanted my name in lights and my face plastered on billboards all over Vegas. Instead, I ended up shaking my ass in a titty bar off the strip called the Kontiki Lounge. Dancing was all I did for the first six months. Then I saw how much money the other girls were making by spending time with the high rollers after work, and I started doing it, too. I got addicted to the money. Then I got addicted to drugs. Not hard drugs, mind you. Mainly painkillers. Anything that would dull the pain." She paused to light up another cigarette.

"I got pregnant by one of my regulars. Some married insurance salesman from Phoenix. He flipped out when I told him he'd knocked me up. Said it couldn't be his. Gave me five hundred dollars for an abortion. Never saw him again. I couldn't go through with it. I used the money to buy a crib and stuff for the baby. After my daughter, Lilly, was born, I got an office job that paid four bucks an hour. That got old real quick. By the time Lilly was a year old, I was back at the Kontiki. Back to stripping, turning tricks and popping pills."

"It must have been really hard for you raising a child under those circumstances." I couldn't break the tie but I felt it start to stretch and loosen.

"Babysitters were hard to come by. I could find someone to watch her during the day. But at night I had to bring tricks home with me. I'd lock Lilly in her room. I didn't want any of those lowlifes near my baby. And believe me, some of those dirt bags thought if they paid me enough, I'd let them have Lilly, too."

"What happened to Lilly?" I asked coaxing her to continue. Stephanie's face collapsed and she turned to stare at the wall.

"One night I brought home this real high roller. Everyone called him Doc because he was a walking pharmacy. Every kind of pill you could think of, he had. That night we drank, fucked, and popped pills until we passed out. Next day, when I woke up, I found Lilly on the floor in her room. She was dead. I'd forgotten to lock her bedroom door when I got home the night before. She was only four. She must have seen the pills lying out on the living-room table and thought they were candy."

"It wasn't your fault, Stephanie. It was an accident," I said.

"That's what I tried to tell those cops," she sobbed crying hard now. "But they arrested me anyway. Charged me with involuntary manslaughter, child endangerment and drug possession. They sentenced me to five years. When I got out I changed my name. Thought I'd try to be an actress. That didn't work out, either. All I got was a talent agent husband whose favorite hobby is knocking me and his son around."

"How did Vivianne find out about all this?" The plastic tie around my wrists hadn't broken but was stretched out enough that I could slip a hand out. But there was still the matter of my ankles.

"She told me she hired a private investigator to dig into my background and Cliff's. Found out I'd changed my last name from Blackman when I got out of prison. Wasn't hard to find out anything about me after that."

Blackman. So, the title, *The Onyx Man,* wasn't just referring to Cliff.

"When did you find out about her book? Right before you killed her?"

Stephanie laughed. "I went to see that smug cow in her dressing room that morning to beg her to take that part Cliff wanted her to do. He needed her to take that part. His agency was going under. Kurt and I were catching hell because he was always in a foul mood. I thought it was the least she could do for all he'd done for her career. She was being a diva as usual. I called her a selfish bitch. That's when she pulled the check from that publishing company from her purse. She had a letter opener and opened it all dramatic like and waved it in my face. Told me when the book came out everyone would figure out it was about me and Cliff and would know about what happened to Lilly. I just lost it. She put the letter opener down and turned her back on me. And I grabbed it and stuck it in her back over and over again until she was dead."

"So you're the one who set off the fire alarm?"

"I wiped my prints off the letter opener and ran. Then I remembered the check and went back to get it, but I saw your sister. She was standing over Vivianne's body holding the check. I went into the men's room and lit up a cigarette and waved it under the sprinklers and then threw it in the trash. When the alarm went off, I saw your sister running away. I was hoping she'd dropped the check but she still had it in her hand."

"And you had to get it back, which is why you tried to

break into my grandmother's house and broke into my apartment and set Diamond Publishing on fire. To destroy all traces of the book."

"I had to. I didn't want anyone to know about the damned book."

"How did you know I had Vivianne's computer disk?"

"I didn't even know there was a disk at first. I figured she must have a computer that the book was saved on. Kurt still had a key from when he used to spend summers with her. I took his key and searched the entire house when Harriet was out. No computer. But I did find a receipt in Vivianne's room from a typing service for a word-processing job and it referred to a copy saved to a disk. I knew she had to have hidden the disk someplace. But I never found it. Then I saw you at the service with that beaded purse. I saw a picture of Vivianne with that same purse when Cliff dragged me to that creepy man's memorabilia shop to see his stupid display. I knew Kurt had sold some of her things recently. I'm the one who encouraged him to sell her stuff in the first place years ago. Cliff had us both on a strict allowance. Sometimes Kurt would share the money with me. I wondered if the disk was hidden in the purse. It was really just a guess. I figured even if it wasn't in the purse I'd give you enough time and motivation to find it for me."

"Then you weren't the one who broke in and trashed Cabot's Cave and chased me?"

Even as the question left my lips, I knew it couldn't have been Stephanie who trashed Cabot's Cave. The shop had been broken into and trashed *after* Stephanie had noticed me with the purse at the memorial service. She'd have had no reason to break into the shop because she already knew I had the purse. So, who chased me?

"Now, it's time for me to tie up some more loose ends." She set her still-lit cigarette on the edge of the desk, picked up the gas can, and unscrewed the top. I could hear a sharp intake of breath coming from Lynette.

"Is that why you killed Noelle? Just tying up another loose end?"

Stephanie stopped what she was about to do and set the can on the floor. She walked over to me and leaned down. Her face was quite calm for someone who'd killed two people already and was about to kill two more. In other words, we were screwed.

"She managed to get hold of that manuscript and figured it all out. She tried to blackmail me. She knew I was the one who killed Vivianne. Told me she was dating Kurt and would tell him all about me and what happened to my daughter. Well, I couldn't have that, could I? I went to her hotel room to try and reason with her. She started reading me passages from that manuscript. She wouldn't shut her mouth. So I shut it for her. Bashed her face in with a crystal ashtray. That shut her up all right. I stuffed her body in a duffel bag and hid it in the trunk of Cliff's rental until tonight. She'll be joining you both in your tragic fire deaths," she said, looking up at the top bunk.

Not if I could help it. When she turned to walk away, I lunged for her legs. She fell forward, knocking over the gas can. The smell of gasoline filled the air. Stephanie's shirt was soaked in gas. The impact of her hitting the floor also caused her cigarette, which was teetering precariously on the edge of the desk, to fall into the pool of gas, instantly igniting it.

Stephanie was on fire. She'd gone up in flames like a torch before I could blink an eye. And so had the cabin. I untied my ankles and quickly untied Lynette as the cabin filled with thick black smoke. Stephanie lurched around in flames screaming like a banshee. My eyes were burning and I was coughing, but I managed to pull Lynette to her feet and grab a blanket from the bed. I threw the blanket over Stephanie and shoved her out the door behind Lynette. A couple of nearby campers were already rushing to our aid. One man threw Stephanie to the ground to pat out the remaining flames. Most of her hair was gone and her clothes and skin were a blackened mess. Another camper called 911 as Lynette and I clung to each other in shock.

They kept Lynette and me in the hospital overnight for minor smoke inhalation even though, except for having almost been killed, we were fine. Stephanie, on the other hand, was in the burn unit in critical condition with third-degree burns over thirty percent of her body. If she survived, she'd be charged with the murders of Vivianne DeArmond and Noelle Delaney and the attempted murders of Lynette and me. After we each gave statements to Harmon and Mercer, and I gave them the dog tags and told them where to find the copy of the disk, our families descended upon our room and a small party ensued until the nurses shooed everyone home so we could rest. Allegra had insisted on spending the night in our room until Mama dragged her home. Before she left, Justine even gave me a big hug and thanked me for saving her daughter.

"Girl, thank you, thank you, thank you for saving my baby," she said wrapping her arms around me. The drama that had occurred between us in the parking lot was instantly forgotten, much to my relief because Justine is legendary in Willow for how long she can hold a grudge.

"Yeah, Kendra, thanks for being such a wonderful friend. I don't know what I would have done without you this week," Greg said, coming over to give me a peck on the cheek.

"No need to thank me," I said looking around "I'm sure any of you would have done the same for me, right?" There was a chorus of yeses but Justine's in particular sounded a little half-hearted.

Carl and Greg were the last ones to leave. Carl pulled the curtain between our beds for privacy and kissed me on the forehead.

"You know nothing happened between me and your sister, right? I mean, she's a beautiful woman but she's gotta be one of the most self-absorbed people I've ever met. All she does is talk about herself," he said, shaking his head. I burst out laughing.

"I know nothing happened. But it's good to hear anyway. And you know nothing happened between me and Morris Rollins's at the Heritage Arms, right?" I asked.

"Of course I do. I know I can trust you, Kendra," he said, pulling me into a tight embrace.

He trusted me. Great. I thought back to my lip-lock with Rollins. Well, that made one of us at any rate. I happened to look over Carl's shoulder at the door to the hospital room and there filling the doorway with his tall frame was the man in question. Our eyes met for a moment and then he grinned and gave me a devilish wink before disappearing down the hall.

EPILOGUE

Lynette and Greg's wedding went off without a hitch. Morris Rollins performed a beautiful ceremony after which we all ate, drank and danced at the reception hall until late into the night. My best friend and her new husband got a honeymoon send-off they won't soon forget. I didn't even mind wearing the hideous Smurf-blue maid of honor dress. I was actually damned happy to be alive to put the ugly thing on. I shook my bow-covered ass all night long. When it was time for Lynette to throw her bridal bouquet, Justine charged through the crowd of single women, knocking them down like a line-backer to catch it, and every unmarried man in the room scattered like crumbs in the wind. The way Lynette and Greg held each other on the dance floor and gazed into each other's eyes left no question in my mind as to what kind of honeymoon they were going to have, though I doubt she's going to be letting him tie her up anytime soon.

Allegra apologized profusely for lying to me about the check. She'd been planning an exclusive story to get back into *Hollywood Vibe*'s good graces and somehow thought holding on to the check would make her exclusive, well, even more exclusive. Whatever that meant. After the wedding, Allegra went back to L.A. She did the talk-show circuit and told the story of finding Vivianne's body, her arrest and being unjustly accused of murder to anyone and everyone who'd listen. For a while there wasn't a day that went by that I wasn't watching her on TV or reading about her in newspapers and magazines. I knew my baby sister was loving every minute of it. As traumatic as the whole experience had been, it all paid off for her in the end. She finally got her big break, the starring role in a major made-for-cable-TV movie. The name of the movie? *The Vivianne DeArmond Story.*

Stephanie Preston was severely disfigured in the fire and is still recovering from her burns. She was officially charged with murder, attempted murder, kidnapping and arson. Margo Diamond also sued her in civil court for the fire at Diamond Publishing. Her trial is set for sometime in the fall. Lynette and I will have to testify. I'm praying she'll save the state the cost of a trial and change her plea to guilty. But since she's denying she did anything wrong, I'm not holding my breath. The media circus surrounding the case is played out daily on TV. Stephanie's finally in the limelight, but somehow I don't think she's ready for this kind of close-up.

In order to beat the media to the punch, Cliff Preston announced in a press conference that he was born Jasper Hairston to a black family in Indiana. Just like in Vivianne's book, the real Cliff Preston was a white army buddy of his who was declared missing in action during the Korean War. But unlike the book, Jasper Hairston hadn't murdered Cliff Preston, at least not as far as any investigation has been able to discover. Vivianne had just wanted to cast a shadow of suspicion on Cliff. The dog tags she had weren't even real. She had them made and planned to use them in case Cliff threatened to report Blackie being alive to the police. Cliff's talent agency went belly-up when the few loyal clients he had left defected to other agencies. He was also publicly lambasted by everyone, including comics, politicians and even the NAACP. But Hollywood being what it is, Cliff was able to capitalize on his notoriety by selling the rights to his story. And in the ultimate attempt at distancing himself from future scandal, he filed for divorce from Stephanie, which will ultimately leave her with no health insurance.

Kurt Preston has written off both Cliff and Stephanie. He never had much use for Cliff, who had abused him since he was a child. Cutting Cliff out of his life had been no big loss. But he had really loved Stephanie. What had happened to Stephanie's daughter, Lilly, and her role in the tragedy, wouldn't have changed Kurt's feelings for his beloved stepmother. However, murdering Noelle, the woman he loved, was something he couldn't forgive Stephanie for. Kurt is living with Harriet at Vivianne's farmhouse, which she left to him in her will, and is attempting once again to kick his drug and alcohol problem. He felt he owed it to Noelle, since she was never able to overcome her demons. Harriet made sure he knew the truth about Vivianne and that she really did love him.

Kurt is also writing a book called, of all things, *Little Black Lie*. I hear it's a mystery.

And speaking of mysteries, the mystery of who had broken into Cabot's Cave and chased me with that hammer was solved one evening when I saw the news report that a man had been arrested for trying to sell collectibles stolen from Cabot's Cave. The thief claimed that Donald Cabot had hired him to break into Cabot's Cave and steal a few of his heavily insured collectibles so he could collect the insurance money and save his failing business. The plan went horribly wrong when the thief took it upon himself to bust up the place to make the robbery look more authentic. When the unfortunate Mr. Cabot walked in and saw what was being done to his precious shop, he dropped dead of a heart attack.

Blackie Randall quietly disappeared from Woodlawn Nursing Home. I didn't tell the police, or anybody else, about him being alive. Whether he was guilty of robbing that bank was something we'd probably never know, but in his current condition he was beyond anything the law could do to him. Cliff reported seeing him to the police out of spite and to deflect some negative attention away from himself. I don't know where Harriet is hiding him now. She isn't talking, and she swore Cliff was lying and trying to make trouble for her when the police ultimately showed up to search the farmhouse.

But I had a good idea of where Blackie might be, and while I was out taking my new car for a spin I decided to test my theory. My Nova hadn't been worth repairing and

I was now cruising around in a silver Toyota Celica—used, of course. I toyed with the idea of reporting Winette Barlow to the police. Since I hadn't actually seen her trash my car, and didn't feel like dealing with any more drama, I decided against it. Much to Rollins's relief, Winette has since set her sights on a new conquest and has given up her pursuit of the reverend, though she still tosses venomous looks at me whenever I see her out in public.

Anyway, I found myself in front of Morris Rollins's brick ranch. I saw his car in the driveway and pulled in behind it. Rollins emerged from the backyard at the sound of my car door slamming. His expression was neutral and I couldn't tell if he was happy to see me.

"Is this a bad time?" I asked. He shook his head and silently opened the gate for me come through.

I stepped into the backyard, looked up onto the deck and saw an elderly man with long silvery-white hair sitting in a wheelchair with an oxygen tube in his nose staring off into space.

"Who's that?" I asked.

"My uncle," he replied simply. I could tell by the set of his jaw that that would be all the explanation I was going to get.

I smiled at Rollins. He smiled back.

tangled
ROOTS

A Kendra Clayton Novel

ANGELA
HENRY

Nothing's going right these days for part-time
English teacher and reluctant sleuth Kendra Clayton.
Now her favorite student is the number one suspect in a local
murder. When he begs Kendra for help, she's soon on the road
to trouble again—trying to find the real killer, stepping into
danger...and getting tangled in the deadly roots of desire.

"This debut mystery features an exciting new
African-American heroine.... Highly recommended."
—*Library Journal* on *The Company You Keep*

*Available the first week of May
wherever books are sold.*

KIMANI PRESS™
www.kimanipress.com

KPAH0680507TR

A soul-stirring, compelling
journey of self-discovery…

journey
into My Brother's Soul

Maria D. Dowd

Bestselling author of
Journey to Empowerment

A memorable collection of essays, prose and poetry,
reflecting the varied experiences that men of color face
throughout life. Touching on every facet of living—love,
marriage, fatherhood, family—these candid personal
contributions explore the essence of what it means to
be a man today.

**"*Journey to Empowerment* will lead you on a
healing journey and will lead to a great love of self,
and a deeper understanding of the many roles we
all must play in life."—*Rawsistaz Reviewers***

Coming the first week of May
wherever books are sold.

www.kimanipress.com   KPMDD0290507TR

BETTYE GRIFFIN

A LOVE for All Seasons

Alicia Timberlake was the woman of Jack Devlin's
dreams, but Alicia had always kept people at a distance,
unwilling to let anyone close. Still, Jack isn't about to give
up without a fight. But when a family tragedy reveals a secret
that makes Alicia question everything she's ever known,
she's suddenly determined to reassess her life and learn,
finally, how to open herself to love.

Available the first week of May
wherever books are sold.

ARABESQUE®
www.kimanipress.com

KPBG0100507TR

Celebrating life every step of the way.

YOU ONLY GET *Better*

New York Times bestselling author
CONNIE BRISCOE
and
Essence bestselling authors
LOLITA FILES
ANITA BUNKLEY

Three fortysomething women discover that life, men and
everything else get better with age in this entertaining
three-in-one anthology from three award-winning authors!

Available the first week of March wherever books are sold.

KIMANI PRESS™
www.kimanipress.com

KPYOGB0590307TR